THE SARACEN

Tom Frye

Copyright © 2022 Tom Frye

All rights reserved.

ISBN-13: 978-1-958557-08-2

Dedicated to
the Police Departments
that incorporate
Pit bulls to be
Service Dogs.

And to the folks
that still believe
Pit bulls are
a heart that walks
around on four paws.

1

Lucas Holland raced down the hallway toward the Boy's rest room at Havelock elementary school. 12-years-old and in 6th grade, the slender reed of a kid was already late for class. Having made a mad dash from home, his shaggy blond hair looked like he'd taken an eggbeater to his wild tangles. In the space of four blocks, he'd managed to inhale a strawberry Pop-tart and swigged down a small carton of orange juice even as he ran.

He wiped frosting from his upper lip, and belched quite suddenly, tasting a remnant of the juice he'd so hastily guzzled. "Whew!" he gasped. "That OJ backwash tasted like monkey butt!" Before rounding the corner into the rest room, he heard a solid thud! It was followed by a pain-filled gasp. As he entered the room, he saw a small boy drop to the ground, his knees striking the tiled floor, while three bigger boys surrounded him.

"Assimilate," one of the boys said as he towered over the smaller boy clutching his stomach. "Is that what you're telling us?"

The boy on the floor peered up at his three tormenters, tears blurring his vision. "My father," said the boy, "claims we are guests here. There is a certain protocol of honor when a host takes in a guest. Are we to repay that guest by doing him great harm, Jabar?"

Jabar kicked him then, his tennis shoe connecting with the smaller boy's chest, sending him back against the tiled wall behind him. The little dark-haired boy struck his head, leaving a bright red spot on the white wall. "Your father speaks of honor, while denying the commandments of the Quran that say we are to annihilate these enemies of our god, not assimilate, stupid fool!"

Ali said, "My father says there has been enough bloodshed for 1400 years to last a lifetime. What principles are in place when Sunni kills Shiite? Why must we kill any infidel who offers his hand to us?"

"Hakeem? Aaban?" Jabar snapped, and like automated robots, the two other Muslim boys reached down, roughly yanking Ali to his feet. "You," Jabar growled, "will fulfill your vows! You will carry out jihad as Allah commands!"

It was then that Lucas intervened.

He reached out, grabbing Jabar by the long curls of his hair. He pulled back, turning the kid's face just enough to land a solid punch on his left cheek. Jabar cried out and sailed back against the same wall Ali had left a spot of blood on. As the tall, lanky boy struck the wall with considerable force, something small and black fell out of the waistband of his pants and clattered on the bathroom floor.

Lucas glanced down and saw that it was a small .22 Ruger pistol. He hurriedly bent down and scooped it up. Jabar scrambled to his feet. "Give me my gun!" he hissed. "It is mine! It belongs to me!"

"Nope," Lucas said. "Not a chance, idjit!"

The three Muslim boys were furious. Lucas had not only interfered in their recruitment activity, he had taken away their advantage. Their plans had been ruined by an American boy who had absolutely no give in him. "If you don't give me my gun," Jabar hissed, "we will come to your house and kill everyone! Your mother! Your sisters! Your brothers! Your father! We will behead them in front of you!"

At this, Lucas actually laughed. "Coming to my house? I'd like to see that! Don't got no mother, but my dad would love to meet you, since you threatened to cut off his head! And if all three of you came, he might let one of you live so he could let others know how the Den deals with people like you! Be. My. Guest."

Jabar muttered something in Arabic then, and Hakeem and Aaban each gave Lucas and an enraged glare before stepping past him to leave the bathroom.

Giving Ali one last kick, Jabar snarled, "We will finish our conversation another time, dog turd!"

"Shut up," Lucas said, knowing at that moment he had nothing to fear from the mean-spirited boy. "Go. Leave. Now."

Jabar moved to the door. He glanced back, fixing Lucas in his furious gaze. "You are dead, kaffir. Dead. Mark my words."

Lucas lunged forward so fast that Jabar had no chance to escape. Tossing the pistol to Ali, he latched onto the lanky boy's shirt, and said, "Don't. Ever. Threaten. I am Den, and Den is death to you. If I even see you sneer at me in the halls, you will meet Den justice. And you will have no future. Now, get out of here!"

Jabar was gone within seconds. Lucas snatched the pistol out of Ali's hands. Ali gingerly touched the slight wound he'd received on his head. When he brought his hand back in front of his face, he grimaced at the droplets of blood on his fingertips. Lucas said, "Go to the nurse. That might need a butterfly to close it."

Ali stared at him in puzzlement. "A butterfly?"

"Butterfly Band-aid," Lucas said.

The two studied the pistol for several moments. It was formed of a smoky black metal with twin scorpions engraved on both of its pearl-handled grips. The most unique feature about the weapon was the engraving of a dragon on the end of its barrel, with the muzzle creating its open mouth.

Tucking the gun into the waist band of his jeans, Lucas met the kid's tear-filled gaze. "Thank you," Ali said, his hand held out to him.

Lucas glanced down at the outstretched hand. "Don't mention it."

Without shaking the hand Ali offered him, Lucas latched onto his shoulder and guided him toward the door. He could feel those black, sorrowful eyes boring into him even as Ali exited the bathroom.

Two minutes later, Lucas headed past the main office. He saw the three Muslim boys all seated in the reception area talking to Mr. Headlee, the principal of Havelock elementary. Jabar leaped up out of his chair, wildly gesturing at him, then pointing to the large red welt on his left cheek where Lucas had punched him. Lucas cringed and his stomach did flip flops when Headlee looked out past the office window. The middle-aged, balding man beckoned for Lucas to join them. "Holy Dogs!" Lucas whispered as he bolted down the hallway. Racing past the office, he deliberately defied the school principal who was all too familiar with the belligerence of Lucas.

The gun! thought Lucas as he sped down the slick linoleum tiled hallway, his tennies screeching like tiny Irish Banshees as he put space between himself and old man Headlee. No way was I gonna sit through an interrogation by that old fart, trying to keep this pistol hidden! And it's not like those three reported me for stealing their gun! No, they were probably crying over the beat-down I gave to weasel face! Hoping to get me in trouble!

He skidded to a stop, plowing into his metal locker when he reached it. His heart pounding, he hastily spun through the numbers on his combination lock, pulling it down open. Lifting his shirt, he clawed at the butt of the pistol and snatched it from the waistband of his jeans. He placed the gun inside his backpack hanging from a hook at the rear of the locker. Slamming the locker door shut, he locked it.

"Lucas Holland?" came blaring out of the speaker above his locker. "Lucas Holland? Report to the office this instant!"

Peering up at the speaker as if it were a drone hovering there in the hallway, ready to blast him out of his Keds, Lucas resigned himself to deal with the trouble. Now that the gun was out of the equation, he was confident he could put on his usual charm and worm his way out of the bad situation presented by the Muslim boys.

In seconds, Lucas passed by the three boys seated across from him in the principal's office. He sneered at them, interrupting Headlee as he said, "Saracens. That's what my dad, an ex-Army Ranger, said about them when he discovered there was a mosque in Havelock. Iran. Iraq.

It doesn't matter where they come from. Sunni? Shiite? In the fifth century, Saracens were descendants of Abraham's older son Ishmael, having come from Abraham's wife Sarah, instead of his slave Hagar. In the Middle Ages, Saracens were followers of Mohammad and they were involved in the Crusades."

Headlee said, "Well, these three Muslim boys belong to a fairly rigid assimilation program, and as such, Lucas, a little tolerance and acceptance would go a long ways. You and I need to sympathize with these poor refugees exiled from their war-torn country—"

"Ah," Lucas said. "Dad says they are sleeper cells, just waiting for the call to rise up and takeover America."

Lucas had to keep from launching himself across the conference table as Jabar lied through his teeth, saying, "I just finished using the rest room when this wild-haired maniac viciously attacked me. Hakeem and Aaban also bore witness to the golden-haired demon who so maliciously yelled racial epithets at me. And then after a tirade, he told me to leave his country and struck me directly in the face. Didn't he, Hakeem and Aaban?"

By the time all three boys had told their side of the story, Lucas was made to look like a racist bigot, determined to make life hell for any good Muslim who only wanted to assimilate into this country. He was after all, the kid that no one messed with. He'd grown up with violence as an ever-present influence in his life. He'd seen too many of his dad's club issues settled by fists to ever allow himself to back down from any confrontation. If his dad, president of the Elder's Den, ever heard he'd pussied out of a violent situation, there would be hell to pay at the Holland house. He knew his dad would not be pleased that he'd helped Ali, but he would at least respect the fact that it was three against one, and not something Lucas could easily ignore.

Lucas, with the sparkle in his blue eyes, often charmed his way out of consequences for confrontations he'd had in the past. From 2nd grade on, he had been sent to the office for each slug fest he'd started. Three times during 2nd grade. Five during 3rd. Seven times in 4th and 5th, and now in 6th grade, only once, which is why he still remained in a normal school setting as opposed to the school for behaviorally challenged students. When his violent outbursts had escalated during 5th grade, Lucas had been court ordered to attend the school for kids who could not function in an ordinary school setting. And Lucas had hated it so bad, he put every effort into getting himself out of the alternative setting, even if it meant controlling his red-hot temper.

He had been in 6th grade for three solid months with "no fists" used to deal with adverse situations. No, Lucas knew there was a line he dare not cross. He had been removed from his home and placed in foster care, with parental contact terminated. He wouldn't like being separated from his dad, as he'd already lost his mom this past year in a car accident. He'd spent the past year in foster care with Lakota dog handler, Ben Black Bull, helping the Native deal with troubled dogs at his rescue ranch, Wounded Arrow.

During his stay with Ben, Lucas had learned a lot about anger management. Although half of the population there at the school were annoying brats who deserved a punch to the face to set them straight, Lucas vowed not to be the guy who delivered that punch. He had enough of the alternative school to know he never wanted to be sent there again. All he had to do is abide by a few stupid rules. Tolerate his fellow students. Get himself from point A at 9AM to point B at 3PM, to put another day behind him.

By the time the meeting ended that day, the whining weasel Jabar made himself out to be the victim of the incident, and when Lucas refused to shake the boy's hand and apologize for striking him, Headlee threatened to send him back to the alternative school setting.

2

When school ended, Lucas was in a real huff. As he walked down the sidewalk toward home, he muttered, "All because I was helping that little kid!"

"Hey, Lucas!" came an excited voice behind him. "I have Skittles to share for your earlier kindness you showed me!"

Lucas turned, rolling his eyes in exasperation as Ali came running down the sidewalk toward him, a big smile on his face.

Lucas said, "Save your Skittles. Those morons were out of line for triple teaming someone as wimpy as you. Hell, those morons are all in 6th grade and in old lady Dawson's room, and not in my class."

Ali said, "I, too, am in Mrs. Dawson's class. Not once did she see Jabar walking by my desk and punching me this day."

He forlornly held up his skinny arms, peeling back both sleeves of his blue T-shirt to show the purple bruises on both of his shoulders.

"Ouch," Lucas said, wincing. "I suppose," he said, patting the straps of his backpack, "he wants this back, right?"

Ali studied the green backpack slung over Lucas's right shoulder.

"The gun," Lucas said.

"Oh," replied Ali, understanding causing his dark brown eyes to look like two shiny marbles. "No. He wants me to use it."

Lucas's brow furrowed as he tried to determine what the kid was talking about. "Use it? How?"

"No," Ali said, falling in behind him even as Lucas quickened his stride, putting distance between him and the little kid. "Jabar wants me to do jihad. To shoot kids in our classroom."

His head lowered, his eyes downcast, Ali muttered, "Yes. Jabar says it is my duty as a good Muslim. I love and serve Allah, but I do not wish to die for him. Which makes me a very bad Muslim."

Lucas snorted, "What the hell does that make you as a person? To hell with any god who commands you to kill someone just because they don't believe in him! If a god is so powerful, let him kill people who offend him himself! If you ask me, that is a real lame move. This god of yours sits safe in heaven, while you take all the risks here on earth? Sounds just like Bones Bridger to me."

Ali asked, "Who?"

Lucas said, "An old club member. One of the OG's of the Elder's Den, my dad's club. Bones Bridger is a chief manipulator with all the trickery of a Mafia don. He speaks. Other cons listen. He orders something done. It gets done. Anyone who disobeys Bridger's command, they get punished. Been sixteen unexplained knifings in the past ten years out at the State Pen, and not even the guards dare point a finger at Bones. He is that all powerful. My dad says Bridger rules behind the scenes like a vindictive, vengeful, wrathful god. If I was a god, and all that powerful, I'd do my killing myself, not command wimpy men to do it for me!"

Ali said, "My father says—"

"You say that a lot," Lucas said, cutting him off. "Who cares what you father says? What about how you think? My dad says a lot of things and yet I don't blab about it to others. I suppose you try winning arguments by bring up what your mother says, too, right?"

A stillness came over Ali, a deep sadness filled his dark eyes. "My mother is gone from us. She died in a car crash."

Lucas glanced back at the forlorn little boy and offered him a look of sympathy. "Yeah, mine, too. She got run off the road by someone my dad is still trying to find."

Ali, much to Lucas's annoyance, trailed behind him for the next four blocks. Two more blocks and Lucas would have to ditch the kid, for they would be approaching the Holland house, which also served as club house for the Den. No telling who might see Lucas walking with Ali, and there would be hell to pay when Stone Holland heard of it later. Or worse, his dad might be out working on a bike in the driveway, and he would freak when he saw his son walking with an Arab boy. The two of them had just crossed the sidewalk over to Logan Avenue four blocks away from the school, when suddenly Lucas's eyes went wide with alarm. He latched onto Ali's left shoulder and roughly pushed him to the ground behind a row of shrubbery.

"Ouch!" burst from Ali's mouth as Lucas dug his fingers directly into the fresh, painful bruises left by Jabar during class.

"Down! Stay down!" snapped Lucas, pushing him one last time to make sure he lay sprawled behind the bushes, and out of sight of the two burly men exiting the Ford van a block down the street.

Diving for cover behind the shrubbery, Lucas ignored Ali's pain-filled grimace as he lay there writhing in the grass and holding his arm. "That's my Uncle Nate! He sees me with you and I am dead!"

Ali held up a hand in a pathetic gesture to keep Lucas from manhandling him again. "Okay," he said. "I understand."

Feeling sorry for the kid, now that he knew he'd hurt him by grabbing onto his already bruised arm, Lucas said, "Sorry, but you have no idea how badly the Den despises you and your people. Dad and Uncle Nate claim you're all just a bunch of spies, infiltrating for a takeover. Nate would pummel me senseless if he saw me with you. Dad would tell the entire club that I was a traitor!"

Ali stared at him for long, silent moments. Then quietly he said, "We would not want that now, would we?"

Lucas noted his sad look. "If only your people were more outspoken about the whacked terrorists belonging to your religion. All we hear here in America is how all Muslims want to blow us up."

Ali nodded. "I and my father are not these same kind of Muslims. It would break my father's heart to even bring harm to any living creature, let alone blow you and your father and his gang to pieces."

"Club," Lucas corrected him. "It is called a club, not a gang. Big difference between bikers who just want to ride and enjoy the road compared to gangsters who do drive-byes, sell drugs, and kill each other over petty squabbles. Bikers are cool. Gangbangers are the scum of the earth."

Slightly angry that Lucas had lumped he and his father in with Islamic Extremists, Ali said, "Moderates! Reformists! Extremists! Big difference there, too! Yet, you claim we are all the same! Sunnis believe that Abu Bakr, the father of Mohammad's wife Aisha, was his rightful successor. Shias believe that Mohammad ordained his cousin Ali Ibn Abi Talib in accordance with the command of Allah to be the next caliph, making Ali and his descendants Mohammad's successors. Both share the holy book of the Quran. The difference in practice is that Sunnis rely on the Sunnah, a record of the teachings of the Prophet Mohammad to guide their actions while Shiites rely on their ayatollahs, whom they see as a sign of God on earth. Jabar, Hakeem and Aaban are Sunni, while my father and are I are Shias. Their home country is Syria. Ours is Iraq."

Lucas slapped his forehead mockingly and said, "Wow, Islam in a nutshell, right?"

3

A loud slamming door caused both boys to fall silent. Scooting forward and pushing their faces into the bushes in order to see down the street, Lucas and Ali lay shoulder-to-shoulder looking like two turtles straining their necks in order to feed. They both watched the scene unfolding before them.

Lucas's uncle, Nate Holland, was a huge bear of a man. He was bald, with the tattoo of a dragon dominating the left side of his shiny skull, and a long, braided beard trailed down to his thick chest. The cut-off jean jacket he wore, revealed his many tattoos inked up and down his forearms and wrists. There was a worn, weathered look in his dark eyes. For a moment, it appeared he was staring with those tired eyes directly at the two boys hiding behind the shrubbery down the street. Lucas froze. Ali closed his eyes.

Nate turned his sultry gaze on his companion.

"Mange," he said in a gravelly voice, "how much dope did you put in the tranq gun? He's still out, barely breathing. Hell, you shot him over an hour ago. What's up with that?"

Mange, a biker even larger than Nate, ambled over to the open passenger's side window, peering in and looking toward the back of the van. "He'll come to in an hour. I put in just enough to keep him from coming to and surprising us. There would be hell to pay if he did that in the middle of us getting him to the Barn."

Nate peered in the driver's side window, studying the interior of the van. "Well, we don't get paid if he dies on us," he said.

Mange snorted, "We don't get paid, if he comes to, and we're forced to put a bullet in his head either!"

Nate walked around the front of the van to join him. "Hope you tamped the dosage down for this one. We want to put him to sleep, not kill him."

The two men walked up the driveway and headed toward the house's backyard. The moment they vanished from sight, Lucas slung his backpack more snugly over his shoulder and ran toward the van. Ali hesitantly followed behind him. "What are you doing?" he asked as he sprinted down the sidewalk. "These are very bad men. Who do you think they shot? What do you think they are planning to do with him? Put him to sleep? And what are you planning to do? Help him?"

Ignoring his annoying babble, Lucas approached the back door of the van. "Crazy loons!" he gasped, breathlessly.

Creeping across the grassy lawn between the sidewalk and the street, Ali tip-toed his way over to the Ford van, his wide eyes fixed on Lucas. "And you say, my people are bad," he cautiously said.

Lucas reached out and latched onto the door handle. He pulled both doors open. "What in the holy hells is that?" came from Ali, who stood there peering into the van, his brown eyes grown large.

Lucas climbed into the van, moving directly up beside the large Pit bull sprawled on the carpeted floor. It was a beautiful dog, with black fur masking his face, and the same black fur trailing down his back, blending with his broad white chest. All four of his paws were black, as well. The dog was out cold, due to the tranquilizing drug injected into his system by way of the gun Mange had used on him.

Running his hands through the dog's thick fur, Lucas showed no fear or hesitancy in trying to rouse the sleeping canine. He glanced back at Ali, angrily explaining, "A bait dog! Uncle Nate and the ape with him go all over town stealing people's pets! They use them as bait dogs to stir pits up inside the fighting rings! They are disgusting and horrible, and if I had a gun, I would—"

He stopped mid-sentence, his thoughts and his words frozen.

I do have a gun! he suddenly realized. *It's in my backpack.*

Slinging the pack off of his right shoulder, Lucas hastily unzipped the pack and reached inside for the gun. "We're gonna save this dog!"

he cried, looking outside the van to Ali.

"Why?" Ali asked. "Dogs are prohibited animals. It is traditional among Muslims all over the world to regard the dog as a dirty animal that when touched would infect the one who touched it with dirty impurity! The Prophet, Mohammad ordered the killing of dogs and gave numerous hadith that prohibit the keeping of dogs! Hadith tell us that angels won't enter a room where there is a dog. Hadith tell us that if we touch a dog we become impure, that we have to wash seven times. Some hadith say that we must kill all black dogs, especially black dogs, because they are devils. There are five animals that can be killed at any time; a snake, a vicious dog, a crow, a rat and a scorpion. I cannot touch that dog. Allah forbids it."

The dog slowly raised his head, his large green eyes fixed on Ali. Lucas gave Ali a hard stare. Still looking at the dog in open disgust, Ali quietly admitted, "I am obligated to help you because of your help you gave me this morning, but do not make me touch this dog."

"I wouldn't dream of it," Lucas said. "I want you to run two blocks down the street. When you get to 67th, you'll see a chopper mailbox sitting on the left side of the street. That's my house."

Looking confused, Ali asked, "Chopper?"

Lucas said, "A Harley, with chopped forks. The club all ride Harleys, the best bike ever made. We have a mailbox with ape-hangers at the top, and chopped forks with a wheel at the bottom. That's my house. Check the garage, my dad might be working."

Ali looked uncomfortable. "Your father is not going to like me."

"True," Lucas said. "You tell him I'm getting jumped by a bunch of Outlaws. Start crying if you have to. Just get him down the street!"

Ali locked gazes with Lucas. "What if your uncle returns?"

Picking up the pistol with one hand, Lucas said, "If you run fast enough, Uncle Nate won't end up with a bullet in his butt."

Tears sprang to Lucas's eyes. Patting the dog affectionately, he sobbed. He loved dogs. He would never throw one into a fight. Nor could he understand how his father and his uncle could ever do such a thing. Growing up around the Den, he knew Stone and Nate Holland were deeply involved with the fights.

In fact, they had ended up with a notorious pit bull who had won over fifty fights in his career. A month after Lucas's mom had been killed, the courts had returned him to his dad's house there in Havelock. Ben Black Bull had insisted that Lucas take Grunge and Goblin with him. The dog therapy he had included Lucas in had done wonders for the rage-plagued kid, and his time at Wounded Arrow rescue ranch would have a lasting impact on the troubled boy. Lucas's dad had willingly taken in Goblin, a friendly gray pit puppy, but Stone was well aware that Grunge, the older, Brindle, had been legendary in the dog fighting circuit.

Lucas had begged his uncle to let Grunge retire, but Nate had told him to quit being such a pansy. Failing to save Grunge from any more heart-breaking, bone-crunching, brutal bloody battles, Lucas resorted to dropping a dime on both bikers, calling Crime Stoppers to report that they planned to involve Grunge in another fight. He spilled the beans, too, telling the dispatcher that Stone and Nate had a habit of fighting dogs. As a result, Ben Black Bull had paid Stone an unpleasant visit.

Afterwards, the president of the Elder's Den had brought Nate to church, the term for biker council meetings, and demanded that he stop throwing dogs in the ring. He made it clear to the club that blowback would be headed their way by law enforcement who certainly knew the Den was involved in the outlawed sport.

Stone told the club he'd heard rumors that a lot of undercover work lately centered around dog fights, not drugs and guns, the usual work involving informants. The majority of the members of the Den sided with Stone. However, Nate had a circle of loyal followers, and they demanded a fight between the two brothers to settle the matter. Stone won that particular fight, so the matter should have been settled. Months went by and Nate stayed beneath Stone's radar, but not without Lucas finding out about several of his covert dog thefts. He'd told his dad that Nate was defying him, to which Stone had said, "I can't do nothing about it without proof, Little Luke."

Proof? Lucas thought as he sat there, nervously waiting. Get here fast, Dad, and you'll have that proof!

Thump! Thump! came from directly beside him. Lucas actually fell back against the wheel well, trembling in alarm. Thump! Thump! Thump! The sound filled the entire van.

Lucas actually grinned, wiping tears from his eyes as he watched the pit bull wag his tail. "Good boy," he soothed quietly, running his free hand through the fur behind the dog's head.

The dog let out a soft whine, peering up at him with green eyes that would hardly open. "It's okay," Lucas said as if the dog completely understood him. "You've been doped up by two crazy loons. They took you from your home. Carted you here. They don't have good plans for you. But I do. I'm going to save you."

A soft whine came in response to his gentle tones, and several more solid thumps of the dog's stubby tail. The pit bull tried to rise, but it could barely open its eyes let alone lift its head.

At a sudden noise from outside the van, Lucas took the pistol in a two-handed grip, launched himself over the dog, and planted his back on the opposite wheel well. Outside the van, Mange appeared, carrying a small gray pit puppy in his hands. The dog began to anxiously whine the moment he spotted Lucas. "What the hell," he growled, "are you doing with Goblin, Mange?"

The big, burly man stopped, nearly dropping the smaller pit bull when he spotted Lucas seated there not six feet away from him, aiming a gun at his face. "Lucas?" he grunted, placing Goblin down on the carpeted floor next to the larger pit bull. "Goblin ran away. Nate and I just rescued him from this house where some guy took him in. Get that gun out of my face!"

4

Gun?" said Nate as he moved into view, stepping off the curb to reach the back of the van. "Little Lucas has a gun? Holy Jesus! Put that down before someone gets hurt!"

Using his free hand to fend of Goblin's excited greeting, Lucas said, "Uncle Nate, you're not taking this dog! I will shoot you!"

Nate nailed him with an intense gaze, his rage boiling just beneath the surface. "You stick a gun in my face, and threaten me?"

"Not a threat," Lucas said, settling Goblin at his side. "A promise. Push me. Go ahead. I'll send you the way of Trailer, Ox, and Mighty Mike Morgan! All three of them can welcome you to the gates of hell, Uncle Nate! I swear!"

At the mention of the three former Den members, Mange and Nate exchanged uneasy looks. The three bikers had died in a shoot-out over drugs just outside of Omaha last summer. Nate had ridden up there, with the three men as backup to settle a score against a rival club. Nate was the only one who rode away, leaving behind him three dead members of the Den. An investigation had followed, with no arrests ever being made. Nate had not only dodged a bullet during his confrontation with the Dodge Street Apaches, he had avoided a long prison sentence, due to the fact that six members of the rival club had died, as well. With nothing to connect him to their murders.

Stone, though, had shared his thoughts on the matter one night at the fire pit in the Holland backyard. Unaware that Lucas was above him silently listening in his tree house nestled in the branches directly above the fire, Stone had quietly told his warlord, Gypsy, "Find out what you can about a lucrative deal Nathan made with the Apaches after the shooting took place out there along the Platte. Instead of settling a score with Crow Harper, president of the Apaches, Nate supposedly cut a deal with him. Rumor is, Crow and Nate eliminated Trailer, Ox, and Mike, along with those six other members of Crow's club, so as to make a two-way split over a million dollar cartel deal."

Recalling every second of that hushed conversation that he had no business being privy to, Lucas boldly said, "Uncle Nate, I need to ask you something."

Mange let out a growl and started forward.

Click! Lucas thumbed back the hammer of the pistol, aimed it up at Mange's face, stopping the big biker in his tracks.

Trying his best not to flinch, Lucas asked, "Did you betray the club out there on the Platte River?"

Lucas could see by the look in Nate's eyes that he'd hit him hard with the question. If indeed Nate had outright murdered fellow club members, Lucas was sure there was a place reserved for him down there with the Devil.

Nate said, "Stop with the crazy talk, Little Luke."

Mange growled, "Enough of this, you little Moonbat!"

The big, brawny biker started to climb into the van, determined to retrieve the pistol, but Nate latched onto the collar of his jean jacket and pulled him back. "No, the kid is pissed, Mange. He's got anger issues, been that way since his mom died. He may shoot you."

Nate smirked at Lucas. "How about I buy you a new Playstation?"

"Damn!" Lucas cursed. "You can't bribe me, Uncle Nate. How about I go get Dad? Let's see what he has to say about this."

Nate stiffened at this. Mange looked down the street beyond the front of the van. "Oh, hell!" he said. "Stone's coming, Nate!"

Nate said, "If you cost me the loss of this dog, Luke, I will put you in the ground!"

The two bikers walked around the van, and Lucas scooted himself across the floor and out onto the street. If his dad caught him with the gun, he would not be able to sit down for a week. Almost going into panic mode, he peered down at the drain sewer beside the van. He hastily tossed the pistol down into its open mouth, hearing a slight clunking sound as the gun landed down in those dark depths.

Stepping out around the open doors of the van, Lucas looked past the two bikers to Stone Holland striding down the street, trailed by Ali. They made a strange pair, small, shaggy-haired Ali trying to match the big man's long strides. Stone moved with catlike grace as he came purposely toward the van, his collar-length black hair trailing back from his bearded face, twin Celtic hoops glinting in the lobes of his ears. He wore faded jeans, scuffed boots, and a black T-shirt that fit him like a second skin. His beard was trimmed, his hair neatly combed. But there was a ruggedness to his face that reminded Lucas of a mountain man.

"The Golden Boy," Nate called out to Stone, "pulled a gun on me! You had better rein him in, Brother! He's out of control!"

Stone reached out and ruffled the long strands of Lucas's hair. "You want to tell me what's going on, son?" he said.

Lucas said, "They were stealing dogs again, Dad."

Stone stood there peering into the van. "Damn you, Nate," he growled. "Do you know who this dog belongs to? Award-winning sniffer dog of Reason Nelson. The biker who became a K9 handler. Reason was the former VP of the Outlaws. You looking to start a war, Nate? Anything happens to this dog, Outlaws will be gunning for us."

Nate responded, "I'm selling this dog to Crow for ten grand—"

"Crow Harper?" Stone asked. "You telling me you cut a deal with the Apaches over this dog? You've gone very dark, Brother."

Mange said, "It's on account of a six-million dollar shipment that the Juarez cartel was sending to the Apaches up in the Big O. Lobo alerted to the drugs and now the Juarez cartel want to see this pitty torn to pieces this Saturday night at the Barn."

"So," Lucas said, causing the three bikers to turn their gazes on him, "the rumor about you betraying the club is true then, right?"

Nate snarled, "Enough with the rumors, Demon Child!"

Stone nailed Lucas with a stern look. "What rumor?"

Lucas knew he's said way too much. If he spoke his thoughts out loud his dad would know he'd been eavesdropping that night he'd shared his thoughts on the matter with Gypsy at the fire beneath his tree fort. He shrugged. "Nothing," he said, barely above a whisper."

Stone looked over at Nate. Unable to meet his brother's somber gaze, Nate looked away. Stone quietly said, "What rumor, son?"

After letting out a long sigh, Lucas said, "Nothing, Dad."

Stone strode purposely over to Nate standing on the curb. Raising one hand, he coldly said, "Hand me your keys."

"What?" Nate said, his hands balling up into fists. "If you think you're gonna leave us stranded here, we've got business to finish."

Stone stood there, his hand outstretched. "Keys. Now."

Muttering angrily, Nate dug into the pocket of his grubby jeans and retrieved the keys to his van. Tossing them to Stone, he said, "What about the gun? It ain't right that your behaviorally disordered son threatened to shoot his beloved uncle. What if Health Services got wind of that? Little Luke is already being shadowed by the courts, right? So, what about that gun?"

Lucas blurted, "Where would I even get a damned gun?"

Stone started toward the driver's side door of the van. "Lucas? Hop in the van. We'll be taking the dogs to our house."

Gesturing at Ali beside him, Lucas said, "What about him, Dad?"

Pulling open the driver's door, Stone gave a heavy sigh. "He can ride with you and the dogs, but once we get to our house, he goes his own way. He is not your friend, son."

Ali lowered his gaze to the street and said, "I will go my way now. I cannot be in the presence of unclean dogs. Especially, black ones, for they are of the Devil."

Stone slipped into the driver's seat, saying, "Nate? You can pick up your van five minutes after we get these dogs settled at the house."

Stone started the van, glancing back once to make sure Lucas was inside with the dogs. He drove away, without looking in the rearview mirror to see his brother standing there focusing on Ali striding away as fast as his small legs would carry him.

5

Khalid Karim was waiting for his son when he returned that day from school. He smiled warmly at Ali as he came through the front door of their residence five blocks from Ali's school. Khalid said, "Welcome home, my son."

A man of average height, with broad shoulders, a narrow waist, and thick, muscular arms, Khalid was not your typical Shiite Muslim. As in keeping with tradition, he kept his beard trimmed short, yet he wore his silky raven hair past his ears and to his collar. Iraqi by birth, he was a handsome man, with dark brown penetrating eyes. His late wife jokingly called him her, Arab Antonio Banderas.

Khalid's wife, Alisha, had been killed two years earlier in a car accident, and he had vowed to make up for her loss by being a father who adored his son. Ali still talked about her, but he no longer wept when he did so. For many months after her death, he was afraid that Ali, being the fragile boy that he was, had suffered permanent damage due to his mother's unexpected death.

Ali graciously accepted the steaming mint tea his father poured for him from a carafe situated on the edge of his oak desk. Beyond the desk, taking up the entire back wall of the living room were six computer monitors, essential tools to Khalid's trade.

Khalid smiled, tiredly. "Ah, the Hound is spent for the day. I'm afraid the jackals have all gone to ground in their dens, Little Ali."

Ali asked, "Why are you known in intelligence circles as the Hound? Aren't all dogs cursed? Muslims all over the world believe that the dog is a dirty animal, that the touching of a dog would infect the one who touched it with dirty impurity. It is claimed that Prophet Mohammad ordered the killing of dogs."

Khalid responded, "No where in the Quran are dogs prohibited, nor is there any mention of any contaminating effect of these lovely animals who are man's best friend. Consequently, we must dismiss all these hadith that fabricate lies against the Prophet.

"The Prophet said, 'A Muslim man was walking in the desert dying of thirst when he found a well. He went down to drink and upon coming out he notices a dog dying of thirst. So he climbed back in and filled his shoe with water. He gave the dog to drink and God forgave his sins.' The Prophet then said, 'Helping any living thing has a reward!'

"Fabricated hadiths contradict the Quran. Many of them narrated by Abu Hurayra, whose name is translated as, father of the little cat. He hated dogs and from his mouth came many hadiths that cursed dogs. These fabricated hadiths were falsely attributed to the prophet Mohammad. Traditionally, dogs have been seen as impure, and the Islamic legal tradition has developed several injunctions that warn Muslims against contact with dogs. During Ramadan, many Muslims took their dogs to the animal hospitals, to have them put to death by lethal injection. The reason given by the majority of these Muslims was that Islam forbids them to keep a dog.

"Cruelty of animals still occur daily throughout the world. Healthy animals belonging to Muslims are also brought in to be put to death. This is a very un-Islamic. The real tragedy is that many of these Muslims still do this in the name of Islam and openly express such ignorant views. This contributes to propaganda against Islam. All animals are a part of Allah's creation and belong to Allah. Muslims are custodians of this beautiful planet. We will be accountable to Allah."

Ali said, "Can I tell you a story about two dogs, Father? Two dogs I helped rescue today."

Ali proceeded to tell him about his encounter with the bikers. He mentioned Lucas several times during his story session, swearing that he'd never touched either dog during their rescue. He came close to calling Lucas his friend, but decided this was not true, admitting to himself that Lucas really didn't want anything to do with him.

When he finished his story, Khalid sat staring at his young son, shaking his head in disbelief. Ali stood up and showed him the cut on the back of his head. He then told him about the incident in the bathroom with the three Muslim boys. Khalid gestured at the monitors situated on the wall before him. "Do you think their selection of you was random? This had something to do with locating the terror cell of Waziri. I told you before this is like a Chess game, with each player making moves in response to the other. Now that I am closing in on Waziri, wouldn't it be just like him to make a counter move?"

Shrugging his slender shoulders, Ali recited the names of his three tormentors. He then told his father about the gun, telling him about the engravings of the scorpions and the dragon on the barrel.

"Come, Ali," Khalid said, snatching up his dragon-headed cane from beside his desk. "I must speak with this Lucas."

Lucas sat in a lawn chair in the Holland backyard, watching his dad dealing with the two dogs. The large pit bull was walking un-steadily on wobbly legs, slowly recovering from being shot by the tranquilizer gun. He wagged his tail as Stone coaxed him to follow him around the yard. He was a friendly dog and he sniffed at the gray pit puppy sprawled in the grass. "Goblin?" Stone said. "What was he doing over there on Kearney? Did he get out again?"

"Mange," Lucas said, "said some guy had rescued him."

He looked down at the smaller dog and said, "Damn it, Goblin, you can't keep running off like that."

At the mention of his name, the little dog whined excitedly.

"Lobo," Stone said, gesturing down at the big dog as he placed his head in Lucas's lap. "This dog is famous as a K9 sniffer. He's alerted to millions of dollars worth of drugs. No wonder the Mexicans want to see him destroyed in a dog fight. He's cost them many pesos."

Lucas stroked the dog behind his ears. "Nate's a low-life, Dad. Poor Grunge certainly deserves a better master than Nate. Too bad we couldn't give him a better home, right, Dad?"

"Speaking of homes," Stone said, "once this big boy is fully recuperated we have to get him home without getting caught at it. That K9 handler would ask all kinds of questions. I hate to involve you in this. But you are better suited for this than me. We wouldn't want that dog handler to think that the president of the Den was a nice guy. Besides, I figure this to be a covert ops mission: You sneaking him back into his yard without him knowing you were there."

Lucas was just assuring Stone he could get Lobo home discreetly, when a knock came from the front door. Stone silently ushered both dogs inside. Curious as to who had come calling, Lucas stepped onto the front porch to be greeted by a big, blond man in a three-piece suit. A smile creased his gold beard. "Lucas?" the large man said. "Son of Stone Holland?"

Before the man could exchange any more words with him, Stone came outside, closing the inside door behind him. He met the cop's gaze with a cold look, and said, "Detective Tory, ex-warlord of the Outlaws, once known as the Viking. What brings you to my door?"

Beef Tory kept his smile in place and said, "We received a report that two men were seen carrying a dog out to a van over on Kearney Avenue. The dog happens to be that sniffer that put a dent in some cartel's business up in the Big O. Why don't we see what we can do about getting him safely back home?"

Lucas was relieved when Stone said, "Don't have a clue what you're talking about, Detective Tory. Sorry, we can't help you."

The two men stood there long moments sizing each other up. Lucas was hoping his dad didn't take a swing at the blond cop, for this guy looked fully capable of handling himself in a brawl.

"Lucas?" Stone said. "See to those chores. Good-day, Tory."

With that, Stone ushered Lucas inside the house, and without a backwards glance, he joined him, closing the door behind them.

Once Stone had Lobo up and walking around, fully recovered from the tranquilizer in his system, Lucas wasted no time in telling his dad he was ready to launch his covert ops mission to return the dog to his home. Lucas walked Lobo three blocks over to the dog handler's house, an old stone house situated among several ranch-style houses. Lobo had remained close by his side the entire walk over, not once even paying attention to the many squirrels nattering at them from overhead branches during the three-block journey. Lucas was actually amazed at how focused the dog remained, sticking to his side as if his fierce loyalty would allow for no other behavior.

"Welcome home, Lobo," he said, ushering the dog into the yard. Suddenly, Lobo bolted and ran toward the backdoor of the house. He nosed the door open and darted inside.

"Hello," Lucas said, when he reached the open backdoor.

He crept forward, listening to Lobo's toenails clicking on the hardwood floor of the den. He glanced at the display of awards taking up the greater portion of one wall. Next to them were photos of Reason Nelson, showing a steady transformation, starting when he was a young, shaggy-haired biker. In that first picture, he was holding up a leather jacket with the words, "Outlaws, Nebraska Chapter," dis-played on the patch across the top the jacket, while below was a patch displaying the words, "Vice-President," in red letters.

In the next picture, Reason wore his cut with no shirt beneath it, and both his arms and his chest were rippled with muscle. The tatt of a fire-breathing dragon covered his right shoulder, while a leaping panther tatt took up most of his left shoulder. In a third photo, Reason wore jeans and a blue sweatshirt, displaying the words, K9 Handler on the front. His raven hair was tied back in a ponytail, while his goatee was trimmed so he looked like a rakish pirate, and someone had labeled this picture, "The Celt."

A second set of pictures showed Reason seated at a table, a dozen of his books on display before him. Next to this photo was a newspaper clipping with a heading in bold print: Author for at-risk kids becomes Truancy Tracker to state-wards.

Directly across from this was an article about his work as a private investigator, and it detailed how Reason had tracked a runaway kid up to the Big O, where he led police to a drug network involving a street gang. His badge was held in one hand, while a flashy-looking pistol was held in the other.

"Geesus," Lucas said, "how many roles does this guy play? VP of the Outlaws? K9 handler? Truancy Tracker? Author? Private eye?"

Lobo nosed at a small wooden chest situated on the floor before them. Lucas flipped the lid of the chest open, revealing three gold rings resting in black velvet. He gasped when he heard words inside his head: *When my master wields the rings, wonders never cease.*

Lucas stared for long, uncertain moments at Lobo peering up at him. "What the hell?" he whispered. "Did you just speak to me?"

Lobo sent a message inside of Lucas's head: *Everything he puts his mind to, he can do ten times better while wearing one of those rings. The rings help him master many things.*

Blinking in amazement, Lucas scooped up all three rings. He couldn't help himself. He was drawn to them. He had never been a thief as he'd veered into delinquency, but this one time, Lucas made an exception. He wanted these rings. As he slipped them into his front pocket, he heard the front door opening. He headed for the back door, his gaze settling on the chain link fence at the far corner of the yard.

Lucas was just preparing to hurtle himself over the fence, when a voice said, "Hold on there!"

6

Skidding to a halt, Lucas turned to face Reason Nelson. He had dark, shoulder-length hair and a neatly trimmed beard. He wasn't particularly tall, but had broad shoulders and a narrow waist, and wore faded jeans and a black T-shirt. Wow, Lucas thought, he reminds me of Cullen Bohannon from the movie, Hell on Wheels.

Lobo nosed his way out through the house's screen door. Barking a friendly greeting, he darted over to his master, dropping down at his feet. "You beautiful hound!" said Reason. "Where did you go today?"

Lucas lied, "I saw him running loose down at the ball diamond. Someone told me he belonged to the dog trainer guy"

Reason continued to stroke the dog. "Well, you rescued an award-winning Narco dog, responsible for busting millions of dollars' worth of cartel money. You did a good job, Lucas Holland, who hasn't been remaining in school like he's supposed to, right?"

Lucas took a defensive stance. Reason said, "I'm your new truancy tracker. Certainly, you've heard about me from your sister, Celeste? It was my report that got her sent to treatment."

Lucas gasped, "The Park Narc? The Snitch Bitch? Patron Saint of Havelock's Stoners? You're that Reason Nelson? Celeste hates you with a passion, dude!"

Reason nodded. "I imagine she does. How about you and I get off to a good start? In the morning, you be ready for me to pick you up, and I'll buy you Micky D's before escorting you to school. Deal?"

The words, Celtic Houndmaster came to Lucas, for the man reminded him of a character out of a book his sister used to read to him to put him to sleep. Celeste had been gone for the past four months, sentenced by Judge Sully at juvenile court to drug treatment up in Omaha due to Reason failing to get through to her.

Lucas said, "Celeste hated you for getting her to school, but she's read every one of your books while she's been in treatment in the Big O. Now I suppose you got business with me, right?"

"Yes," Reason said, "but you are going to be far less challenging. My dog likes you, and he never lies. Since we're going to be working together, you don't expect me to do all the work in getting you to school, do you? It has to be a joint effort, right? You have a very important role to play in that, too, Lucas."

No wonder, Lucas thought, Celeste didn't like this guy. He's already talking weird. And six more months of this? Yeegods!

Reason opened the screen door, ushering Lobo inside. Lucas remained standing there. Reason stuck out his hand and Lucas had no choice then but to remove his hand from his pocket and shake it. "Here," Reason said, handing him two one-hundred-dollar bills. "For rescuing my dog, how does two-hundred sound to you?"

Two-hundred dollars? Lucas thought. The insult alone would kill Uncle Nate! If the club ever finds out about me messing up his ten-thousand dollar deal, Nate will be the laughingstock of the Den!

Lucas took the two bills, slipping them into his front pocket of his jeans. He asked, "Did it take a lot of training to teach Lobo?"

Reason said, "Sniffer dogs are amazing creatures! They are trained to detect explosives, drugs, money, or blood. Some are trained to search for human remains. Some dogs are trained to search for firearms, cell phones, tumors in humans. Sniffer dogs are able to discern individual scents even when they are masked by other odors. Nose-work is a sport that mimics professional detection tasks. One dog and one handler form a team. The dogs must find a hidden target odor and alert the handler. After the dog finds the odor they are rewarded.

"Not that Lobo ever had behavioral issues, but I picked him up from Pine Ridge rez, and I made sure he was a multitasker. He's not only adept at sniffing out drugs, he's good at finding humans, as well.

Did you know that two police departments in the US have adopted pit bulls as service dogs?"

Without meaning to say it, Lucas said, "My uncle has a pit."

He stopped, unwilling to reveal any more about the notorious killer pit his Uncle Nate forced into the circuit.

Reason noted his sudden silence, and asked, "Is he a good dog?"

"He has the potential to be," Lucas said, yet thinking, *If he hadn't been thrown to the fights, where he's killed over twenty other dogs!*

Lucas said, "Where could I learn how to train dogs?"

Reason said, "I have some CD's put out by my friend Jim Osorio, director of Canine Encounters. He teaches cops how to deal with aggressive dogs. I'll find something for you to carry them home in."

When he returned to the yard, Reason carried an old gym bag with him. He handed it to Lucas, zipping it closed. "Once you think you learned something, come back and we can try it on Lobo. Deal?"

Lucas nodded. "Deal," he said, knowing he would have to sneak them past his dad when he got home.

At 35, Reason still wore his hair to his shoulders, and though it was still dark, his goatee was shaded in salt and pepper tones, a result of years of stressful youth work. The author of 15 books for at-risk kids, Reason had lived for the past 30 years in the Irish Catholic suburb of Havelock. During his career, he'd never considered adding Investigative Journalist to his resume until most recently, due to the story he had published, a well-researched piece for an online magazine he had created, Storm Haven, a monthly publication that resonated with thousands of young people all over the planet. In its first year Storm Haven had won half a dozen awards, and sold over 2 mil-lion subscriptions. Reason contributed 80% of the stories each month, dealing with teen suicide, drug addictions, and issues that kids re-quested. The magazine had been a success only because of his drive to make it work, and his passion to help kids.

His last story about the Den was instigated by Nate Holland's obsession with dog fighting. But the story only came about because of a journal that was mysteriously left on his porch by an anonymous source. Reason, however, figured out halfway into researching the detailed notes in the journal who had written it. He never did know the reason why the source had left it for him.

Celeste Holland refused to tell him.

As he stood there, Lucas realized he was going to be stuck with the long-haired truancy tracker for the next six months. It was a bleak prospect. He hated school with a passion, and since he'd seen how much Celeste had gotten by with before she was hammered by the courts, he figured he could fly under the radar as his older sister had done. Celeste had been wild and unruly. For her, it was all fun and games until Reason had been assigned to her case by Judge Sully. And now, she was locked away in treatment.

Lucas wanted to avoid the same fate, and something in Reason's eyes told him he was going to make life a living hell for him if he did not cooperate with him. He said, "Just before Celeste got sent to treatment, she told me to go and read the words some kid spray-painted down in the tunnels. It said, 'Reason Nelson was right!' It was her way of telling me she wished she'd listened to you. Lots of kids consider you a legend, with all the books you've written. And with your name spray-painted in the tunnels—"

Reason's laughter cut him off. "I have no claim to fame, Lucas. Just been trying to make a difference in my little part of this world. And as such, I'm well known, at least in Havelock. I once was standing in line at the post office, behind four women. I heard them talking in hushed whispers, 'He wrote that book. He worked with my kid when he was on probation. He worked with mine when he was on drugs.' The three women knew me, for I had worked with their kids when each had landed in court. The fourth woman, however, whispered, 'Never heard of him. My son has never been in that kind of trouble.' I so badly wanted to say, 'Bingo, lady! You won the grand prize! I don't know your son. He's never been in trouble! I only know the devious and the defiant on account of lack of parenting skills, on account of misfiring wiring.'

"God only knows why some kids go down in Kamikaze mode. Not looking for fame. Just want to impact kids in a positive way. At my last book signing, I watched more than one-hundred of my readers come to get copies of my books. Bikers, Natives, probation officers, cops, teachers, parents, and even the Red Hat Society. A diverse group. Multi-cultural. Counter-cultural. Common folk. It was good to know my books are demographically sound, meaning ten-year-olds through eighty-year-olds read them. When the last two friends of mine came to buy a book, both dressed in tie-dyed Led Zeppelin shirts, they had with them their newborn son dressed in a tie-dyed Zeppelin shirt! That was the most diverse gathering of folks I've ever seen in one small place."

Lucas wanted to tell Reason that he'd liked his book, but he could not figure a way to do that without it seeming like he was sucking up to the tracker. Finally, Reason said, "When I was a kid bored to death in school with a book I was required to read, I vowed to never write a book that bored kids as badly as some of those that put me to sleep in the classroom.

"I accomplished that goal, too. Eight Ball is the most stolen, lost, missing book in the public libraries. Kids like it, so they steal it."

7

When Reason offered to walk him back home, Lucas had no choice but to comply. As they rounded the corner at the end of Reason's block, Lucas spotted a slender Muslim man and a skinny, black-haired boy approaching them from the opposite end of the block. It was Jabar, the boy he'd taken the gun from at school. Lucas handed Lobo's leash to Reason. "Gotta go!" he said. "Can't be on the same sidewalk with those two!"

Leaving Reason standing there, holding Lobo's leash, Lucas dove through the thick hedges lining the sidewalk.

As the man and the boy approached him, Reason offered them a smile. The man said, "My name is Achmed Waziri. You are some kind of social worker, correct?"

"Tracker," Reason said. "Truancy tracker."

In flat tones, Waziri said, "You do investigative journalism. You write for Storm Haven, a youth-oriented site where thousands of kids log on each week to read about drug use, running away from home, being suspended from school, being placed on probation, and teen suicide. I've read your writings on the Storm, a site created by a panel of drug counselors. I researched you. Your books are nationwide. Your target audience is alternative schools, treatment centers, detention facilities, and AIDS awareness programs. You are not afraid of controversy, your stories often stir up a hornet's nest. Have you not challenged thousands of Muslim youth, criticizing the 'radical vipers' who demand killing in the name of Allah?"

"We are Viper!" Jabar snarled. "The Red Vipers of Syria! And we will see your nation fall! Dirty American, writing garbage about us! And you live with unclean, filthy dogs!"

Watching from behind the thick hedges, Lucas saw Jabar whip out a butterfly knife, working it back and forth with some degree of skill. It clicked and snicked as the kid caused the blade to flash before Reason's eyes. The boy then jabbed at his dog, trying to stab Lobo. Lucas saw a blur of black flash past him on the sidewalk on the opposite side of the shrubbery as a second man darted in front of the dog. The black-haired man struck Jabar across the back of his wrist with his cane. "Ouch!" cried the kid as his knife flipped through the air and landed in the nearby grass. The man moved in front of Waziri, placing the end of his cane against his chest. Waziri gasped, "The Hound come out of hiding!"

Khalid kept his cane snugly planted. "Fear not," he said, "we should not conduct our business with our sons present, agreed?"

Waziri froze for long moments, considering Khalid's words.

It was Ali who broke the silence by nervously saying, "If we were in our homeland, you could fulfill your vows to each other, but this is America, where the laws about such things are much different. There would be consequences I would not wish my father to endure."

Waziri latched onto Jabar and steered him away down the sidewalk, disappearing at the end of the block. Khalid extended his hand. "Khalid Karim," he said. "I know who you are, Storm Writer."

Reason took Lobo's leash in one hand to return his handshake. Khalid smiled. "I have been reading your posts on Storm Haven. You pull no punches when you write about radicalization of my people. Your voice is being heard by hundreds of Muslim youth."

Khalid handed him a business card. "Tomorrow, will you call me? I want to discuss a writing proposition with you."

Reason accepted his card, quietly reading the contact information. "So, I take it you are not opposed to reformation?"

Khalid said, "We have a lot to discuss, my new friend. Do you like coffee? Strong, black coffee sweetened with sugar cubes?"

Reason grinned. "The sweeter the better. Is this your son?"

He gestured at Ali standing there, staring at his dog, a look of disgust on his face. Reason said. "Would you like to pet him?"

"Oh, no sir!" Ali said, a look of horror on his face.

Khalid said, "Excuse him, he is religiously inclined to believe that all dogs are unclean beasts, not worthy of our respect or affection."

Ali started away down the sidewalk. "Father? We should hurry along. Lucas's house is just around the next corner."

Khalid said, "Call me. As for now, I must see to an urgent matter."

"You headed to the Holland house?" Reason asked. "Chopped forks on the mailbox. Just look for those. You can't miss it."

Khalid and Ali were a block away from the Holland house. Ali raised his father's cell phone, focusing its camera on the chopped forks coming down from the mailbox ahead of them. "That is the home of Lucas Holland," he said, impersonating a narrator shooting a docudrama. "In moments, we walk fifty steps to the Holland front door. What you are witnessing, folks, is the Death Walk of young Ali Karim, whose stern father insists I join him."

Turning to zero in on his father's face with the cell phone camera, Ali asked, "Do I have to join you? Could I just go home now?"

With a twirl of his ornate cane he carried, Khalid said, "You must accompany me. I will need you to be a witness. What if your friend lies to me and his father when I confront him?"

"He is not," Ali said, "my friend. Just an acquaintance. Once you confront him, he will hate me with a passion."

Panning to both left and right, taking in the view of the sidewalk, filming his father walking past him, tapping the ground with his cane, Ali started to follow him. Khalid stopped in his tracks. Ali bumped into him. Father and son stood in the shadows cast by an ancient oak tree as a man pulled up in front of the Holland house in an old Buick half a block down the street. Raising the cell phone to focus it on the beat-up car, Ali continued to film as a white man with dark dreadlocks exited the car.

In his hand, he carried a fist-sized bag of white powder. He crept up beside a red pickup and opened the door. Looking in all directions, he shoved the bag beneath the driver's seat of the Ford truck. He closed the door and turned back toward the Buick.

His gaze flickered for a moment down the street to the shadowy sidewalk where Khalid and Ali stood. Still holding the cell phone camera aimed at the man, Ali actually started to duck.

Khalid said, "Do not move, son. Stay as still as a mouse."

The phone held out before him, Ali recorded the man climbing back inside the Buick. He filmed the car as it sped off down the street. Ali stood there, silently studying what he had recorded. He stopped the images flashing past him on the screen, freezing one image. He said, "Apaches. That word on the man's jacket is Apaches."

Ali cringed each time his father's cane struck the front door of the Holland house. He knew Lucas would never forgive him for telling on him in regards to the gun. At the fifth solid knock on the front door, it opened.

Stone Holland took one look at the Middle Eastern man standing on his porch. His eyes then fell on Ali standing meekly off to one side of the man. "Sorry, but whatever you're selling, I am not buying."

He closed the door.

Khalid stood there, staring at the door, unperturbed by the man's rudeness. He raised his cane and knocked again.

Ali said, "Father, he doesn't like Muslims. He will not talk to us."

Khalid spoke directly to the closed door, saying, "Aren't you concerned about the gun your son has brought home from school?"

The door swung back open. Stone's large framed took up the space directly beyond the threshold of the porch. "This is the second time today that I've heard about this gun. What's up with that?"

Khalid told Stone the story of the assault in the bathroom at the boys'school. He explained how Lucas had intervened, preventing Jabar from recruiting Ali for a supposed attack on his fellow classmates. Why Lucas took the gun was up for speculation.

Stone started to close the door again, but Khalid shoved his cane inside the door, preventing it from closing. "It is not just any gun."

Sighing heavily, Khalid slipped one hand beneath his black suit jacket, removing a leather billfold. He flipped it open, holding it out so that Stone could see the badge it contained. "Have you heard of the Phantoms?" he asked as Stone started intently at the badge.

Stone said, "I served two tours in Iraq, special forces with Delta. I know Phantoms are counter-terrorist agents whose purpose is hunting down and arresting terrorists. But I heard a different story on your Shadow agents. You and I both know there is no cure for these radicals, eliminating is the end result when the hunt is over. Am I wrong? You find them, you kill them?"

Glancing over at Ali, Khalid said, "I've carried out dozens of successful missions for my country. In each of them, the perpetrators of horrendous acts of terrorism, have been legally arrested. It would be against the law to simply assassinate a known terrorist. Perhaps, too many spy novels in your past has led you to believe otherwise?

"My plan is to track down a terror cell that is determined to carry out a brazen act of terrorism. This particular cell is here in the states posing as a Syrian film crew producing a docudrama. These Islamic terrorists are known as the Red Vipers. Waziri, the leader of this cell, has come to your small suburb of Havelock due to an imam who has ties to a mosque here. Yesterday, this same imam gave Waziri a special-made pistol. Sources report that his son took it to school with him this morning to cause mischief. Your son now has it."

Stone used his booted foot to force Khalid's cane outside his door and said, "I did my fair share during my tours to your god-forsaken country. You people need to help yourself, Shiite and Sunni. You know, all the News ever reports is about the conflict between Jews and Palestinians, while missing the bigger picture of the wars be-tween all of you Muslims all over the Middle East."

Stone was just preparing to close the door again, when a black Suburban pulled up in the street, followed by a Sheriff's cruiser.

"Now," Stone muttered in irritation, "what the hell is this about?"

8

Lucas slipped back inside the backdoor of Reason's house, the gym bag in hand. He'd nearly carried the bag home when he realized Stone would throw a fit if he brought it with him. He'd decided to simply return it, leaving it in Reason's den so that he wouldn't have to be responsible for the dog training tapes.

Stepping into the den, he heard a voice echo throughout the entire house, "Narcotics would like to give El Lobo one final send off!"

"My dog is retired, Beef," Reason said. "In light of that new opiate out there that has caused the deaths of several sniffer dogs, my plan is to have him die a ripe old age. Having served faithfully, he deserves that, wouldn't you say?"

Detective Tory said, "One more job, live and televised! Backed by the warrant I obtained, all we need is a legitimate cause, and Lobo could provide it. It would certainly even out that run-in you had with Nate back in your Outlaw days. Remember when Nathan brought a shipment of meth into Havelock, and you burned it?"

"Yes," Reason said. "Stone can't control his brother, but I've never known him to deal in drugs."

Beef said, "These drugs are inside of Stone's truck. It will be a slam dunk, with Lobo alerting to narcotics and being filmed while doing so. What do you say?"

Reason remained adamant. "Lobo's registration as a sniffer —"

"Runs out in two months," Beef said. "Lobo might be officially retired, but he's also still registered for active duty, Reason!"

Inside the den, Lucas so badly wanted to defend his dad. Drugs? he thought. Dad doesn't deal drugs! He's blocked Uncle Nate every time he's tried dealing drugs! The Den does not deal in drugs of any kind! I best get home and warn Dad.

The doorbell rang a second time. Lucas paused, curious about this new arrival. Against his better judgement, he crept down the hallway to peek at the African American lady entering the house. Dressed in a tailored suit of dark green, she was tall and slender with short-cropped hair. She said. "I'm Agent Gloria Raynes from Homeland."

Reason said, "Homeland? What brings you here?"

Agent Raynes said, "No bombs. No drugs. Homeland has granted a Syrian film crew visas to produce a docudrama here in the states. A terrorist cell, the Red Vipers, are posing as the producers of this film, led by a man named Waziri, drawn here by a radical imam determined to pass on his next mission to him. This imam gave a pistol to Waziri during an awards ceremony at a mosque last night. A thumb-drive was inserted into the gun with directives on it for Waziri. And now this morning, his son took it to school with him. The pistol was stolen during an altercation. During questioning of the school principal the name Holland came up. I wish to use your dog to deal with a matter of national security."

By the time Lucas ran the four blocks back home, the Holland residence was surrounded by a small army of cops. Local uniformed cops were stationed at either end of the block. Several cops formed a perimeter guard around Stone's truck, while others stood some distance away, regarding the truck as if it was about to blow up at any second. Taking cover behind a nearby tree, Lucas took a sneak-peek at his dad walking through a group of officers in the front yard, but when he approached his Ford truck parked in the street, a cop stopped him from going near it.

Ali seemed to materialize beside the tree Lucas was using for cover. "Lucas?" he whispered. "My father needs to speak with you."

He gestured to a space between two houses on the opposite side of the street. Lucas narrowed his eyes as Ali's father gave him a friendly wave, gesturing at him with his cane. "Tell your dad," he spat, "I've got problems of my own right now!"

Ali remained persistent, nodding emphatically. "Yes, that is what my father would like to talk to you about. Will you join us?"

Lucas watched as Detective Tory detached himself from a small circle of cops gathered next to the driveway entrance. He walked directly up to Stone, offering him a smirk. Lucas used the gym bag he held to push Ali out of his path. He cut across the street and ran down the alley leading to the Holland back gate, lugging the gym bag with him. He ran to his bedroom window. He often used it to sneak out at night and was relieved to find it unlocked. The moment he tossed the gym bag inside and wormed his way through the window frame, Goblin leaped up on Lucas's bed, licking his face repeatedly.

"All right!" Lucas chuckled. "Glad to see you too, Cornball!"

Goblin nuzzled him beneath the chin, then rolled over, wanting his belly rubbed. Lucas complied for several seconds, placing the gym bag on the bed beside them. He told Goblin, "All those cops outside! Come on, let's go take a look!"

Lucas darted to the front window, Goblin scampering along behind him. Both boy and pup poked their heads in between the closed curtain shades to peek outside. They watched with keen interest as Tory and Agent Raynes began a heated debate, the word, "Jurisdiction," echoing down the street. While the white detective and the black agent continued their red-hot exchange, Reason walked up the sidewalk across the street, Lobo at his side.

Detective Tory shouted in the center of the street. "Put that dog to work, Reason!" Raynes snapped, "That is not how this is going to play out, Detective! My mission takes precedent over yours!"

Reason gave a gentle tug on Lobo's leash. Before the two were even halfway across the street, Agent Raynes interposed herself be-tween Lobo and Stone's truck, saying, "Proceed to the house. Do not bother with the truck, Nelson!"

Detective Tory shouted orders to the Cameraman from Channel 10 in the middle of the street. "Get a shot of me searching the truck! Keep your camera trained on that truck!"

Beef opened the truck's door and pulled out the bag he found beneath the seat. "Busted!" he cried. "Holland, you are under arrest!"

Tears sprang to Lucas's eyes, trickling down his cheeks as he watched his dad being placed inside a police cruiser. Sensing his anguish, Goblin nuzzled his leg. Lucas kneeled down to embrace the affectionate dog. Goblin whined, and Lucas wept.

A voice from the front yard alerted him to a new danger. "We're covered by the warrant! Let's go check inside the house!"

Scrambling to his feet, Lucas was nearly to his bedroom when the front door flew open and crashed against the living room wall. Goblin, two steps behind him, gave a soft growl. Lucas scooped up the pup and scurried down the hall and into his bedroom. Tossing Goblin on his bed, Lucas closed the door, and heard Reason say, "Raynes, put that gun away! Holland's got a kid living here with him!"

Raynes shot back, "These Hollands own a killer pit! I've seen that dog fight! Besides, I heard a dog growl when we stepped inside!"

Reason said, "Wrong residence. Nate's the one who owns the pit, not Stone. Just put the gun away, Agent Raynes!"

Lucas and Goblin settled on the bed in the far corner of the room, both of them staring intently at the bedroom door. Muffled cursing came through the walls. The voice of Agent Raynes came from some distance away as she came through the front door.

"What are you doing, Raynes?" Reason's voice came from the front room: "Look, Holland's got two kids living here with him. An older girl in treatment right now, but a younger boy who doesn't deserve to be terrorized by a cop with a gun. Stand down, Gloria. Let Lobo and I conduct our search."

Goblin growled as Raynes pounded on the bedroom door. The agent shoved the door open. Goblin sprang off the bed and barked at her as she stumbled into the room. The small pit bull took a protective stance in front of Lucas, growling fiercely. Raynes raised her gun. "Damn!" she shouted. "It's a damned pit bull!"

Lucas sprang off of his bed, screaming, "No! Don't shoot!"

Raynes snapped, "Stay back, kid! I've got no choice but to shoot the damned dog!"

She took careful aim and began to squeeze the trigger.

Reason, coming up the hallway behind Lobo, had a clear view into Lucas's bedroom. He looked on in alarm as the agent prepared to shoot the pup. Still moving forward, Lobo stuck his cold, wet nose on the outstretched wrist of her gun hand. Agent Raynes let out a scream, overcome by sheer panic. Cursing, she crashed into the nearest wall, and slid to the floor.

Reason reached down and removed the gun from her grasp. After sliding her pistol into her shoulder holster, he said, "You had no business charging in here, your gun drawn. Your moronic behavior put the kid in your line of fire, and the dog was posing no threat. Simply doing what dogs do when someone breaks into their home."

"She was going to shoot my puppy," said Lucas.

Rising back to her feet, Raynes stepped past Reason. "You've got quite a mouth on you, son. Now, why don't you use that mouth to tell me where that gun is you carried home from school?"

Lucas said, "Like I have a clue what you're talking about."

Raynes stood there, slowly shaking her head. "And here, I thought you would work with me, Lucas. Dad goes to jail on drug charges. Sister is in treatment. The kid can't stay here all alone. What options do we have? Youth services? Emergency foster care? And here if you cooperated with me, I was going to allow you to pick where you wanted to stay, young man. Now what do you say about this gun?"

Sniffling, Lucas bowed his head and muttered, "Still not a clue."

9

Reason and Lobo conducted a thorough search of the house. When they were finished, Lobo located two hunting rifles and two different drugs, one for high blood pressure, the other for allergies, in the bathroom medicine cabinet.

All during Lobo's search, Agent Raynes remained in Lucas's room grilling him relentlessly about the pistol. Lucas had perfected playing dumb over the years with every administrator and counselor his problem behavior put him in touch with. His dumb act had infuriated the best of them, and Raynes was no exception.

During the thirty minute interrogation, she had gotten nowhere. She was nearly at her boiling point, when Reason came back into the room, Lobo trailing him. "Sorry, Raynes," he said, "the second search turned up nothing. No exotic pistol is to be found on these premises."

Lucas was just saying, "See? I told you all I know nothing about any damned—" when Ruff! Ruff! burst from Lobo's mouth as he stuck his nose inside the open backpack Lucas had tossed down on the floor earlier. The dog burrowed his nose deeper inside the pack, then turned to peer up at Reason, an excited look in his dark eyes.

Reason produced a treat from a pouch at his belt. Handing it to Lobo, he looked down at Lucas seated on the bed. "You are good, I'll give you that, but my dog's nose never lies."

Lucas snatched up the backpack and dumped out two books on

the floor. He smirked at Reason. "Lobo must have got his wires crossed!"

Reason said, "It was in there earlier. The kid must have removed it. Lobo alerted to it, and he has not been wrong yet."

Lucas said, "Your dog knows the specific smell of one particular gun? I carried my BB pistol in there, not the gun Cop Lady is after!"

Raynes exchanged an uncertain look with Reason.

Reason said, "He got a hit. Just not sure it was your gun."

Raynes nailed Lucas with a hard stare. "This is what happened this morning at your school. You walked in on a Muslim boy brandishing a gun with scorpions engraved in its pearl-handled grips, and a dragon along the barrel. The boy, Jabar, threatened you with it, shoving it in your face. So, you hit him. Before he could recover, you snatched the gun out of his hands. Before leaving school, you put it in your pack."

Lucas said, "Who is Jabar?"

"The boy who first had the gun."

"What gun?"

"Lucas! We are so far past that at this point!"

"Point? Is there even a point to any of this?"

"Gawd, kid! How in the hell do your teachers deal with you?"

"Why? Getting annoyed? Maybe you need anger management, Cop Lady. Lots of anger is bad for your blood pressure."

"Enough of this, Lucas! You think this is some kind of game?"

"Game? I don't know, is it?"

Agent Raynes snapped, "Stop it!"

She shot Reason an enraged glare and muttered, "Watch him for me. I'll be right back!"

Once Raynes left the room, Lobo planted his head in Lucas's lap and whined, fixing him in his sad-eyed gaze. "He's empathizing with you," Reason said. "He knows you are distressed about your dad."

Lucas lowered his head, so that Reason could not see his tears. "There's been some kind of mistake. My dad hates drugs."

Reason kneeled down behind Lobo, politely keeping his face turned from Lucas so as not to humiliate him. "That was a lot of powder, Lucas. How do you explain it being in your dad's truck?"

Lucas wiped tears from his cheeks. Goblin placed one paw on his back, while Lobo burrowed his head into his lap. Keenly aware that both dogs seemed to be picking up on his sad vibes, Lucas said, "This is about Uncle Nate. Nate set Dad up as payback."

"Payback?" Reason asked, slightly puzzled. "For what?"

Lucas was so tempted to tell him that Nate had stolen Lobo and that he and Ali had rescued him, foiling Nate's deal, but he did not want to be a snitch. His dad would not approve. Even if it got him out of jail. He knew the biker code, the one that said you never snitched, that you would rather die than snitch on your fellow bikers. There was no way Lucas would tell him anything in regards to Nate.

Lucas shrugged. To change the subject, he asked, "How come you didn't want Lobo involved in any more searches, Reason?"

Reason let out an exasperated sigh. "A new danger has been introduced into the drug war: Opiates mixed with fentanyl, so lethal that several sniffer dogs have died after inhaling a small amount. Departments have been required to carry an antidote for this toxic residue, known as Narcan. It counters the nasty effects of the opiates. Cop canines are vulnerable because of their smelling skills, and because they're not decked out in protective gear as their human handler. And fentanyl is so toxic that even a tiny amount is all that's needed to kill. Fentanyl poses a problem to officers, too. One cop doing a field test on what he thought to be heroin, went into opioid intoxication. The high potency due to man-made procedures has made it a heroin substitute. As a result fentanyl is more frequently encountered by law enforcement. Have you heard of Deep 9? It's also an airborne toxin. It is more lethal than fentanyl. It has a chemical compound that tells the brain to shut down, demanding its user to stop breathing."

Khalid and Ali were preparing to leave the Holland place. Ali had watched the entire arrest with wide eyes. He looked up at Khalid. "Father, what about the pictures I took on your phone?"

Khalid nodded casually. "In due time, son. However, this needs to be turned down a notch. They are so keyed up over this arrest, it would take a lot of convincing on our part to get them to take another course at this point. Besides, which one would we be able to trust?"

It was then that Detective Tory came storming out of the house.

The detective rushed over to two uniformed officers standing outside their cruiser. "Where's that damned packet I gave you?" he snapped. "Did anyone determine exactly what it is?"

Ali stopped there on the sidewalk, watching the officer retrieve the packet of white powder from inside the cruiser. Khalid tapped his cane on the walk. "Come, my son. Let us return home."

But Ali remained where he was, keenly interested in whatever was inside the packet. Out in the street, Beef took the bag from the officer and plunged his pocket knife into its center. The moment his knife penetrated the plastic of the bag, a fine white mist sprayed out of the cut, and drifted up into the detective's face.

Detective Tory suddenly dropped where he stood.

Agent Raynes, who had been back on her way inside, a laptop in her hands, had witnessed the bizarre way Beef had simply fallen to the street. Shocked by the suddenness of his reaction, she still had the presence of mind to safeguard the other officers rushing directly into the cloud of ghostly white particles floating through the air.

"All of you, stay clear!" Raynes ordered, firmly. "Agent Talbot, get our men in hazmat suits here at once! Tory is in serious trouble!"

Minutes later, paramedics loaded Beef Tory inside an ambulance and rushed him to the nearest hospital.

10

Inside the house, Reason looked up as Raynes walked unsteadily into Lucas's bedroom. "What's wrong?" he asked her in alarm.

Placing her laptop down beside Lucas on the bed, Raynes told him about the situation out front. Reason listened in deep concern, his eyes straying over to Lobo. He said, "This is exactly why I didn't want my dog involved, Raynes!"

Raynes picked up her laptop from the bed and turned to place it on Lucas's desk in one corner of the room. While her back was turned, Lucas made his move. He had been thinking of his open window all through her questioning. It was wide open, and would provide a perfect escape route for him. Besides, he knew with Stone headed to jail and Celeste in treatment, he would end up in some wacky foster home. Lucas bounded up onto the bed, placed his steepled fingers before him, and performed a perfect dive out through his bedroom window. He tucked and rolled, for it was a four-foot drop to the lawn below. "Ooof!" burst from his lips as Goblin landed directly on his back as he lay there in the yard. Both then raced across the backyard.

As Lucas ran, he didn't even bother to look back to determine whether he was being pursued or not. He figured with how relentless Raynes had been, she would not just let him go like this. He knew that she and the cavalry would be coming to snag him off the streets. He was after all, a fugitive from justice. He had something she wanted, and she would not give up until she had it.

He wasn't going to give her a chance. She had wanted that gun so badly it now made Lucas more than curious as to how important it was. All during her interrogation, Lucas had decided he was going back to reclaim the pistol he'd tossed down through the drain sewer.

Ali and Lucas collided just as he and Goblin exited the alley at the end of the block. Lucas peered up into the amused-looking face of Khalid. Placing his cane before him, leaning on it with both hands planted on its dragon-headed hand grip, Khalid smiled warmly.

Ali told Lucas, "This is my father, Khalid. He wants nothing more than to help you. Come home with us."

"Home?" Lucas said. "To your house? Why would I do that?"

Keeping the smile on his bearded face, Khalid said, "Why not? Do you have other pressing matters to attend to, son?"

Refusing to shake the man's hand, Lucas stuffed his hands in his pockets in a defiant gesture. "I'm not your son, good sir!"

Khalid's look of disappointment caught Lucas off guard. "Why the hostilities, young Lucas? Is there any reason to show such defiance?"

Lucas began to say, "My dad says—" then stopped himself when the loud thunder of a Harley came rolling down the street from the opposite direction of the Holland house.

Nate Holland, his bald head gleaming in the sunlight, rolled on past the mouth of the alley. Lucas hoped his uncle would be more concerned with what so many cops were doing a block down the street. He was hoping Nate would then go investigate what was taking place at his brother's house, and leave Lucas alone. But Nate pulled his Harley to the curb, killed the rumbling engine, put his kick stand down, and dismounted.

"Dad got arrested, Uncle Nate," Lucas said, hoping to distract him.

"Yeah," Nate said. "I heard about your dad."

Lucas stared at Nate suspiciously. "Who told you about it?"

"Gypsy," Nate snapped. "Gypsy called me, Little Luke!"

The thunder of a second bike filled the air, and a hulk with dreadlocks pulled up to park his Harley beside Nate's. "Crow Harper," Lucas said, grimacing at the sight of the president of the Apaches.

Nate said, "We ain't done with this. And you're gonna help me."

"No," Lucas said, quite firmly. "I'm not. You are dirty and evil,

Uncle Nate. Far as I am concerned, your compass is broken."

Crow Harper shook back his dreadlocks as he walked up beside Nate. He gruffly said, "Told you I would handle this."

Staring at the large biker, Khalid said. "A ten-thousand dollar deal with an MC out of Omaha, involving an award-winning dog that put a big crunch on the narcotics business of a cartel? Surely, I thought, this had to be a farfetched tale. But then, I happened to get evidence that lent credence to what my son was telling me."

Khalid shifted his cane to his other hand so that he could reach inside his suit jacket and remove his cell phone. The Muslim man held the phone up so that Lucas, Nate, and Crow could clearly see the screen, which showed Harper planting the bag in Stone's truck.

Lucas gasped, "Did you help set him up, Uncle Nate?"

"Shut up, Luke!" Nate growled. "Give me that phone, Arab!"

Khalid closed his phone, slipping it into his pocket.

Nate ordered, "Take that phone away from him, Crow!"

Khalid struck Crow in the forehead with his cane, sending him floundering down to the curb. Nate was on him a second later. Lucas heard a whoosh of sound coming from the swinging cane, and then Crack! Nate was struck in the solar plexus. Khalid moved so swiftly that Lucas stood there, wide-eyed and watching him deliver a series of well-aimed blows with his cane.

Snick! Snack! Crack! The man moved like a fencer, his cane held out before him as he landed sharp blows to Nate's chest, stomach, and groin. Nate was already falling when, Crack! Khalid jabbed him in the forehead, sending him landing in the street beside Crow.

While Crow simply sat there, looking like he was trying to figure out where he was, Nate was out cold.

Khalid said, "I would advise that we move away from here."

Lucas and Ali fell in behind him as he moved down the opposite alley. Goblin stayed close on Lucas's heels. "Nate did this to Dad," he said, fighting hard not to sob. Ali said, "I recorded it. It is proof that it did not belong to—"

"Dad!" Lucas snapped. "So, why didn't you guys turn it into one of those cops swarming my place?"

Khalid answered him, saying, "Which one can we trust?"

Lucas used the ends of his T-shirt sleeves to wipe the tears from his eyes. "I need to show that to Gypsy and the rest of the club."

Khalid said, "But right now, I must ask you a serious question, Lucas? You will be tempted to lie. You must not. I know you have no reason to trust me, but you acted honorably today when you defended Ali from the three little thugs. Do so now. I assure you it is imperative that I get that gun you took from Jabar this morning at your school. Jabar's father, Achmed, is on a terrorist watch list. He is here in America, posing as a film maker, but he has nefarious plans. It is my duty to stop him. You can go on lying about this gun, but why would you do so, if I'm the only person who could help your father?"

Khalid patted the cell phone inside the pocket of his suit jacket. "You need to see the bigger picture here, Lucas. Revenge by this club might be sweet, but this needs to be seen by a person of authority, such as the county attorney who is in a position to help your dad."

Pulling a handkerchief from his back pocket, Khalid said, "Here, blow your nose, son."

Accepting the handkerchief, Lucas nosily blew his nose. Wadding up the cloth, he passed it back to Khalid. "Watch it, it's snotty."

"I can deal with snot," Khalid said, placing the wadded up handkerchief back in his pocket. "You will retrieve the gun, then we will find a way to secure your father's release."

Khalid smiled slipped off his wristwatch and handed it to Ali. "Keep track of the time with this, just make sure you boys are headed for home long before it gets dark. Understood, Ali?"

Slipping the watch into the front pocket of his jeans, Ali nodded affirmatively. "Yes, Father. Home before dark."

Ten minutes later, they stood before Reason Nelson's house where Nate and Mange had abducted Lobo and Goblin from. Lucas had told Ali about dropping the gun down into the drain sewer, but when they got there, the heavy metal lid leading to the sewer would not budge. Ali wanted to just knock on the door and ask Reason for his help in lifting the lid. Lucas wanted to simply be gone before Reason even knew they had been there. And yet, even as the two boys argued over which strategy to take, Goblin gave an excited, "Whuff! Whuff!"

He then bolted up the driveway toward Reason coming through the back gate, Lobo trailing behind him. He kneeled down to catch the dog as he leaped up into his arms. "Goblin!" he said.

Reason asked, "Where did you find this little rogue, Lucas?"

Lucas lied, "Uh, my dad found him. He's actually my dog."

Reason said, "Goblin belongs to you? Glad the pet rescue placed him with me. Glad he's back with you. I tried to call your dad earlier, but some lady, Agent Raynes, answered your phone. She told me your dad had been arrested. I told Raynes I was your court ordered truancy tracker, and asked her if there was anything I could do to help you. All she told me is, if I saw you, I was to turn you in."

Lucas said, "So, is that your plan then? To turn me in?"

Reason narrowed his eyes slightly. "Are you a danger to yourself, or a threat to your community?"

Lucas narrowed his own eyes. "Is this a trick question?"

Reason said, "My role is to see you make it to school the rest of this year. Your business with Raynes has nothing to do with me. Your dad was arrested, right? So Raynes was determined to place you in emergency foster care, correct? Too bad Raynes didn't consult with me. I take in emergency stays all the time."

Lucas asked, "You would take me in?"

"Yes," Reason said. He stood, beckoning to his dog to follow him up onto his wrap-around front porch. "I'll need your address, Ali."

"What for?" Lucas asked, defensively.

"To pick you up for school," Reason said.

Lucas said, "Oh, yeah, right. Almost forgot."

Ali rattled off both his address and his father's cell phone number.

Reason bid the boys a good night and slipped inside his house.

"What about the gun?" Ali asked. "You promised my father."

Shooting him an annoyed look, Lucas kneeled beside the manhole in Reason's front yard, just adjacent to the drain sewer along the curb. Sticking his finger into the hole of the metal cover, Lucas grunted, "This thing weighs a ton!"

Ali said, "Maybe we could ask Reason Nelson for his help?"

"Yeah, idjit," Lucas snapped. "Tell him I tossed a gun down there and that I need help retrieving it! That should work! We're just gonna have to bite the bullet and go down to the tunnels by Ballard pool. I hate walking the sewers at night, but it's the only way to get the gun."

He added, "But we're gonna need a flashlight."

11

Chapter Eleven

Lucas decided not to return to his house to get a flashlight. He did not want to take the chance that he would have a run-in with Agent Raynes. Instead, he resorted to car-shopping. As he tip-toed up to a car parked along the darkened street, Ali was appalled that he was taking such a risk. He had never heard of snooping through a stranger's car and taking what did not belong to him.

Lucas was likely to get them both arrested for pulling such a risky prank. On the search of the sixth car, Lucas found a Maglite. It was a long-handled light, and though the batteries were a bit weak, it put forth enough light to see in the darkness of the tunnels.

Five minutes later, they stood before the tall and wide opening of the Havelock storm tunnels. The ceiling was nine feet above them with a ten-foot passage between the cold, dark walls. Ali stood gaping at the large black opening as if it were the entrance to hell. Goblin sniffed at the darkness apprehensively. He let out a weak, woof! and backed away from the tunnel mouth to take a stance behind Lucas, obviously using him for a front line defense.

Lucas said, "Nothing to be afraid of. The bats have too good of radar to smack into us. And if we do see a coon, they will likely run from us. Five blocks in and five blocks out, and we'll be home safe.

Once we get inside, you can look at all the graffiti on the walls. It's where I learned all about sex."

By the weak light of the Maglite, Lucas, Ali, and Goblin trudged along in the dark depths of the tunnels. The first three blocks, Lucas had entertained the young Muslim kid by shining the light on the colorful spray paintings taking up the walls on either side of them.

Some of the artwork was very graphic, and left Ali blinking like an owl in bright sunlight. He could not believe his eyes, that American kids had so crudely left such dirty images on the walls. Ali was just thankful his father was not there to see what he was seeing. His face burned with shame to even think that his father would see such vulgar images. Fifteen minutes into their journey into the tunnels, Lucas said, "This tunnel we are in, runs another four blocks to the railroad yards. Once, Mike Truax and Jamie Price were butt-surfing in the culvert leading into these tunnels. It had been raining, and the concrete in the culvert was slick with moss, so that they could slide down it on their butts. What they didn't expect was a flash flood to come sweeping in behind them. Danny managed to snag onto the side of the culvert and pull himself out of the water, but Mike got swept into these tunnels.

"The water was so high Mike was in nine feet of water, with only his nose between the water and the ceiling. He should have drowned, because at the end, down there at the last three blocks of the tunnel it turns to three-by-four-foot around. He got swept through there, moving so fast that later he swore he got caught in an air pocket. He went sailing along at about 60 miles per hour and got shot out of the tunnels, and into the pond at the railroad yards! And Mike lived!"

"Wow," Ali said. "I wonder was he thankful to God afterwards?"

Lucas turned to look at him in the shadows. "Don't know. I just know he never went butt-surfing ever again after that."

"I would thank Allah daily," Ali said, "if he brought me safely through such an ordeal."

"Daily?" Lucas said. "Wouldn't once be enough?"

Reason sat at his desk, Lobo snoozing peacefully on the floor behind him. He reviewed a clip from his surveillance tapes recorded from his front porch security cameras. He watched as Nate Holland opened his gate beside the house and entered his yard. He then watched as Mange scooped up Goblin from the yard. Both bikers headed to the van parked in the street. A second later, the bigger biker placed Goblin inside the open door of the van. The moment Lucas appeared on screen, waving a pistol at his uncle, Reason sat straight up in his chair.

Seconds before Stone appeared on the screen, Lucas tossed the pistol into the mouth of the drain sewer.

Reason sat there, wondering where Lucas might have nabbed the gun from, when he heard a soft knock at his front door. Lobo barked and darted into the front living room. When he opened the front door he was surprised to find Khalid standing on his porch. Khalid patted Lobo as he followed Reason outside onto the porch. He removed a device from the pocket of his jacket. "Up until fifteen minutes ago, I was keeping track of my son. Little did Ali know, but my wristwatch he carries has a GPS device inserted into it. I suppose you deem it extreme that I keep track of my son like this, correct?"

"Hey," Reason said, "I know a lot of parents who wished they could afford to run 24/7 surveillance on their defiant kids. It reminds me of the joke I used to tell many of my truant kids when I tracked them down. They asked, 'How did you find me?' And I responded, 'Your mom sewed a tracking device in the band of your underwear. I just followed the blip on my machine. It led me right to you!'"

Reason stared thoughtfully at the Muslim man. "Does this have anything to do with a gun that the two may have stumbled upon?"

Somewhat surprised, Khalid said, "Why, yes, it does."

Reason said, "I think they are in the Havelock tunnels."

Khalid said, "Do you know these tunnels well?"

Reason laughed. "Been playing in those tunnels since I was a kid."

He smirked and added, "And that GPS device? I've got a dog who is far more reliable than that."

Ali froze when a sudden sound came from the tunnel behind them. Startled by the sound of footsteps echoing off the cold cement walls, Lucas swung the Maglite up, shining its weak yellow beam down the corridor. Goblin let out a soft growl.

The foot falls ceased at once. Only silence came back at them. The flashlight beam was far too weak to pick up any shapes or forms.

"Hello?" Lucas said. "Someone back there?"

The sound of silence came back at them, and a hollow echo of, "back there . . . back there . . . back there . . ." that bounced from one side of the corridor to the other.

They traveled another ten feet when Ali said, "You seem surprised that I would thank Allah so profoundly. The reason why is, Islam is a religion that professes there is only one God, Allah. Mohammad is his messenger. It is the world's second-largest religion with over 1.8 billion followers. Islam teaches that God has guided mankind through prophets and the Quran, the verbatim word of God, and the teachings called the sunnah composed of accounts called hadith of Mohammad.

"Muslims believe that Islam is the universal faith. The Quran is considered to be the unaltered word of God. Islam originated in the early 7th century in Mecca. The Islamic Golden Age was from the 8th century to the 13th century when the expansion of the Muslim world involved caliphates and empires. Muslims are of one of two denominations: Sunni or Shia. Muslim, the word for a believer of Islam, is one who submits. Islam was once called Mohammadism, but that was offensive because it suggests that a human rather than God is central to our religion. My father prefers Saracen, as all Muslims are descended from Sarah, the wife of Abraham, and not from Hagar, his slave wife, as many claim."

They walked another two blocks, their tennis shoes slapping on the cement floor, Goblin's paws creating a soft tapping. Lucas could see a shaft of moonlight slanting down from a drain sewer ahead of them. "That is the drain I dropped the gun in."

Ali asked, "Is it loaded? Does it even have bullets in it?"

"Don't know," Lucas said, even as he used the beam of the light to study the iron rungs embedded in the wall just beneath the manhole cover nine feet above them. Off to one side of these steps was the recessed section that was situated two feet below the drain sewer opening. By the sounds of the gun clunking earlier when he'd tossed it down into the sewer opening, he figured it landed on the ledge above.

Blue moonlight seeped down from the opening above. Whipping the Maglite up, Lucas used its beam to search the darkness behind them to examine the seemingly empty corridor. He could see nothing.

"Here," he said, passing the Maglite to Ali. "Shine its light on me so I can see where I'm climbing. Goblin? Stay put. I'll be okay."

Ali raised the light beam so that it illuminated the nine iron rungs embedded in the wall leading up to the manhole cover far above them and very near the recessed ledge where Lucas figured the gun to be.

Springing up from the floor, Lucas latched onto the rung a foot above his head, and planting his feet on the rung below, he clambered up the wall. He reached into the recess, searching for the pistol. His hand closed on cold metal. He took a hold of the gun. Clinging to the one rung with one hand, he aimed the pistol down the corridor behind them, and pulled the trigger. Click! Click! Click! The cylinder turned three times, the hammer falling on empty chambers inside the gun.

Click! Click! Lucas continued to pull the trigger, hoping to at least hear a thunderous roar. But the gun held no bullets. Even if Jabar had forced Ali to take the gun from him in the bathroom, Ali would have simply pulled out an unloaded gun on his fellow students.

"Jabar is a terrorist wanna-be!" Lucas said. "He took his dad's gun to school, without even checking it for bullets!"

A low snicker drifted up the corridor toward them. Achmed Waziri pressed the trigger on the taser he held as he stepped out of the dark-ness. Sparks of blue light illuminated the narrow features of his face. His gray-streaked hair and his ratty V-shaped beard gave him a goat-like appearance. He growled, "Give me the gun!"

Clambering down the rungs to the floor of the sewer beside Ali,

Lucas shoved the pistol into the waistband of his ragged jeans. Goblin fiercely growled at Waziri as he closed in on the two boys. He raised the taser and blue sparks sizzled within its metal prongs. "Hand it over, or I zap you with this!"

Ali stood there, terrified, just thinking of drowning in his own urine. Lucas's defiance disorder was kicking in big time. This Muslim man may have been terrifying Ali, but his crude bullying tactics were setting off a rebellious rage inside of Lucas Holland.

The moment Waziri lunged at him, Lucas darted to one side, barely dodging a strike from the crackling prongs of the taser. Waziri crashed into the cement wall in the place Lucas had just vacated. Lucas ripped the Maglite out of Ali's grasp. Ali and Goblin yelped in alarm and wheeled around, fleeing down the corridor they had traveled to get there.

Pup and kid came face to face with Lobo silently slinking up the center of the tunnel. The big pit ignored the two as they cowered on the floor before him, and totally focused on the dark-clad man attacking Lucas.

Lucas's eyes widened in surprise when he saw Lobo. Attack him! his thoughts screamed. Bite him!

And though he knew it wasn't possible, he imagined he heard the pit bull say inside his head, *I find things. I find drugs. I find guns. I find things that blow up. My handler has never directed me to attack. He instructed me to find you. I have done so. My task is over here. If I injure this man, there will be consequences. I will be listed as a vicious dog. I will be quarantined, maybe even put to sleep. There are some things even my handler can't protect me from.*

Waziri moved in for what he assumed would be his last and final strike with his taser.

12

Lobo launched himself up and off the cement floor, the soft scraping of his toenails the only sound he made as he opened his jaws to bite Waziri. Having watched many seasons of Animal Planet, Lucas was quite familiar with how well-trained police dogs took down an aggressive assailant. He fully expected Lobo to clamp his powerful jaws down on the wrist of the hand that Waziri held the taser in and promptly bring his attack to an end.

What he didn't expect was Lobo to bite the Muslim man directly in the butt. Waziri screamed. The taser flew out of his hand. He hop-skipped directly into the cement wall. Lucas latched onto the dog's collar. "Okay, boy, enough. You put a damper in his hamper."

Lucas guided him away from the man, now writhing on the floor.

Ali peered down the corridor, whispering, "Someone is coming!"

Reason's voice came some distance down the passage: "Lobo? You up there, boy? Where did you get to?"

Lobo gave a soft whine. Lucas released him, whispering, "Go, boy. Go meet up with your master. Sounds like he's worried about you."

Lobo took off down the tunnel, barking a greeting even as he ran.

Lucas, Ali, and Goblin whirled around, racing in the opposite direction of Reason. Three blocks ahead of them, a circle of white light marked the exit of the tunnels. If they ran in silence, perhaps they could enter into the railroad yards and slip away into the night, without the dog handler even knowing they had been there.

As they ran, Lucas adjusted the pistol he'd crammed into the waistband of his jeans, making sure it didn't fall out.

If Lucas hadn't of latched onto Goblin when they came to the end of the tunnels, the little pup would have plunged into the pond that lay directly before them. As it was, he tottered on the rim of the concrete tunnel, fighting to keep his balance. The scummy waters of the pond stretched before them thirty feet out from the tunnel exit. One more step and Goblin would have been swimming.

"Skirt the pond," Lucas instructed Ali as he scooped up the pup and darted in front of him, leaping down to the bank to the immediate right of the exit point. He landed solidly on the grassy bank. A second later, Ali came down beside him, barely avoiding a fall into the green waters of the pond.

Lucas tossed down the Maglite as the moon was bright overhead. "Stick to this path. It leads past several sets of railroad tracks and over to a hole in the fence. Been in and out of there hundreds of times."

Ali screeched in terror when Waziri suddenly shoved him out of his way to get to Lucas. The Muslim man punched Lucas in the center of his back, sending him down to perform a painful face plant on the hard ground. Goblin flew from his hands, the gun slipped out of his waistband, and for long moments, Lucas struggled to breathe. Blackness swirled at the edge of his mind, and he nearly passed out.

Goblin scampered out of his way as Waziri scooped up the gun, then headed for the opening in the fence forty feet ahead of him.

"He has the gun!" Ali cried.

"Jesus!" Lucas snapped, clambering slowly to his knees. "To hell with that damned gun! Did you see how hard he hit me?"

Ali bolted after Waziri, a determined look on his face. Waziri was just approaching the hole in the fence when Ali made a running leap, wrapping his arms around his legs. Waziri glared down at the little Muslim boy, grappling at his legs. He raised the gun, preparing to send it down into Ali's upturned face.

Poof!

The sound caused Lucas to stare up at Waziri's face in bewilderment, his eyes fixed on the red-feathered dart stuck in the center of the Muslim man's forehead. And then, Khalid was there, the bottom end of his cane emitting a slight cloud of smoke from the opening the dart had obviously came from. The sudden strike startled Waziri and forced him to stumble away from Ali, a dazed look on his face.

"You are done now," Khalid said. Waziri fell unsteadily to one knee. Khalid reached down and removed the pistol from his grasp. Waziri produced a knife, came back to his feet, and staggered back into the tunnel, keeping Khalid at bay with the knife.

"Butthole!" Lucas spat as the man vanished into the dark depths.

Catching him by one shoulder, Khalid turned Lucas away from the tunnels. A little surprised to see Reason there with Khalid, Lucas picked up Goblin and headed toward the hole in the fence. Scrambling through the hole in the chain-link fence, Ali and Lucas reached the sidewalk running adjacent to the Havelock yards. Reason and Khalid checked to make sure Waziri was still inside the sewer, then followed the boys out of the rail yards.

It wasn't until they were three blocks away from the yards that Lucas gestured at Khalid's cane and said, "What are you? Some kind of Muslim James Bond?"

Stifling a laugh, Khalid nodded. "I had my cane patterned after a fleshette. During the Kennedy assassination in 1963, there were rumors that a fleshette had fired the fatal bullet. I dismissed this because a high caliber firing device installed in the unstable casing of an umbrella defied logic. And the bullet that blew through Kennedy's head had definitely not been a mere .22. Based on the designs of a fleshette, I paid a gunsmith in Iraq to fashion a similar device inside my cane. He installed a CO_2 powered device to send a dart down its barrel at over 120 mph. Most assassins use lethal substances on their darts shot from similar devices. I chose to use powerful tranquilizers."

Lucas said, "Would you ever sell that sucker to me?"

By the time, they reached the Karim house, Lucas was dead on his feet. Ali led him into his bedroom, where he graciously offered him his bed, saying he would take up a place on the floor since Lucas was a guest of honor. Lucas did not argue. He had no energy to do so. He simply slipped into the single bed, watched Ali gather an extra pillow and blanket from his closet. Just before spreading the blanket on the carpeted floor beside the bed, Ali picked up Goblin, placing him on the bed beside Lucas. Lucas was asleep within seconds of his head hitting the pillow. Goblin curled up beside him.

In the kitchen, Reason studied the pistol with the engravings of the scorpions and the dragons on the gun's butt and barrel. He handed it over to Khalid.

His dark eyes fixed on the single screw keeping the ivory piece in place on the butt, Khalid retrieved a set of screwdrivers from a kitchen drawer. He chose one, removed it from its case, and carefully removed the ivory piece, exposing a hollow opening in the butt.

"There you are," he said, staring down at the small black thumb drive resting inside the hollow of the butt. Placing the gun back on the counter, Khalid held the drive up. "Let's find out what's on this."

Seated beside Reason, Lobo whined as if in solid agreement.

The next morning, Khalid led Agent Raynes into his kitchen, where Reason, Lucas, and Ali were already seated at the table. Beef Tory, still recovering from his inhalation of the chemicals, joined them all a few minutes later. Looking pale and haggard, the detective was determined more than ever to get the Deep 9 off the streets. His own brush with the dust nearly took his life.

Khalid said, "First I shall lay the groundwork. The Quran contains 109 verses that speak of war with non-Muslims. Muslims who do not join the fight are told that Allah will send them to hell. Verses of violence in the Quran are known as sword verses. These passages come from a loving God, and though there are few verses of tolerance to balance out those calling for non-believers to convert to Islam, there are more Muslims who do not take the lives of unbelievers, than there are who do. As an anti-terrorist agent I prevent extremists from killing unbelievers. I'm known as the Hound because of my dogged persistence in tracking down terrorists."

Khalid held up the thumb-drive he'd retrieved from Waziri's gun. "On this, is an article entitled, Havelock, Home to Dogs of War. Until two years ago, thousands of service dogs were discarded in foreign countries. Too expensive to ship them back here, the military did not have the resources to care for them. And yet, now all US dogs are sent back here and adopted or used by law enforcement agencies.

"The article involves the Thunder Dogs, a litter of pups born on

Pine Ridge on a night the Thunder Beings were active. A Lakota holy man, Colton Lone Wolf, gifted these pups to an elite company of Cheyenne K9 handlers, who led dozens of bomb-finding raids in Iraq. No one can explain how they survived so many missions, yet they walked away, unscathed. Wolf claimed they had brushed up against the Otherworld like Crazy Horse who rode into hundreds of battles and was never struck by bullets. They became the Ghost Company.

"On the day the Islamic State overran Mosul in 2014, a deadly weapon was left behind: A cache of cobalt-60, with high levels of radiation inside a therapy machine, ingredients of a dirty bomb. The Ghosts were sent into Mosul to find it. They played a game of cat and mouse with the Vipers, securing the campus where the machine was found. Rather than alert the Vipers to what they were guarding, the Ghosts led them on a chase and ended up trapped at a dead end in the city. They were rescued by my Phantom agents and I.

"ISIS never did find the cobalt-60. One official said, 'They are not that smart.' Those words reverberated throughout the Muslim world, stinging ISIS badly. When they discovered it was a unit of K9 handlers who humiliated them, ISIS determined to exact revenge on the unclean dogs causing them to be the laughing stock of the world.

"The Vipers put out contracts on the dogs of the Ghosts. The dogs were shipped out of the war zone and placed in quarantine at a dog rescue ranch. The Ghosts now work at the compound, helping service dogs transition here from other war zones. Currently, they are caring for two-hundred dogs at Wounded Arrow, owned by Lakota dog handler, Ben Black Bull. The directives on this drive indicate Waziri is to use chemicals in the ventilation system where the dogs are kept."

Lucas sprang out of his chair. "Someone should let Ben know about this terrorist! I lived out at Wounded Arrow this past year, and I should warn Ben of the threat by Waziri!"

"No one," Raynes said, "is taking this information outside this room! This is a matter of National security! Khalid, you know the stir this will cause among Islamaphobes. Americans emotionally attached to their dogs would get highly offended if extremists targeted these service dogs. This is a powder keg! This will only turn up the level of hatred of millions of peaceful Muslims."

"My own people," Khalid said, "should be just as offended by such an attack. As an honored guest here, my assimilation includes protecting my people. Your people. Your dogs. If I can prevent these few from causing harm on your soil, for the love of Allah, I will."

Lucas turned to pick up Goblin. He handed the pup over to Ali, whispering, "Take care of him for me, will you?"

Ali made a sour face as Goblin turned his head to sniff and lick at his face. "Dirty!" he gasped. "Unclean!" Lucas patted Ali on the head and said, "That's the spirit!"

He whispered, "Take care of him until I can sneak back here."

Raynes said, "This information must remain strictly confidential!"

Beef said, "Like they did in Europe, keeping the citizens in the dark in regards to the radicalized? This plot to kill service dogs needs to be stopped. The information on the thumb-drive should start an investigation as to what an imam was doing giving Waziri instructions like those on the drive. These dogs served our country. The psycho-logical damage would be harmful to the handlers. Extremists like Waziri use any means to destroy their enemies once they have infiltrated a country. And the hurt this would our cause, would have a harmful impact on those who loved these dogs."

At that point, Lucas bolted and ran out the door.

13

Chapter Thirteen

By noon that day, Lucas was amazed that Reason managed to track him down; more amazed that the long-haired truancy tracker got the jump on him. He was hiding out in his tree house after ditching Raynes. It was located in an oak tree beside the Holland house. When Reason knocked on his door, Lucas sprang out through the window, scrambling to the ground ten feet below.

The moment he did, Reason dropped to the ground and took him down with a flying tackle. So stunned by the move, Lucas failed to even put up a fight. He said, "Ain't that child abuse or something?"

Reason simply smirked. "I was obligated to catch you. After Agent Raynes put an ABP out on you, I asked Judge Sully if I could provide emergency foster care for you, as I don't think Raynes has your best interest in mind. Sully agreed, and so here I am."

As Reason walked him toward the Holland house to pick up extra clothes for his temporary stay, he appeared to be deeply troubled.

"What's wrong?" Lucas said. "Is it my dad?"

Reason said, "Beef Tory took Khalid's phone recording to the city attorney. He wants to question Crow before they release your dad. They still suspect he may have been involved. Beef tried to convince the county attorney that your dad detests drugs, but he is keeping your dad in custody, especially since the powder contained in that packet was laced with Deep 9. Beef drove out to Wounded Arrow and warned Ben about Waziri's plans. To safeguard the dogs, Ben contacted the American Vets, asking them to ride out to the ranch. Raynes is having a fit because of the News folk doing stories on why they are now guarding this ranch. She is furious with me."

Lucas offered him a confused look. "You? Why you?"

Reason said, "Despite the fact she tried to stop me with a gag order, I uploaded the story of this potential attack online. Due to my story on Storm Haven, more biker clubs are now volunteering to stand guard duty at Wounded Arrow to prevent these Vipers from taking revenge on the Ghosts. In case any more extremist operatives receive directions to attack these service dogs, they are locked and loaded."

Lucas stared at him. "This is all good, right? So, what's wrong?"

Reason said, "Someone broke into my house and stole Lobo."

As Lucas hastily shoved clothes into a backpack, he felt really bad for Reason. Of course, he knew who had taken the dog, he just wasn't able to share with Reason that Lobo had already been stolen once before by Nate. Biker code would not allow him to snitch on his uncle. Tears came unbidden to his eyes. Although he shared no bond with Lobo, he still felt really bad for him, knowing he was to be heartlessly thrown into the fighting ring as a bait dog at the Barn. His shoulders shook and he sniffled, then he broke down and outright cried for the loss of Reason's dog.

A sudden rumble came from the front of the Holland house. Lucas sucked in a ragged breath and listened keenly to the Harley approaching from the west. Slinging the backpack over one shoulder, he ran down the hallway, using his free hand to wipe the tear streaks from his face. As he neared the front door he heard Reason say, "Sweet Jesus!"

Peering out through the screen door, Lucas watched the rider park his Harley in front of the Holland house and shut it down. He was tall and rangy, his long, gray hair reminding Lucas of a wolf. He thought, Sam Elliot from Roadhouse, or Aragorn from the Lord of the Rings.

The man approached Reason, the ghost of a smile on his

weathered face. "Why are you standing on Stone Holland's porch, son? I thought you didn't like big, bad bikers."

After a heavy sigh, Reason responded, "Hi, Dad."

Lucas stepped out onto the porch, stunned. "Rain Nelson is your dad, Reason? President of the Outlaws? Why didn't you tell me this?"

The grizzly biker gave Lucas a curious look.

Reason said, "Dad, this is Stone's son, Lucas. He's been placed in my custody while Stone is in jail."

Lucas said, "Dad told me that long ago the Angels came to Lincoln to settle a fight between the Screaming Eagles and the Association. During that meeting, the Angels disbanded the Association, creating Nomads, who later became the Den. The Angels tried to shut the Den down. Hell's Angels reign over Nebraska. Dad said you went and had a face-face with the president of the Angels in Omaha, asking him to sanction the Elder's Den here in Havelock."

Rain looked over at Lucas with a rueful grin. "This is touching, the history of the Den and Outlaws, but I've no time for chit-chat."

Rain ran a hand through his gray hair, feathering his shaggy bangs. "Got a call from your dad. You are on the radar of the Apaches. Crow Harper is in business with the Juarez cartel, and they are pissed at him over the cancellation of some dog fight you interfered in."

Reason said, "Cops are looking for this president of the Apaches. They won't release Stone until they hear Harper's side of the story. Maybe you could put out a biker ABP on Crow. If Crow is serious about harming Lucas, just get the guy off the streets!"

Lucas wished he could zip Reason's lips shut. Rain should have been angry with him for making ignorant suggestions on how to eliminate this Apache problem, yet he grinned, amused that his son was schooling him on how to handle this issue.

He looked up at Rain and said, "You want to go to church with the Den? Their council table is behind the house in the barn in our backyard. But the two of you might not be welcome there."

The three of them walked behind the Holland house and to the big red barn at the back of the property. In a gravel-covered parking lot adjacent to the alley were thirty Harleys, some fully dressed, others chopped and sporting ape-hanger handle bars. The door of the barn was closed as church for the Den was in session. Lucas pounded on the door with one small fist. The door of the barn opened and the warlord of the Elder's Den stepped outside. Tall and slender with shoulder-length raven hair, due to his Romani blood-line, Gypsy was Cingane with a family heritage that stretched back to Wallachia when Gypsies roamed that countryside in painted wagons. Lucas had heard tales of Vlad the Impaler so many times from Gypsy that he knew them by heart. The dark-skinned man had been his dad's right hand man for twenty years and there was no one that Stone trusted more. And yet, Gypsy also had a history with Rain of the Outlaws, having once rode with them long ago.

Gypsy's black eyes flickered over to Reason, while Rain made his case to be allowed into the Den's council meeting. "Yes," he said, "I grant you permission to attend church, Rain. And you, Writer, I'm going to make an exception. If you'll tell us about this plot to kill service dogs."

Gypsy then reached out and ruffled Lucas's tangles of golden hair. "Sorry, Little Luke, church is not for you."

Lucas said, "President of the Outlaws comes to speak to the Den about me, and I am not allowed? I got a right to hear this. Besides, Reason's dog was stolen by Uncle Nate. I came to get him back!"

Despite Gypsy's objections, Reason, Lucas, and Rain followed the Den's warlord into the barn, and then stood before the large, oak council table, and due to protocol, waited in silence. At the sight of Rain standing in Den territory, Nate lurched to his feet, clutching a wooden gavel in his fist. "What the hell, Gypsy?"

Taking a seat at the table amidst twenty other Den members, Gypsy said, "Didn't Stone make a ruling about your bait dog business?"

Nate stood there, gripping the gavel. "What the hell does that have to do with allowing trespassers into church, Gypsy?"

"We're about to find out," Gypsy responded, flatly.

Upon seeing that the rest of the club members were intrigued by the Outlaw president invading their space, Nate yielded the floor to him. Rain said, "Stone called me from jail. He was worried about his son. Seems he got himself in the crosshairs of Crow Harper, Apache from the Big O. I'm here to put the Elder's Den on full alert."

Nate said, "Message received. Little Luke can stay with me until Stone gets released. The Den will place him on a 24/7 watch."

Lucas opened his mouth to protest, but Rain said, "Stone doesn't want Lucas staying with you. Instead, he wants you to confront Crow, and get things settled with this cartel. This deal you made with this Apache set things in motion to go very wrong for your nephew."

From his place at the end of the council table, Lucas said, "You broke Dad's rule, Uncle Nate. This dog fighting is a cruel sport. Only heartless men throw two dogs together to have them tear each other to pieces! You stole Reason's award-winning sniffer. But I stole him back! And now you have the Juarez cartel pissed at you for spoiling a dog fight that they had investments in."

Rain said, "I'm here at Stone's request to see that you settle things up with the Apaches and the Juarez cartel, Nathan."

Lucas scanned the faces of the Den members, expecting to see them all glaring at the Outlaw in rage, yet finding instead, that they were all staring at Nate, unreadable expressions on their faces. Rain glanced at Nate. "You dug a hole, Brother. The Angels have their own problem with this particular cartel at the moment. We don't need any sparks flying between the Outlaws and the Den. If the Angels go to war, they're gonna need all of us on board. Any petty squabbles right now is unacceptable. You understand?"

Giving Rain an ugly sneer, Nate slowly nodded.

Lucas said. "Do you have Reason's dog?"

Nate replied, "Do I look like I have a dog on me?"

Gypsy said, "Lucas? Go out to the kennel. Get the dog there."

"Damn you, Gypsy!" snapped Nate.

"No," Rain said, "damn you for what you do to these dogs!"

Lucas exited the barn through the back door and immediately spotted Lobo. He opened the kennel gate, receiving a good dose of attention from him. Lobo then trailed him out to the street to Reason's van.

Lucas opened the side door, ushering Lobo inside. Closing the door, he returned to the barn.

The moment he stepped inside, Reason said, "Got my dog?"

"Yep," Lucas said. "He's safe inside the van."

Suddenly remembering the reward that Reason had given him for returning Lobo, Lucas said, "Uncle Nate, Grunge is fighting this weekend, right? Would two-hundred dollars buy him a pardon?"

Nate snorted. "Hell, no! I've got five-hundred placed on Grunge to win against some killer cross-bred wolf dog! You got five-hundred squirreled away in those pockets of yours, Little Luke?"

Lucas dug into his pocket and withdrew the hundred dollar bills. He slapped them down on the table, "There, I'll owe you three!"

Nate picked up the money. Slowly, he unfolded it, his eyes widening in surprise. "Where in the hell did you get this, Little Luke?"

Rain said, "You're talking about Grunge, right? It's a shame what has become of such a noble dog." He removed his billfold from a back pocket of his jeans. He opened it, pulled out a one-hundred dollar bill, and placed it on top of the other two on the council table. Nate snorted, "Three-hundred? Don't quite cut it, dude."

There was a stir amongst the Den club members, and seconds later, Gypsy, Toker, Big Charlie, and Ratchett had placed their own money on the table directly in front of Lucas. The gesture brought tears to his eyes, and he quickly wiped at his cheeks before they ran down his face, making him look like a baby before his father's club.

Gypsy slid the pile of bills over in front of Nate. Nate picked them up and counted them. He said, "Seven-hundred dollars? What I am supposed to do about the fight?"

Rain said, "Scrap this particular fight. Besides, if you and the kid were playing Chess, he put you in Check. I admire his spunk. Keep that same attitude, kid, your dad will make you a prospect by the time you're fourteen. Look me up one day. I'll tell you Grunge's story. Ironically, Lobo is of the same blood line, just different litters."

Gypsy looked at Reason. "Writer, some members of the Den read your books while serving time at county. A few read your books at treatment. Two of them read them serving Federal at Yankton."

Reason looked around the table and was relieved to see curious looks rather than hostile glares directed at him. Lucas was slightly impressed to think that so many members of his dad's club had read Reason's books.

"Tell us, Writer," Gypsy said, "about this terrorist threat to destroy service dogs."

14

Nate Holland opened his front door after Agent Raynes rang his doorbell three times in rapid succession. "Raynes," he said. "The answer is no. You saw what that powder did to Tory, and I am not putting myself at risk. Period. End of story."

Raynes said, "I need you. I researched Waziri. He's a known terrorist, and yet he has committed no crimes here. The consensus at Homeland is to give him enough rope to hang himself. Khalid intervened last night, foiling plans regarding US service dogs. But Waziri contacted the imam who first sent him directives to destroy those dogs. I know you are an informant, who has infiltrated this particular cell, and you know Waziri plans to assassinate Khalid."

Placing her purse and laptop on the wooden picnic table on Nate's front porch, Raynes rummaged around in her purse, producing a handheld GPS device. "I know you met with Waziri. With the GPS device you managed to install in his pistol, I've been keeping track of him throughout the day."

Nate said, "You've just been following this blip all over Havelock? You didn't actually have eyes on the target all this time?"

Raynes said, "My superiors considered our options. Since Havelock is such a small suburb, they did not put a tail on him, knowing he could easily spot an agent shadowing him. If the gun gets near Khalid's residence, then agents are waiting on standby. My superiors suggested that since you grew up in this area, you would help us keep track of the—"

"The beeping gun," Nate said, interrupting her, "before it becomes the smoking gun? Is that it, Raynes?"

Rayne's gaze fixed on the GPS device. She handed it to him. Nate tapped the Program button and read the times and locations to determine where Waziri had been so far. Raynes removed the thin thumbdrive from the GPS device and slipped it into the port of her laptop. They studied the screen together, reading the coordinates. "Odd," he said, "this indicates he frequented the playground of the park all four visits. You sure that's Waziri carrying that gun? Why would a grown man visit the park playground four times in one day?"

Khalid had just placed a pistol on a shelf in the kitchen, when Ali stepped through kitchen doorway, Goblin trailing behind him.

"Father," he said, forlornly. "The pup is hungry again."

"Okay, my son," Khalid said, forcing himself to smile as Ali entered the kitchen. "I shall feed you both."

For several moments, Khalid busied himself placing a glass of milk and a box of graham crackers on the kitchen table. He then placed a bowl of milk on the floor for Goblin. The phone rang on the kitchen counter. Ali, dipping a graham cracker in his glass of milk, noted his father's rigid stance. Khalid answered the phone, saying, "Agent Raynes, I already know Waziri has obtained another of the Viper pistols. And you think the tracking device inside the gun will give you warning before Waziri makes his move? I appreciate your surveillance, but I have prepared for a possible visit by him."

Khalid eyed the pistol he had just placed on the nearby shelf. It was a Mosin Nagant, complete with a sound suppressor. The Hound was an experienced hunter. He had stalked dozens of extremist prey to their lairs and safe houses. Each time, he'd been fortunate to catch his targets unprepared for his sudden, deadly attack. He had succeeded on each of these missions only because the terrorists had become careless, a carelessness that had worked in Khalid's favor. He would not make the same mistake they had. He was armed and ready.

Hanging up the phone, he said, "You, my son, must go and visit Lucas at Reason's house. Authorities have not yet released his father.

Perhaps the boy might enjoy your company. Besides, returning Goblin would be a nice gesture. He likes you more than he lets on. Besides, I want you to get acquainted with Reason's dog—"

"His dog?" Ali blurted. "Unclean beast?"

Khalid said, "I am considering getting one for our household."

"But," Ali interjected, "the Quran says—"

"My son," Khalid said, "Allah looks kindly on those who care for the creatures he has created. Many great followers of Islam have owned noble hounds throughout history. Some to guard their houses. Some to hunt with. Others to just grow fat and lazy. A dog would compliment our house."

Khalid picked up two large envelopes. "Make certain Reason gets these. They are dossiers of Waziri and his operative. If I am forced to eliminate the two men, those dossiers should prevent me from ending up like Lucas's dad when the smoke has cleared in this situation."

Ali said, "I listened last night to your phone call to Iraq. You asked about a green light. What did you mean by that?"

Khalid wanted to end their conversation on a good note. It could be the last time on this earth that they spoke to each other, and he did not want to send his son away thinking he was disappointed in him.

Forcing a slight smile, Khalid said, "Ali, you do know Waziri is a very bad man, right? The threat on the service dogs is bad enough, but this particular two-man cell that he leads is responsible for the bombing of a mosque back in Iraq. One that killed not only the imam of that mosque but dozens of men, women, and children. It was an indiscriminate bombing that was not carried out on enemy insurgents, but upon innocent Muslims there that day to worship Allah. Waziri is an evil man. The worst of the worst.

"And yes, I have been given a green light to take him out, my son."

For a kid with such low self-esteem, Lucas felt good about himself. Reason said, "Rules were broken to allow you in church, yet the diplomatic skills you showed maneuvering your uncle into that deal over that dog were awesome. If some ghostly scribe is keeping track of biker history somewhere beyond the clouds, I'm sure his ink was barely dry on the page when you brought Grunge's fight to the council table. Amazing, kid, simply amazing!"

Most of his life Lucas had put up with his dad's constant belittling, figuring that it just came with the territory of being the son of a biker president. Any time he got into trouble at school, Lucas knew he had coming whatever punishment his dad dealt out to him. Stone had no parenting skills, nor was he the nurturing type, and yet rarely did he lay a hand on him. But still, he did a lot psychological damage addressing his son's behavior problems with angry tirades that rolled around inside of Lucas's head for days afterwards.

Lucas often sat in school, listening to his fellow classmates complaining about a scolding they received from their parents. Yeah, he thought, boo hoo! Try these words on, you big cry babies! Twisted! Mental! Wrongly-wired! Stupid! Retarded! Betcha never hear that coming from your mom or dad. Happens all the time at my house. My dad is a real motivational speaker when he wants to be! Lucas had never had anyone talk so positively about him like Reason did.

"Thanks," he finally managed to say, turning his head so Reason couldn't see how red his face was turning at such high praise.

Kneeling in the back of the van, Reason laughed. "And no dog had a better advocate for his cause, Lucas. You did good, kid."

Lobo nosed Reason's left hand, while Goblin wormed his way beneath his right one. Reason hugged each one, then turned to exit through the open side door.

Rain approached the van. He said, "Heading out to Wounded Arrow to make sure the boys have a welcoming party set up in for these damned terrorists."

Upon seeing Gypsy walking toward Reason's van parked along the side street, Rain turned to leave. "See you later, son."

Reason quietly said, "Yeah, see you, Dad."

He turned to face Gypsy as he walked up to the van. The warlord said, "You made it clear that Lucas has been placed in your custody while Stone is locked up. Now let me make this clear, the Den is parking an RV in your driveway in the next ten minutes. We are posting two club members inside for a 24/7 watch on Lucas. Anything less with this threat by Crow, and Stone will take it personal that the Den did not take this seriously enough. Agreed?"

Reason said, "Fine by me."

On the drive back over to Reason's house, Lucas eye-balled him. "Do you have a gun?"

"That," Reason said, "is a long story. It all started on my tenth Birthday. Mine was July 9th. My friend, Tommy Wolfe's was July 4th. Our moms used to have our parties together. They invited about a hundred kids so Tommy and I would get a ton of presents.

"On our tenth Birthday, I got a bow and arrow. Tom bet me that I couldn't hit a running target. He ran. I fired. And I hit him on the nose! He screamed like an Irish Banshee! His dad broke my bow over his knee, and ended our friendship."

Lucas gave a chuckle. "That sucks."

Nodding, Reason said, "Not as bad as what Tommy Wolfe pulled ten years later. I grew up to be a drug counselor. He grew up to be a drug dealer. He got busted one night for breaking into a pharmacy. He gave the arresting officer my name and my date of birth. When he didn't show up for court, they put out an arrest warrant on me. Luckily, Captain Jake of the Narco squad knew me from my youth work. He walked me up to the City Prosecutor's office. I was given his card to use in case I was ever stopped. I had to use that card several times after that. Captain Jake suggested I get a pair of handcuffs and track Wolfe down. His exact words were, 'Cuff him to a telephone pole! Call us! We'll come and get him!' I never did find Wolfe. But I met a lot of dealers in my search. Many of them associated with a murdered narc named Kelly Drake. Later, I wrote a book about her."

Reason let out a long sigh. "My dad, an Irishman to the core, claims this whole story is like a Celtic Hoop, one strand of fate interweaves with another, and like a snake chasing its tail, it keeps circling back to impact my life. You see, when I was a kid, I stumbled across the evidence to solve her murder. I actually had a run-in with the man who killed her: Jack Holland, your grandfather. And your uncle Nate vowed vengeance for his death. He may come and visit me one day. And that's the reason I got a gun."

Lucas thought about it some more, and finally concluded, "I never knew my grandfather. Sounds like Grandpa Jack was a bad man."

Reason laughed. "Too bad I was such a good shot with that bow. If I had missed, none of those other things would have happened."

15

Chapter Fifteen

Ali sat there on the front porch, looking up to greet them as Reason pulled his van into his driveway. Lucas noted the little Muslim kid's forlorn demeanor as he peered at them with tear-glazed eyes. "What's up?" Lucas asked, clambering out of the van and kneeling down to greet Goblin who was glad to see him.

Reason busied himself let Lobo out of the van, then led him to his fenced yard at the back end of the driveway. When he returned to the front porch, Ali handed him the two thick envelopes he'd carried from home. "Here," he said, "from my father. So that he does not end up in jail like Lucas's father."

Puzzled, Lucas said, "Why don't you start making sense, Ali?"

"Shhh," came from Reason as he gestured at Lucas to remain silent. "What's wrong, Ali? Has something happened to your father?"

Ali sniffled. His small nose scrunched up as worry lines creased his brow. "It is not what has happened, but what is soon to happen."

Tucking the envelopes under his arm, Reason said, "Your father is in danger?"

"Yes," Ali said. "But not the danger you are thinking. He is the Hound, a title he earned as an Agent of Phantom. He is a dangerous man. He portrays himself as a kindly man devoted to his faith, one who is scholarly, educated, and well-refined. But he is a badger when cornered. And if Waziri invades our house to assassinate the Hound, it is he who will die."

Reason said, "So, what is your fear, Ali?"

"Having a future," Ali said, "with my father. If he kills this terror cell, what will your courts do with him?"

Reason had to be strict with the two boys, sternly telling them they were to remain inside where they could play video games. He told him there was nothing they could do to help Khalid, who had sent Ali there, expecting Reason to keep him safe until he was done with his business. Lucas turned defensive, calling Reason a big pussy.

By Ali's account, he knew that Khalid may be facing two men sent to kill him because of his role as an anti-terrorist agent. He admitted that he should not care, telling Reason, "My own dad would be ashamed of me for even wanting to defend a Muslim, but he didn't see how Khalid handled himself when Nate and Crow attacked him. Nor did he see that encounter with Waziri at the train yards. Hell, he shot a damned dart into his forehead, using only his cane! And if you weren't such a pussy, you'd let me go get Big Charlie and Ratchett from their guard station out front in the RV. We could then go over there and deal with these stupid fools! Charlie and Ratchett are armed, I can guarantee you, and they could—""Have a shoot-out?" Reason said. "Great idea, Lu

In a huff, Lucas stormed off to the backyard, Ali and Goblin trailing behind him. As a safeguard, Reason stationed himself in his den where he could keep an eye on the two boys as he read the files inside the dossiers Ali had given him.

Lobo nosed him and whined, knowing that Goblin had gone outside with Lucas and Ali. Soon, he began prancing around. Looking up from the files spread on his desk before him, Reason checked to make sure the boys were playing ball with Goblin in the yard, then told the dog, "Let him sort this out. Take a nap."

Lobo whined again.

"Lobo?" Reason said, not looking up from reading. The big dog turned and with a grunt of displeasure, sprang up, planting his front paws on the windowsill so he could peer outside.

It only took Reason five minutes to discover just how dangerous Achmed Waziri and Fariq Abdullah actually were. Their terror attacks took up an entire page in the files. The two men had grown up together in Syria, where as young boys they had had Islamic verses instilled within them by radicalized mullahs. As Boy Warriors, they had vowed to become Jihadis, taking the fight to any one who opposed Islam in any way. While America was always front and center in their warfare to please Allah, France, Germany, Spain, and Morocco also felt the burn of their righteous wrath. Many bombings in those countries were attributed to the two Muslim men.

Two minutes after viewing the files, Reason tried getting a hold of Khalid on the phone. But his call was sent to voice mail, and Khalid did not answer. Frustrated at feeling so helpless, and with Lucas's words ringing in his ears, Reason sat there fuming in silence.

Lucas sauntered over to the back gate. He shot a wary look toward the house, where he saw Reason seated at his desk in his den. When certain he wasn't looking his way, he gestured to Ali as he opened the gate and darted out into the alley.

Nearly tripping over Goblin who eagerly followed Lucas out into the alley, Ali said, "Have you no sense of honor? Reason has opened his home to you, and this is how you repay him?"

For a moment, Lucas actually felt bad. Ali was always one to do the right thing in any circumstance, even when two mad-dog killers might be headed for his house and gunning for his dad. And Lucas did appreciate the fact that Reason had stepped up to the plate, intervening when Agent Raynes had wanted him locked up. In a way, he felt bad that he was breaking Reason's trust, but his defiance disorder overruled those feelings.

"Do you want to save your dad?" Lucas asked Ali. "If we show up over there, there ain't no way Waziri would carry out a hit on him."

Ali stepped into the alley, closing the gate behind him. "Have you not heard anything I have said, Lucas? I do not fear for my father. He is capable of dealing with these assassins. Besides, these Muslim men would not hesitate to kill you. In fact, they would enjoy doing so."

Lucas continued on down the alley, Goblin loping behind him. "I'm going over there. If it was my dad, I would want to do everything I could to save him. Or don't Muslims believe in loyalty?"

Spurred to anger by the remark, Ali said, "Do not question my loyalty. I love my father as much as you do yours, Lucas Holland!"

Lucas quickened his pace, his sights on the end of the alley three garages away, when suddenly, Goblin skidded to an abrupt halt, his gaze fixed on the last garage at the opening to the alley.

Lucas attempted to step out around the pup, but Goblin wheeled around and planted himself directly in front of him. He peered up at Lucas, then turned his head to look back down the alley, a mixture of growls and barks erupting from his tiny mouth.

Once again, Lucas moved to go out around the pup, but Goblin leaped up, planting his front paws on his knees. His tiny claws made soft scraping sounds as they slid down the fabric of Lucas's jeans.

"What in the hell's with you?" Lucas said, slightly alarmed by the pup's behavior. Goblin sprang back to his paws, took a rigid stance, and peered down the alley to the last garage, growling fiercely.

Ali stared at the alley opening. "Look," he whispered, "there's a shadow! Someone is hiding there beside that garage!"

Lucas said, "You're just trying to scare me from going over to your dad's. There's no shadow—"

Yes, there is! came a soft voice inside his head. *There is danger there! Do not go any farther! There is a man waiting there!*

Lucas sucked in his breath, his eyes gone wide, his mouth hanging ajar. Goblin? he thought. Are you speaking inside my head? Can I hear you just like I did Lobo in the tunnels? Is this some sort of mind trick, pulled on a human by a dog?

No trick, came the soft, child-like voice inside his head. *I am trying to warn you of danger. There is a man at the end of the alleyway who means to do you great harm. Trust me. Go back inside the yard. Go back inside the house. Now!*

Lucas gasped, "Holy crap! This pup is talking to me!"

Ali kept his gaze fixed on the shadow darkening the alley opening. "So am I, Lucas! Let's just go back inside Reason's house!"

Snorting an astonished laugh, Lucas said, "That's what Goblin just said . . . inside my head! This happened once before with Lobo back in the tunnels. I can hear dogs? Either that, or I am losing my mind!"

Reason hurried into his den, where he removed his 9 millimeter Ruger from his gun safe. He tucked it into the back of his jeans, draping his shirt over it, for fear some neighbor would become alarmed by an armed man running down the streets of Havelock.

Before closing the safe, logic kicked in, and Reason seriously thought about what he was about to do. When he'd first purchased his gun, he had checked the laws in regards to shooting a home invader. If the invader had broken into his home and was armed, then it would be justified to shoot him. The key words being: Inside the house.

He had read several stories of home invaders getting shot before or after they had entered a house, and the law was specific when it came to shooting them then. There was a good chance the shooter, whether he owned the property or not, would be cited for homicide if he shot and killed someone merely trespassing on his property.

Thinking of another way to deal with Waziri, he removed the handcuffs he kept in the safe. As he turned to exit the den, he looked out the window and saw that Lucas, Ali, and Goblin had vanished.

16

Performing a quick shuffle, Lucas managed to dodge to one side of the persistent Goblin as the pit puppy tried one last time to keep him from proceeding down the alley. He saw before him a clear path to the end of the block and he bolted ahead of the pup.

Nooooo! came Goblin's voice inside his head.

Unnerved by the spooky way he could actually hear the pup's thoughts, Lucas glanced back in bafflement. The next thing he knew a burly biker with dreadlocks stepped out from beside the last garage at the end of the alley. Running at full bore, Lucas ran right into him, performing a painful face-plant on the big man's mid-section.

"Gotcha!" Crow Harper said, grabbing at him.

Shoving himself away from the Apache president, Lucas back-pedaled, ducking beneath his grasping hands. Before Crow could close in on him, Goblin darted boldly between them, placing himself directly in front of Lucas. The pit pup growled fiercely at the grungy biker glaring back down at him.

"Shut up!" Crow snapped as he reached down and snatched the pup up into his grasp. Grabbing onto the scruff of his neck, he drew a gun from beneath his sleeveless jean jacket. Even as Goblin began to desperately squirm, Crow planted the muzzle of his pistol against the pup's head. "Lucas?" he growled. "Come with me or I will put a bullet in this flea bag's head!"

Click! echoed across the alley, causing Crow to freeze.

"I've never shot a man before," Reason said, taking a firmer grip on his pistol as he shoved the muzzle up against Crow's left temple. "But if you don't drop your gun and lower that pup to the ground, Harper, I swear I'll send you to see Jesus!"

Lucas stood there, totally caught off guard by Reason appearing from around the side of the garage and behind the ruthless biker. Lucas sprang forward and snatched Goblin out of Crow's grasp. Crow attempted to wheel around, but Reason struck him forcefully in the side of his head with the butt of his gun, dropping him to his knees. Crow groaned and his gun fell from his hand, even as blood spilled from the cut on his head.

"Lucas! Ali!" Reason said, removing his cuffs from his back pocket. "Take Goblin and get back inside the house! Now!"

Without bothering to see if the boys obeyed him, Reason snapped one cuff on Crow's right wrist, then forced the dazed biker over to a metal dumpster beside the garage, his eyes fixed on the iron handle on the side of the metal container. Reason snapped the cuff around the handle, and Crow slumped down beside the dumpster out cold.

Goblin followed Lucas as he ran down the street. "I'm heading to your house!" Lucas said over one shoulder.

Running beside the pit bull puppy, Ali said, "Next time, listen to me, Lucas! You are bullheaded always!"

Lucas said, "And your point?"

"Point is," Ali snapped, "if we get to my father's house and Waziri is there, listen to me, or you might die from your own stupidity!"

Lucas continued to run. "Don't call me stupid, Idjit!"

To which Ali responded, "Don't call me Idjit, Stupid!"

Reason scooped up Crow's pistol and headed back to his house. Inside the house, he placed a call to the Lincoln police, informing them that a man who had a warrant out for his arrest was now waiting for them to pick him up out in his alley. He then searched the house for Lucas and Ali. Unable to find the two boys, he opened the screen door to step outside. In a mad dash, Lobo shot past him and headed directly to his van parked in the street. Reason ushered the dog into the van and drove off, his tires screeching.

Khalid sat in his reclining chair in the living room of his house. Beside him on the end table was his Mosin Nagant. It was a powerful weapon and would do considerable damage to a human target. Khalid was confident he would only need one shot to eliminate the threat that Waziri posed. As an agent of Phantom, he was an ex-pert with firearms, and knew exactly where to place a bullet in an enemy, to either wound or kill. In the case of Waziri, he had determined his one shot would be fatal.

As an Islamic Extremist, Achmed Waziri had left a trail of blood and tears in his wake on his own personal jihad, and there was no chance of de-programming him. And yet, Khalid glanced down at his dragon-headed cane resting on the other side of his chair. Yes, he thought, I can justify taking a mad dog's life, considering all the tragedies in his lame belief that causing such catastrophes is pleasing to Allah. But allowing him to live may result in gaining a treasure trove of pertinent information in the war on terror.

Khalid had always been conflicted when it came to his sworn duty to take another man's life. He often thought it ironic how easily some Muslims could kill in the name of Islam. He was never certain Allah condoned such killings. Having been a devoted believer in Islam, he knew there were millions of faithful Muslims who had never taken the Quran so literally that they took someone's life.

What separated these Muslims from the Extremists was something Khalid referred to as 'Good Sense,' meaning that despite the sword verses, if he'd devoted himself to be a jihadist, where did that leave him in regards to other aspects of his life? Islam had inspired him to be a good person. A good husband. A good father. And that had been where he drew the line, not feeling obligated to carry out senseless killings. And now that he had two men possibly coming to his house to eliminate him, what choice did he have?

Khalid heard a noise. It came from the back patio. Earlier, he had considered moving out there to await the arrival of those coming to kill him. Any confrontation he had with Waziri was going to be messy and bloody. Slowly picking up the pistol beside him on the end table, Khalid now wished he had taken up a defensive position out-side on the patio. He was confident. As an expert marksman, he would place his bullets skillfully with head shots to avoid sending hot lead flying.

He did not wish to place any of his fellow neighbors in danger. He had brought this fight to the suburb of Havelock, and the last thing he wanted to do was to create a tragedy in an American city he had chosen for their home.

The noise came again.

It sounded like someone had bumped into one of the three metal lawn chairs situated on the open air patio. The scrape of metal on concrete was barely audible, and yet Khalid was sure he'd heard it. He looked toward the two glass doors leading to the patio. He'd opened the shades as an open invitation to Waziri to try the unlocked door. Flicking off the safety on his pistol, he arose and swiftly moved down the hallway and into his bedroom. Holding the gun out to one side, he peeked outside through a crack in the curtains. Movement came from the back of the garage. Khalid spotted the large figure of Fariq Abdullah trying to blend in with the thick shrubbery at the back of the patio.

Fariq, second in command of Waziri's cell, was an expert in hand-to-hand combat. The man could move with lightning speed, using fists, feet, or knives to exact damage on his victims. But today, Khalid saw that the big man was armed with a silenced pistol. He could even see the dragon engraved on the end of its barrel from his place at his bedroom window. Fariq was lean with a hawkish nose, resembling a weasel. He gestured at someone near the house. He wasn't, however, signaling his accomplice to advance, but rather that he stand down. Which seemed very odd to Khalid.

A faint whoosh! of sound came from the kitchen. Khalid knew at once the sliding glass door had been opened, and seconds later, footsteps could be heard as someone entered the house. Khalid took his pistol in a two fisted grip and started toward the kitchen. He said, "Achmed, if Allah is willing, I will give you a quick, clean death. If it is me who walks away from this, I assure you I will get a message to your son, letting him know your passing was swift. How odd isn't it, that we both traveled here to America, and our sons end up in the same school? And yet one being Sunni, the other Shiite, they could never get along. If us fathers had adapted here and assimilated, maybe our sons could have one day played together as most boys do."

The voice that came from the kitchen startled Khalid: "Shut up, you Shiite dog! Come to me! Be prepared to eat a bullet!"

Khalid entered the kitchen, his pistol raised. He looked into the dark eyes of the assassin that had come to kill him and froze, unable to pull the trigger.

After finishing off two pots of black coffee there on Nate's front porch while keeping track of the blip on the GPS monitor, the moment the blip crossed the boundary line designated as the hot zone, Gloria sprang to her feet. "It's on! Waziri is at Khalid's!"

Nate sprang up, staring curiously at the device. He examined it. In seconds, an image appeared on the screen. Nate said, "68th and Kearney. Three blocks away from here. And Waziri's is there! Time to call in for backup!"

Shooting him a nervous look, Raynes said, "We are the backup!"

Suddenly, her cell phone rang. She slipped it out of her pocket and answered it. Raynes stood there fuming as she conversed with the caller. A few seconds later, she closed the phone and said, "That was Detective Tory. He claims Waziri is headed to Ballard ballfield to buy the chemical Deep 9 from a source."

Nate asked, "If Waziri is at the ballfield who has his gun?"

Khalid lowered his gun. "If you were my son, he would ask him-self if I would really want him to do this thing. Taking a life is a serious matter. If you end my life, all you will accomplish is placing sorrow in your father's heart by being separated from him when the US courts sentence you to prison."

Jabar puffed up his chest. "I am not Waziri's son! My father was killed by American soldiers in Iraq! I am a Jihadi Warrior! Waziri is my handler! I failed him badly when I took his gun to school unloaded. This one is not unloaded now. Prepare to die, Shiite!"

A stern voice came from the other end of the kitchen: "Jabar? This is not what Achmed intended. Give me the gun."

Khalid exchanged uncertain looks with Fariq who aimed his own gun directly at him from across the kitchen. It was obvious then that Jabar was acting on his own, not on a direct order by Waziri. "Yes," Khalid said, "listen to him, Jabar. Walk away from this, son—"

"I am not your son!" Jabar snarled so savagely that even Fariq blinked in concern at how unhinged Jabar was.

The lean Muslim man said, "If you kill the Hound, that will merely bring unwanted attention on all of us. Would you like to see our operations fail because you used that gun seeking revenge?"

"You did not lose a father!" Jabar snapped. "Achmed recruited me to come here posing as his son! When I have accomplished my task, I will be a legend! Others will name me a hero! Now drop your gun!"

The gun clattering on the floor at his feet, Khalid offered Fariq a heated glare. "Do you see why it is a mistake to involve children in your terror attacks? Your imams and mullahs have created ticking time bombs, recruiting innocent children who should have been playing kick ball in some dusty field. Children who should never have been infused with so much hatred, bitterness, and such self-righteous condemnation of anyone who does not accept our faith. You have nothing more here than a brain-washed child who lamely believes that killing pleases Allah. Now, how do you reel him in?"

17

When they reached Ali's front porch, Lucas guided Goblin through the door, while Ali darted inside and ran past Khalid standing at the kitchen doorway. It took the little Muslim boy seconds to realize Jabar and Fariq stood there, guns aimed at Khalid.

"Stay back, Lucas!" Ali cried out in alarm. "Don't come in here!"

In that instant, Jabar latched onto Ali, looped his free arm around his neck and drew him against him. Planting the muzzle of his pistol against Ali's head, he snarled, "You win, Fariq! If you advise me not to kill this Shiite dog, then I will cause him pain by killing his pup!"

"No!" came from both Fariq and Khalid as both men took one step forward to prevent such a tragedy from taking place.

Jabar placed his back against the kitchen wall, holding Ali tightly in his grasp. "Both of you stop! Or I will shoot this scrawny maggot!"

Khalid immediately moved back to his place at the kitchen doorway. Fariq stepped back, as well. "There must be no killing here today, Jabar. Any shooting will bring the authorities to investigate. This does not fit into our plan."

Sliding the muzzle of the pistol up against Ali's left temple, Jabar snapped, "The revenge I seek, has nothing to do with your mission, Fariq! Allah commands me to kill heretics, and this is the son of the biggest heretic to our faith! It would please Allah to kill him!"

Ali's warning caused Lucas to latch onto Goblin and steer him away from the kitchen doorway. As he tugged on the pup to guide him into the livingroom, he noticed Khalid's dragon headed cane resting against his couch before him. "Stay!" he whispered to Goblin, forcing the pup to sit, while he reached for the cane.

He listened intently to the terse words being spoken in the kitchen, his eyes on Khalid's backside in the doorway. He examined the trigger mechanism on the cane, switching off the safety to one side of the trigger. He then tried to work up the courage to bolt into the kitchen and arm Khalid with his cane. Before he could move, Goblin shot forward and ran into the kitchen. "No!" he whispered.

At the sight of the small pup, Jabar gave a startled cry of dismay, peering down at Goblin as if he carried the Plague. The pup caused the Muslim boy to lose his composure as he rambunctiously sniffed at his shoes. Goblin leaped up, planting his front paws on Jabar. Ali latched onto Jabar's wrist, forcing the pistol away from his head.

It was then that Lucas entered the kitchen, prepared to shove the cane into Khalid's hands. However, he skidded to a stop, watching in alarm as Fariq raised his gun. Khalid moved like lightning. He slapped his right wrist down against his thigh. At once, a slender knife shot from the spring-loaded device attached to his wrist and into his hand. He buried it in the tender flesh of Fariq's right shoulder. Fariq frantically clawed at the knife, causing the pistol to fall from his hand.

Lucas raised the cane and aimed its tip directly at Jabar, who was so busy trying to avoid contact with Goblin that he did not notice the danger he was in. Hisssss! A breath of air released from the CO cartridge inside the cane sounded like the hiss of a mad viper. A second later, a dart appeared in Jabar's forehead. He fell back against the kitchen wall, still holding onto the gun and Ali. Lucas slammed the cane down hard on Jabar's right wrist, sending the pistol flying from his hand. Jabar peered up at him with glazed eyes. He swooned, and slumped to the floor, unconscious.

Fariq painstakingly drew the knife out of his shoulder. With a grunt of disappointment, Fariq wheeled around and exited through the open sliding door. Agent Raynes was just approaching Khalid's house from the front when Fariq came running directly at her. She had a fraction of a second to notice the bright red blood leaking from the man's shoulder, when he backhanded her.

Raynes sailed backwards, crashing into the bole of a tree at the center of the yard. She struggled to rise, but the blow to her head had knocked her senseless. Fariq hovered above her fallen form, the knife in his hand raised to strike. He found himself facing a large dog.

Lobo growled and Fariq lunged backwards. Reason appeared in front of him, nailing him in the nose with a palm strike. Thrashing his arms, horrified to be so close to such an unclean creature, Fariq fell back, landing hard on his butt, the knife tumbling from his grasp. Fariq sprang back to his feet. An expert at Martial arts, the large man was not only swift, he packed a lot muscle behind his devastating attacks. Performing a flurry of hand strikes, Reason got in three solid punches on Fariq. He then let loose with a round-house kick that left a gash in Fariq's forehead. Lobo lunged at him. The big man flew backwards, landing on his back. "Lobo!" Reason called to him.

The dog broke off his attack and sprang back inside the van. As Raynes snapped her handcuffs onto Fariq's wrists, she watched as Waziri raced past them in a Ford van, speeding down the street.

Reason turned to Raynes. "Check on Khalid! I'll go after Waziri!"

Reason followed Waziri into the Ballard field parking lot. The Muslim man skidded to a stop beside a lone biker seated at the end of the lot on a chopped Hog. Even from the entrance of the parking lot fifty-feet away, Reason could see the man's bald head gleaming in the late afternoon sunlight. It was Nate Holland, the red lettering on his leather jacket depicting the words, Elder's Den.

Reason recalled their childhood days, playing baseball down at this field. He had never considered Nate a friend, but the guy could sure hit a ball, helping their Little League team win a champion ship when they were kids in the golden days of their summers.

Reason turned off the van and climbed out. Suddenly, the rumble of four Harleys came from the street behind him. Nate dismounted at once. "I'm gonna take a swing at you," he whispered."

Reason glanced back at the four bikers entering the ballfield parking lot. He felt Nate's fist clip him on the shoulder. He latched onto Nate's shoulders and spun him around, forcing him against the side of his van. "Deck me! he said. "I'll explain later!"

Reason looked to the bikers pulling in behind Waziri's running van. He knew most members of the Den, and where he expected to see at least one familiar face, he saw four complete strangers. He then read the patches on their black leather jackets: Apaches.

Nate lurched back, putting up a half-hearted struggle for the sake of the four bikers, even as Lobo leaped out through the open window of the van. Although Lobo wasn't trained in arrest tactics or dealing with violent prisoners, the pit bull interposed himself between the raging Nate Holland and his master. Nate fell back against the van with enough force to put a dent in the rear wheel well. Lobo lunged at him, but Reason stopped the dog.

The four bikers shut down their machines. The largest member of the Apaches, a giant with red hair and a braided beard, nailed Waziri with a cold stare. "Where's Crow?" he growled.

"Late," Waziri said. "I expected him by now, but he's not here."

The red-haired giant slowly turned his head, his dark eyes settling on Reason. "You're him, aren't you? The Outlaw they called the Celt. The VP fallen from grace."

Reason eyed him back. He was six inches shorter than the giant, and the red-head outweighed him by two-hundred pounds. The giant glanced back at the three Apaches standing behind him, letting Reason know he had their backing should things go south between them.

Long tense moments passed. Waziri drove away.

"Red," said the rat-faced Apache with greasy blond hair to the left of the giant, "what about his dog? That's El Lobo!"

All four of the Apaches looked past Reason to Lobo staring at them in the front seat of the van. "Celt," Red said, "the plan was for your award winner here to be pitted against the Beast, a crossbred wolf dog. Owned by the Juarez cartel, he's the main attraction this Saturday night. You might have quit riding with the Outlaws, but surely you would want to make ten-thou if Lobo kills the Beast."

Reason held up one hand. He kneeled beside Lobo and at once, the big pit plopped down, rolled over on his back, exposing his stomach to his master. Reaching down to stroke the dog's chest and belly, he said, "Do you know how much trust a dog places in their owner when they roll over on their back, exposing their entire belly to you? A certain honor passes between dog and owner. Before dogs descended from the Gray Wolf, they used this in their pack to establish trust, placing their lives in the teeth of an Alpha male who could easily tear out the submissive wolf's throat if it chose to do so.

"Today, when a dog rolls over on its back, he is saying, 'I trust you entirely. My life is in your hands. You will either harm me or nurture me. I have placed myself in this position, because I love the attention, but also to honor you by making a statement that I trust you.'

"The dog who does this is sharing a bonding moment with its owner, one that stretches back into time when submitting to an Alpha male built trust among the entire pack. So imagine what it is like for those dogs who are thrown into the fighting ring. They are betrayed by cruel-hearted thugs whose only purpose is to force that dog to be savagely mauled, and oftentimes killed. Tragically, these dogs have taken their trust to another level, all for a master who throws their lives away at a whim. I could never in a million years think about throwing my dog's trust away by forcing him into the blood-sport. It would break my heart to have my dog savagely ripped to shreds by another dog who is only trying to please his heartless master. You Dog Men see nothing wrong with having your own dogs savagely killed in the ring. You harm the dogs of this world and Karma's going to be mad bitch in heat one day, all because of the hurt you spread."

He paused, ushering Lobo back into the van.

He turned to face the four Apaches. Red offered him a frown, saying, "Enough of the lecture. We need to find Crow."

The four bikers started up their bikes, and slowly drove away.

18

Chapter Eighteen

Looking over at Nate, Reason asked, "What the hell is this all about, Nate?"

Nate said, "Being an accessory to murder tends to change one's perspective. The shoot-out between the Apaches and the Den up in Omaha this past year? Beef Tory and homicide from Omaha placed me at the scene of the crime. Me and Crow."

Reason narrowed his eyes. "So, even though Beef liked you for the murders of your fellow club members and the seven Apaches who also died in this drug deal gone south, you are walking free?"

"Yes," Nate said. "Tory made us his informants. Either that or Crow and I could go to prison for our crimes. He involved us in a matter involving real live Arab terrorists, too."

Reason could not believe what he was hearing. For any club member to turn snitch and align themselves with law enforcement was the lowest of deeds. One that would result in that biker's death if anyone ever discovered he was working for a cop. That Nate Holland was telling him this, shook him to the core.

Nate said, "I'm also working for Raynes, that Homeland agent. And yet, Beef wants the credit for taking down the Powder King. He's a master chemist who developed that nasty powder, Deep 9. Rumor came from Homeland that there was terrorist cell wanting to buy a large amount of the chemical. In the past, this chemist produced meth for the Apaches, so Beef sent Crow to be the mediator in this sale between the chemist and Waziri. Crow was setting him up for an arrest by Detective Tory."

Reason nodded. "Why are you trusting me? With the information I now have on you, all it would take is one word to Stone, and your days with the Den would be over."

Nate said, "You are my Ace in the hole, Reason. The life span of an informant is pretty short once the wrong people find out about the double life they lead. I am in deep, not only with Tory, doing a service for my country, protecting us all from terrorists, but I have ties with the Juarez cartel that places me in a world of hurt."

He paused, then gave a sad laugh. "And now, because of my little nephew, I can't satisfy the demands of the cartel. And Juan Juarez has put a price on my head. I need a favor from you. Waziri paid me big bucks to retrieve these so-called magic rings from you. He claims the rings allow you to call forth powers. He says there are four of them. All I am asking is you give me one. Because of that story you put online, I figure you owe me at least that. Or you can continue to look over your shoulder for the rest of your life. Magic rings won't help you if you're dead."

Reason stared at him for long moments. He then said, "What have you been smoking, Nate? Magic rings? Like I have a clue what the hell you're talking about."

Shortly after the brutal attack in Khalid's kitchen, Raynes called Homeland and Fariq was taken to a hospital. Khalid's knife had done considerable damage, requiring surgery to properly tend to his wound. A pair of paramedics carted a still sleeping Jabar out of the house, followed by a police officer who would later escort the boy to the detention center.

Seated beside Ali at the kitchen table, Lucas had earnestly listened to all the charges the two Muslims would be facing. Fariq was to be charged for illegally carrying a gun. As a guest here on a visa granted by Homeland, he was also to be charged for impersonating as a member of the film crew, under the guise of producing a documentary, when in fact he had devious intentions as an extremist operative. Fariq would also be charged for his assault on Agent Raynes and his attack on Khalid. Lucas was especially pleased that Jabar would be charged with attempted murder on Khalid. Of the two, his was the most serious charge, and Lucas could only hope Jabar would be sent out to western Nebraska, to the Kearney Youth Detention Center.

He was also pleased to listen to Agent Raynes getting grilled by her supervisor about how far out of line she was by not informing him of her activities, including the GPS tracking device she had some unknown informant install in Waziri's gun. The big, fat balding man spoke rather heatedly about her insubordination, threatening to report her for her rogue operation. During the dressing down her supervisor gave her, Raynes looked once in Lucas's direction, and he smirked at her from his place at the kitchen table. He hoped she got canned for her stupidity, and also for the threats she made to have him locked up in detention.

As the big man was winding down, Reason stepped into the kitchen, greatly relieved to find Lucas unharmed after the ordeal he had gone through. He shook Khalid's hand, tossled Ali's shaggy curls, and drew Lucas out of his chair. "Time to go home, buddy," he said. "Call you later, Khalid. You can tell me what happened here."

Khalid offered Reason a sad smile and said, "Lucas can tell you on his ride back to your house. After all, he and Ali stumbled into the middle of the tragic affair. Why, if it wasn't for Lucas and his pup causing a distraction, things might have gone terribly wrong."

Beside himself with fear, Ali blurted, "Will my father be charged with any crimes involved in this assault upon his person?"

His large brown eyes settled on Raynes, but she gestured to her supervisor. The big, balding man stepped forward and shook Khalid's hand. "Captain Crawford," he said. "As I see it, you acted in self-defense and were justified in your attack on these perps. Although the county attorney is going to want to talk to you about the matter, I will be there to speak on your behalf, Mr. Karim. Before I arrived here, I received a call from your commanding officer in Iraq. He appraised me of your role as an anti-terrorist agent. Perhaps, after the smoke has cleared regarding this mess, we can work together to apprehend Waziri. At this moment, he's in the wind!"

Khalid surprised both Crawford and Raynes by saying, "Perhaps,

Agent Raynes and I could work together on arresting Achmed."

Crawford seemed taken back by the suggestion. He angrily snapped, "For her foolishness,

I'm more inclined to strip her of her badge, her gun, and her credentials to even operate as an agent for Homeland! As far as I'm concerned, Raynes is hereby suspended!"

And as Reason led Lucas and Goblin out of the kitchen, Lucas winked at Raynes and offered her one last smirk.

Reason drove Lucas away from one crime scene only to drive directly into another. He turned the van at the corner leading to his street and braked quite suddenly. "What the hell?" Lucas said, sliding out of his seat, barely keeping Goblin from doing a nose-plant on the dash. Reason leaned forward to peer through the windshield, amazed to take in the scene at the mouth of the alley. Five cop cruisers blocked the street, and two more were parked in the alley.

"Wow," Lucas said, "all these cops just to arrest Crow Harper?"

Reason's eyes went wide when he saw his handcuffs dangling from the handle of the dumpster, a spattering of bright red blood running down the side of the metal container. He followed the blood trail down to the gravel-covered alley and spotted what looked like a hand laying there, severed at the wrist.

"Oh," Lucas gasped in a horrified whisper. "Is that a hand?"

Behind Reason, Lobo growled as a man in a suit approached his master at his driver's side window. "Quiet!" Reason commanded him. "It's just Beef Tory. You know Beef."

The huge, blond detective peered in the window at the dog. The moment he recognized the big man, the dog began to wag his tail. Beef said, "Someone wanted to take Crow with them and had no qualms about leaving his hand behind. Dispatch got a call an hour ago. The anonymous caller claimed he had Crow cuffed to a dumpster in the alley here. Any clue what that was about, Reason?"

Making direct eye contact with the big ex-biker, Reason was reminded of the days he was still a kid and getting grilled by Beef for some infraction he had pulled. "Crow was threatening the kid and the pup, so I thumped him on the head, cuffed him to the dumpster, and put in the phone call. I left him there before taking off for Khalid's place. And Crow had both hands at that point."

Beef glanced back over one shoulder to the crime scene. "It has cartel written all over it. We know Crow was associated with the Juarez cartel, that they were disappointed with him over his foiled attempt to dog-nap Lobo" He paused and looked over at Lucas seated there in the passenger's seat holding Goblin. "Your Uncle Nate and Crow are both on some kind of hit list of this cartel, Lucas. Your deed, rescuing Reason's dog, stirred up heavy consequences for two bikers with bad intentions. Not that I'm blaming you for any of this."

Resting his chin on Goblin's small head, Lucas peered earnestly at Reason and said, "If the cartel snatched Crow off the street, then he's dead, right? How is the county attorney ever gonna talk to him?"

Beef said, "I have differences with the Den, but your dad does not deserve to be locked up. This does put a spin on things, however."

Lucas was close to telling Reason about Nate's scheme to sell Lobo to the cartel, building the case against him as to why he'd paid Stone back by having Crow plant the powder in his truck. Instead, he kept his mouth closed. "Nelson!" called one of the cops hovering on the periphery of the crime scene in the nearby alley. "How about we turn your sniffer dog loose to track down the one-armed bandit?"

Beef said, "Someone always wants to use your dog. Take Lucas to your house. He's seen enough for one day. Feed the kid. Read him one of your stories. And put him to bed, a dog on either side."

Back at Reason's house, Lucas fed the two dogs, then wandered into the kitchen where Reason was making them dinner.

"So," he said, "you trust this big cop, Beef? You two seemed to all be on good terms. I heard both of you used to ride with your dad in the Outlaws. Is that true?"

A rush of memories washed over Reason as he turned from the stove to face Lucas. He remembered the day Beef and Jessie Dalton had been speaking about his late dad in the present tense instead of past tense. He had been 14 then, and he demanded to know exactly what they had meant. He shared bits and pieces of that heated conversation he'd held with the two ex-Outlaws with Lucas:

"What in hell did you mean by," he asked, "if Rain knew about the threat, Beef? Dad has been dead now for the past ten years. I've always been told by Mom and Boone that he was killed on his bike. Did dumb kid Reason hear something he wasn't supposed to hear?"

Jessie said, "Rain's been alive all this time, serving time at the State pen. Your mom thought it best that you did not know about him until you had grown up, Reason. She didn't want you to live with that overshadowing every thing you did in your own life. Rain and I are brothers, same mother, different dads. Our mom left Rain's dad for mine. The two moved away to Callie. I remained behind in Nebraska, and was raised by Rain's dad, president of the Outlaws. Five years after the Viet Nam war ended, drugs began to flow into America. Our dad, Chase Nelson, refused to allow the Outlaws to deal in drugs. It was his hardline stance that eventually caught the attention of the Juarez cartel. The Nomad they sent after him killed our dad.

"Ten years later, Rain and I ended up at a rock quarry to deal with a crooked cop. During this meeting, Jack Holland drew out a gun. He planned to kill Rain, and yet I showed up there at the quarry, providing the distraction Rain needed to pull a gun of his own. Sheriff Clyde Baxster died. I don't know what Beef ever told anyone in this family about why he and I no longer ride with the Outlaws, but after Rain was sentenced to prison for the murder of a cop, Beef, in turn, became one, and I became a private eye. I thought by connecting the dots on Jack Holland's crooked dealings, I could one day exonerate my brother for the shooting that took place at the quarry."

Reason snorted sarcastically, "And how did that work out for my dear old dad?"

Lucas stared directly at Reason. He shook his head, causing his blond tangles to swirl away from covering his eyes. "No wonder," he said, "you never became a biker. Sounds like your dad screwed up by shooting that cop, whether he was crooked or not. And Jessie and Beef leaving the club? One to become a cop, the other a private eye?

"It kinda gives me hope. I always thought I was locked into this thing with the club, you know growing up to be a biker like Dad and Uncle Nate. I love Harleys. I love riding in the wind behind my dad when he takes me out on his beast. But even with my red-hot temper that gets me into all kinds of trouble, I don't like the fights or the taste of beer. Seeing how you didn't follow in your own dad's footsteps, it means I got a choice, too. When it comes time, I hope I make the right one."

19

Later that night, Lucas confessed that he'd stolen Reason's three rings from the chest in his den. Surprised by his calm attitude, Lucas settled next to his computer desk in a gaming chair. As small as he was, the large chair swallowed his lean frame. He sank deeper into the chair as he asked, "Do you know Gus Howard? Celeste does research for him. He's a writer like you. He collects ancient relics. Gus also dredges up stories about ghosts."

Slightly puzzled, Reason allowed Lucas to continue. "Gus told Alex and I about strange activity in Havelock. 75-year-old Lon Dormer told Gus about George Dormer, the oldest son of his great grandfather. Lon's family always referred to it as the Dormer curse. Rumor has it, two boys had gone hunting and were found shot in the head in a corn field with their guns lying by their sides. They are buried in the Havelock cemetery, Fairview, and Lon's relatives tell the story every year on Memorial Day when they visit his ancestors' graves. George was killed at age 9, 1913. Lon's mother once told him there was fire on the two boys' graves and the mother of the Reese boy wanted to pray them out of purgatory, she was Catholic, but Lon's great grandmother, a Lutheran, refused to allow that.

"After hearing this story for years, Lon ventured to the Lincoln Historical Society. He found a fact-based story in the Lincoln News: Sept. 8th, 1913. John Rhys, found dead in a pasture Saturday, fatally wounded George Dormer, his nine-year-old companion, and in remorse shot himself. Powder burns were found upon Rhys, indicating that the weapon had been held close to his breast when the shot that killed him was fired. George Dormer, 9, and John Rhys, 16, were found dead in a pasture one mile north of Havelock.

"Dr. Ballard, the coroner, said he examined the small boy and found a gun shot to his abdomen made by a .22 bullet. The Dormer/Rhys story made news all over the US, and various reporters could not determine how they died. In one story, they were charged by angry, territorial bulls. In another, they shot one another. A third story claims they were murdered. This fact-based story makes more sense. Not a murder. An accident. Lon came back to Havelock to visit the lady who now lives in his grandparents' house, where George once lived. She spoke about the ghost of a little boy wearing a hunting hat seen dozens of times outside the house. It's the ghost of George, trying to get back inside the house where he's no longer welcome."

Lucas paused, then said, "Nine-year-old George has long since passed on, but Lon Dormer mentions the Gypsies from the State Fair. Gypsies have a network. This story is known among Alex Thorn's clan. George's parents went to the State Fair, asking the Gypsies to help locate the missing boys. The Gypsies divined—"

"As a Gypsy child, Alex Thorn," Reason said, "would not tap into the Otherworld. To do so, he might attract an Unseen entity that might be hanging around. One never messes with the paranormal. Did you give my rings to Alex?"

Lucas tried to muster up an indignant look. "What?" he asked.

Lobo from his place on the backseat sent, *He knows you took them, Lucas. I told him about you snooping through his chest. He knows you know they are rings of power. Who else has had access to his den? Stop playing games with my master, and he will share the magic of the rings with you.*

Lucas sighed. He drew a single ring out of his pocket. "I gave the other two to Gus Howard to check to see if they were magical. I'm sorry I broke your trust. You can kick me out if you want to."

"Go to bed," Reason said. "We'll talk about this in the morning."

Five minutes later, Lucas and the two dogs stood before the

Dormer house three blocks away from Reason's place. Determined to try one of the rings out for himself to see if it held magical powers, Lucas slipped the ring on his ring finger, and at once lurched backward. The entire world turned a brilliant shade of fluorescent violet, with tones of bright blue and deep greens. Houses and parked cars were a dull blue. The trees, shrubbery, and hanging plants on nearby porches were all pulsating with emerald light. Tiny bars of multicolored light zipped past the van, moving too fast to resemble any shape other than six-inch bars of rainbow colored light.

Flitterings, Lobo sent. *Paranormal researchers call them rods, for on camera they appear like flying rods of bright light.*

Lucas looked up and saw fairies trailing sparkling dust behind them, their wings fluttering madly as they performed loops and spins above the front lawn. They were tiny magical beings three inches in length. The tiny fairies gave off a violet aura as they flittered about before the house. The entire company of fairies stopped quite suddenly, their gazes fixed on a shimmering at the edge of the yard below them. There, a doorway appeared, blue mist spilling from a plane beyond this one. When the ethereal figures of two young boys sprang out of the portal, the fairies clapped their hands in glee. One boy wore an orange hunting cap. He stood about 4 feet tall and looked to be a child of nine or ten.

George Dormer, Goblin sent. *John Rhys.*

The two insubstantial boys began to run across the yard. The smaller ghost sprinted away from the bigger ghost. The bigger ghost boy had his hands outstretched toward the smaller boy as if trying to get him to stop. Even though his features were smoky, Reason and Lucas could clearly see the anguish in the older ghost boy's eyes.

He wants, Lobo sent, quietly, *to be forgiven.*

"Sweet Jesus!" Lucas said. "The shooting took place over 104 years ago! How many nights has this played out?"

A sudden movement came from the front porch, where the ghost of George Dormer appeared, his hunting hat askew. He darted up the steps leading to the front door, and he began to bang on it. But no one inside could hear him, desperately banging from the Otherworld. The moment the ghost of John Rhys came running from the side yard the chase was on again.

Lobo sent, *They are caught between two realms. One needs to forgive, while one needs to be forgiven.*

Lucas stepped forward. "George? John? I know what happened to you two."

George snapped, "He shot me!"

The spunky little ghost pointed down at his abdomen where John's .22 bullet had entered and taken his life. Lucas nodded at George. "But look there below his left breast, George. He felt so bad about the fatal injury he caused you, he took his own life."

George studied the hole left in John's chest where he had inflicted his own wound to end his life in remorse for what he'd done. John bowed his head, crystal tears welling up in his eyes.

"Your parents, George," Lucas said, "must have forgiven John, for you were buried close beside each other at Fairview cemetery, as a gesture to pardon a tragic mistake. With this ring, I see the realm where you've been trapped for over one hundred years. It's time to let go. Time for both of you to move on."

John said, "I'm so sorry, George. Will you please forgive me?"

Slowly, little George Dormer clasped the older boy's hand in his own, and they went through a five-step handshake performed in 1913, crossing wrists, slapping palms, releasing with their thumbs pointed toward the sky, both were grinning.

John wrapped both of his big arms around George and wept, "Oh, Georgie!"

A moment later, the ghosts of the two boys vanished.

Lucas was in a daze on the walk home. Goblin nuzzled up beside him on one side, while Lobo nudged him with his big head on the other. *Shadow companions,* Goblin whispered softly. *Here to lend you support, Little Luke.*

Lucas muttered, "I used magic to send them on their way. I wielded magic. Wolf was right about me being a Thunder Dreamer."

Stepping out of the shadows beneath a nearby tree, Reason said, "Don't know anything about this thunder dreamer, but consider this a one-time deal for now. I'm going to want my ring back to store it in a safe place. There are others who want them and I'm afraid they would misuse them."

Nodding and still quite shaken by his encounter with the two ghosts, Lucas reached over and dropped the ring in Reason's outstretched hand. "Could I maybe use it again?" he asked.

Reason simply smiled at him, then led him up the sidewalk and ushered him and the two dogs inside his house.

20

The next morning, Reason drove Lucas, Ali, Goblin, and Lobo out to the dog rescue ranch. Only a year ago, Lucas had been placed there with the owner of the ranch, Ben Black Bull. The Lakota dog handler had a gift for working with damaged dogs, broken vets, and troubled kids. If anyone was a kid whisperer, it was Ben.

Before ending up in foster care with Ben, Lucas had stressed out in his first placement with a police officer and his wife, whose structured home environment had been too much for a little biker kid to handle. In a desperate attempt to be removed from the home of the Yardleys, Lucas had blown out of anger management on the first day that his new family support worker, Ben, had taken him there. Lucas had led the Lakota youth worker on a six-block run through down-town Lincoln, rode an elevator to the top floor of a parking garage, and ended up perched on a ledge six-stories above the street.

There, Lucas threatened to jump.

During the middle of Ben's crisis intervention, Lucas had peered down to the street below the parking garage and watched as a man dumped a gray pit bull pup out of his car and onto the sidewalk. That pup turned out to be Goblin.

Lucas had scrambled off the ledge, darted to the elevator, and ended up scooping Goblin up before he could run out into the street. Ben later claimed, it was Goblin that had gotten Lucas off of that ledge, preventing him from following through with his threat to jump. A few minutes after rescuing Goblin, Ben and Lucas watched the driver of the car come screeching around the corner. Squealing to a stop before them, he dumped a large, badly-scarred Brindle pit out of his car and drove away. This was Grunge, a legendary dog who had won over fifty fights in the dog fighting circuit.

At Wounded Arrow, despite his own volatile nature, Lucas had bonded with the aggressive dog. Even as Reason drove them out to the ranch a mile away from Havelock in the country, Lucas remembered that first conversation they had in regards to him working with the badly damaged older pit bull:

"Will you teach me how to whisper?" Lucas asked.

"Don't know about whispering," Ben said. "But you can start working with Goblin tomorrow."

Lucas said, "What about Grunge? Do you think I got what it takes to work with him?"

Ben stared at Grunge. "You might not have the patience, Lucas. Every step with him will have to be measured according how he reacts. He's a damaged dog, who needs a lot of stubborn love to bring him around. That means never giving up on him. Never getting so frustrated you just walk away from him. Grunge will read you like a book. He's far more sensitive than most dogs, because of what he's been through. If he senses you losing your cool with him, you might do more damage to him. Can you manage your tantrums?"

"I don't throw tantrums," Lucas said.

"Yes, you do," Ben said. "If things don't go your way, you turn into the Tasmanian Devil. If you deny that, you'll never change. Grunge deserves better. If you want to heal him, first heal yourself."

Yet in the end, Lucas and Grunge formed a bond that changed both of their lives.

As Reason drove up to the gateway leading to the dog compound, Lucas said, "Stop right here."

Reason brought the van to a stop directly beneath the wooden sign that read, Wounded Arrow. "Ben is gonna be mad at me," Lucas said, readjusting Goblin in his lap. The pup was fidgeting with excitement. He knew where they were and he was eager to be reunited with Ben.

"Mad at you?" Ali asked from his place in the backseat.

Lucas made a sour face. "Everything happened so fast when I got returned home after living out here. Ben said I was going to remain with him at least another year, and then Mom got killed in that wreck, and the judge ruled that I be returned to Dad. Me, Grunge, and Goblin ended up back in Havelock within a week after Mom had her wreck. Dad didn't trust Grunge on account of his years in the fight ring. He let me keep Goblin, but Grunge had to live in the kennels behind Uncle Nate's place."

Lucas looked ahead to the assortment of motorcycles parked in a long line to one side of the three large barns taking up the back quarter of Ben's property. He then saw the many bikers gathered on the ranch, some walking the fence line armed with guns, others positioned in strategic locations, and these were also armed. Any attempt to harm the service dogs residing at Wounded Arrow was going to be a difficult task for Waziri and any members of his extremist cell.

"See," Lucas continued, "Ben promised Grunge when he took him in out here that his fighting days were over. 'Never again,' Ben told him. And I think this is part of the reason why Grunge finally settled down and quit being so cantankerous. You should have seen him when he first got here. Because of all those fights he'd been forced into, he was a spooky beast. It took a lot of magic to heal his heart. Native magic. Ben's a gifted dog whisperer. He's got a special talent for bringing some of the most vicious dogs back from the brink of being outright mean and wild. He invites them into the Sacred Hoop, where spirits of hatred and anger from the Otherworld cannot attach themselves to them and cause them any more damage. You might say, he did the same to me. Maybe we should go back home. Ben has enough to deal with here with all these bikers. I should have called him to let him know Nate had thrown Grunge back into the fights. Ben would have turned Uncle Nate into Cora Red Cloud."

"Cora?" Reason asked, intrigued by Lucas's words.

Lucas nodded. "Cora is an Animal Control officer. Cora's uncle, Colton Lone Wolf, calls himself the Dog Soldier, and he would be even more disappointed in me if he found out I did nothing to stop Nate from involving Grunge in the fights. I really let all three of them down.

Big time. In a bad way."

Lucas was glad that Reason and Ali were not looking his way, but instead of focusing on the tall, long-haired Lakota stepping out of the center barn. Ben Black Bull was dressed in faded jeans, jean jacket, and dusty, weather-worn cowboy boots. His raven hair flowed back and over his broad shoulders, and his handsome features were creased by a grin as he spoke with Beef Tory, who had followed him outside the dog barn. The two men appeared to be amused by whatever they were discussing. Beef, standing there in his suit, towered over the Lakota dog handler by a good six inches, and yet Ben met his gaze, even though he had to look up to do so.

Reason let up on the brake and the van began to roll up the driveway. They were halfway to the dog barns before Ben and Beef looked their way. Beef waved at Reason, and Ben waved a friendly greeting to his former foster son. Fighting hard not to tear up, Lucas placed a hand on Goblin's head and peered off to the buffalo scattered across the field to the north of the ranch. "It will be okay," Reason said as he shut the engine down. Knowing that Lucas was having a meltdown, he reached over and patted him on one shoulder. He said. "You stay here and pull yourself together. Ali and I will go meet Ben. I'll have Beef introduce us, give you some time to gather your wits, okay?"

Lucas nodded, sinking his chin on top of Goblin's head. Seated in Lucas's lap, Goblin sent his thoughts up at him: *Uncle Nate did more than force Grunge back into the fights. One evening while I lay beneath the kitchen table back at your dad's house, I heard Detective Glass questioning Nate and your dad about your mom's car crash.*

Lucas stared in wide-eyed amazement down at the pit bull pup in his lap. Goblin nuzzled him on the chin. *Call it a gift, but yes, you can hear me. Listen close to what I have to say. Your dad was angry over Nate forcing Grunge back into the fights. It was during their heated words about Grunge, that Detective Glass showed up, speaking of the rumor of Nate being involved in your mom's accident. Glass said that in order to get the judge to place you back with your dad, your mom was in the way. He accused Nate of running your mom off the road. Nate denied it, but Detective Glass asked him if he planted an open bottle in her car after she had died, because the police reported your mom's death as alcohol related when she crashed her car in that ditch.

Nate denied it still.*

"How could he," Lucas said, "do something so rotten?"

Goblin sent, *Your dad knew Nate was using Grunge to fight. When he tried to stop him, Nate threatened him, so your dad backed off. When the detective left, Nate shouted, 'I had nothing to do with Maggie's death, but now that she's gone at least you got your son back! How would you like losing both Lucas and Celeste? Because if that detective shows up here again accusing me of causing Mag's accident, one whisper of you being involved, and Glass will arrest us both for her death.'*

Lucas blurted out, "Nate's a dirty rotten bastard!"

Yes, Goblin agreed with him. *He is.*

21

Ben approached the van, grinning at Lucas. Goblin was so ex-cited to see him, he squirmed around in Lucas's lap until Ben opened the door and picked him up. "Goblin," he said, fending off his slobbery greeting. "Good to see you, little guy!"

After a few minutes of getting reacquainted with the rambunctious pup, Ben placed him on the ground, and turned to greet Lucas. "Since I know you don't go in for hugs, how about a good old-fashioned handshake, Lucas?"

Ben reached into the van, clasped his right hand in his, and gently pulled him out of his seat, settling him down between himself and Goblin. "It's really good to see you, kid," he said, a broad grin on his darkly-tanned face. "Did you miss poop patrols out here?"

"Don't remind me," Lucas said, failing to keep his smile in place.

Ben said, "I still haven't found a way to recycle it to create something to make me rich."

That had been a running joke between them ever since Lucas had moved in at Wounded Arrow. Ben had talked about his neighboring rancher's herd of buffalo, explaining to Lucas that buffalo dung was unlike cow dung, in that it replenished the ground wherever it happened to fall. And he'd added that it was too bad dog waste didn't have the same properties. Or they could find a way to get rich off of the plentiful supply they had always been plagued with.

"Where's the big guy?" Ben asked. "Grunge didn't come along?"

"Uh," Lucas said, "there's been some complications with Grunge."

"Nate's taken him back to the fights?" Ben asked.

"Yes," Lucas said. "I'm afraid so."

Despite any disappointment he felt about the sad plight of Grunge, Ben placed a leather thong over Lucas's head. Once settled around his neck, Ben smoothed out the small eagle feather attached to the cord and slipped it inside of Lucas's shirt. "You left this behind," Ben said, "Cora and Wolf thought you should have it."

Lucas reached out and placed his hand over Ben's. "Do you really think I deserve it after I let Grunge down so badly?" he asked.

Ben glanced down at the rare show of affection by Lucas, his hand resting on his own. "Of course," he said, "how else are you ever going to be a Thunder Dreamer?"

Lucas said, "Oh, yeah. I'd almost forgotten."

A flood of memories then washed over Lucas as he stood there:

Wolf settled Goblin at his feet, then withdrew a leather cord from beneath his parka. He slipped it around Lucas's neck and settled the three-inch long feather inside of his shirt. "Ever heard of," Wolf asked, "a talisman? A token of power to ward off evil?"

Lucas asked, "You mean like silver bullets against vampires? Like Kryptonite that weakens Superman? That kind of talisman?"

"Yeah," Wolf said, "That is an eagle feather, once worn by one of the original Shirt Wearers, American Horse. It is a sacred item. In the coming days, I think you're going to need it."

And then onto his memory screen stepped Cora Red Cloud: "My Uncle Colton gave you this to accomplish a mission. He knows you are supposed to be a special mediator."

Lucas asked, "Why me? I'm not too good of a kid. Aren't souls high quality stuff? Like special? Like holy? Like magical? I'm the most unholy kid you'll ever meet. I'm far from special. I know nothing about magic. A mediator? If you could see through to my true nature, you would be terrified. I am a raging demon most of the time."

He then remembered Grunge let out a soft whine:

Lucas looked on in amazement as the big pit slowly got to his feet and walked over to him. He stopped directly in front of him, his head cocked to one side, his big brown eyes fixed on his face. Lucas simply sat there, uncertain of what to do with the head of a 90-pound pit bull resting on his legs. The moment Lucas's hand came to rest on top of Grunge's head, he opened his eyes. Tears welled up in Lucas's eyes as he softly said, "Thanks, Grunge. Thanks for trusting me."

Ben's uncle, Pete He Dog, infiltrated his memories:

Old Pete said, "I am keen to meet this young Thunder Dreamer."

Ben stared at his uncle for long moments. "Thunder Dreamer?" he asked. "How can that be? Lucas is a white boy."

Wolf and Pete laughed at the same time. The two elders offered Ben a look of admonishment. Both said, "Racist!" They then cackled like two old hens.

Pete He Dog offered Grunge a warm smile. "The Pup," he said, "is what I called you when you were just a puppy. The Thunder Beings were active on the night you were born. Thunder. Lightning. Your brothers and sisters were black and white, but you were set apart by your markings. I was sure you were destined to do something special in your lifetime. But the fights?"

Tears streamed down the wrinkled and weathered face of the elder Native. He leaned forward and placed his forehead on Grunge's head. "Ah," he moaned. "Oh, no, you poor, poor puppy. You pretty much had the love beaten out of you. Ah. Oh. Criminy sakes. The things you have suffered. The hurts you have endured. No dog should ever be subjected to the wrongs that were forced upon you."

That connection to him opened up a view of just what had turned him into the killer pit that he was. "Lucas?" Pete said, gesturing for him to join them at the couch. "Are you committed to walking the path on this dog's journey? If so, come. Touch him so that you might know where he's been to reach this point on his long, troubled path."

The moment Lucas touched Grunge's bulky shoulder, he gasped out loud. The images that came to him were laced with such violence and savagery, he wanted to break his connection to the big dog. He saw: A mean-looking Hispanic man snatching Grunge up when he was just a puppy. The same man shoved him into a metal kennel and drove Grunge away from the reservation. After that, the man used cattle prods on Grunge, forcing him to enter the fighting ring where he was forced to kill or be killed. It was a slow-motion view of damaging images, suffered by Grunge as he rose through the ranks to be King of the Ring. And there was blood, blood, and more blood.

And then, Grunge slowly turned his head and looked directly into Lucas's eyes and saw the images of: His dad shaking his fist in his face, cursing at him, shouting at him, chewing him out for some long forgotten infraction. He slapped Lucas, he cuffed him, he wadded up his shirt in his fist and drew him nose-to-nose with him, growling out angry words, his saliva hitting Lucas's cheeks. And then Uncle Nate dealt him a slap on the back, a whap to the back of his head.

Grunge witnessed all that Lucas had been through growing up in such a hostile environment. He empathized with him, pressing his face against his chest, rubbing his head beneath his chin. They each knew at that moment just what the other had suffered in the past.

Pete said, "Angry spirits that should have never been aware of both of you, were attracted to you when you disturbed the fabric of the Otherworld with your bitter outbursts or your savage attacks. You were infected by these wrathful beings, who fed off of your own rage and lent more power to your tantrums and beastly tirades. You must both overcome the influence of these spirits, kick them out, send them packing, or they will torment you the rest of your lives."

Lucas stood there, reminded of the unseen strings that attached Grunge and him together. The two had an emotional bond that could not be broken, and yet Lucas had let the big dog down by not speaking out for him, by not championing him when he should have.

"I tried," he told Ben, "to tell Dad what Nate was doing, but Nate held something over Dad's head, something I can't tell you about."

"Biker code, right?" Ben said, frowning.

"I cannot be a snitch," Lucas said. "But at church yesterday, I gave two-hundred dollars to pay off Nate's obligation to keep Grunge out of the upcoming fight. Some members of the club chipped in, and so, too, did Reason's dad, Rain Nelson, president of the Outlaws. Nate should be bound by the word he gave all of them, plus he walked away with seven-hundred dollars which was two-hundred more than he paid to have Grunge fight."

Ben asked, "Where is he being held?"

"Uncle Nate's house," Lucas said, unable to meet his gaze.

Ben said, "I'll go and get him. This is not what Stone and I agreed upon. Grunge deserves better than this."

"Nate," Lucas said, "won't just let you take him."

Ben gestured over one shoulder at the seven Natives gathered near his dog cemetery on the south side of his ranch.

"I won't ask," Ben said.

He then firmly added, "And I won't go alone."

22

As Ali, Goblin, and Lobo joined them, Ben started walking down to the cemetery. He glanced back and said, "Come with me. Beef is taking your writer friend for a tour of the ranch. I am scheduled to hold a ceremony for a dog who recently passed."

A few minutes later, Ben introduced the Cheyenne dog handlers known as the Ghost Company to Lucas and Ali. Five of them were big men, heavily muscled and over six feet tall, their hair close-cropped and military-style short. The other Native wore his hair in a single braid trailing down his back. All six were dressed in black outfits, that reminded Lucas of martial arts clothes, loose-fitting and easy to move in. All six moved with catlike grace as they gathered around a headstone there in the Wounded Arrow dog graveyard.

Lucas blinked in surprise when he saw a large Native rising from beside a grave to join the Ghosts. The big Lakota's salt and pepper hair was tied back in a braided tail, and he was dressed in dark jeans and a black duster. It was Colton Lone Wolf. He smiled down at Lucas, saying, "Ben informed us that there were some evil men wanting payback. It is a shame that those terrorists followed us back here to exact revenge. In Mosul, our dogs prevented dirty bombs from ever being built by the Vipers. The Ghost Company is now retired. Three of our company's dogs are still alive, getting fat and lazy in the homes of three Ghosts who own them. Two are buried out here. And the sixth dog?"

Wolf gestured at the headstone before them. "Bear served me faithfully, a Brindle given to me by Pete He Dog of Pine Ridge."

"A Brindle?" Lucas said. "Like Grunge?"

Wolf said, "Grunge came from the same line of pits that Bear came from. Same mother and father, just a different litter."

Noting Ali's alarmed look to be standing in the dog cemetery, Lucas said, "By the way, this is Ali. You guys knew his dad, Khalid, captain of the Phantoms when you were all in Iraq, right?"

All six Cheyenne soldiers looked directly at the small, raven-haired Ali standing there nervously fidgeting. Lucas looked on in surprise as each of the Native men stepped forward to shake the young kid's hand, solemn looks on their faces. It was Wolf who surprised Lucas even more as he said, "We would not be here if not for your father. You must be very proud of him and the work he does for both of our countries. Your father is a legend, Ali."

Ali nodded yet remained silent. Sensing how uncomfortable this praise for his father made him, Ben held up a golden urn. "Shall we conduct the ceremony, or continue to chit-chat?"

Wolf's dark eyes swept the landscape to the north. "My sixth sense is telling me that amongst these headstones and these giant pine trees, we are very vulnerable. Hostile eyes watch us."

Ben chided, "Don't be so paranoid, Wolf. We've got bikers from five different clubs patrolling the ranch, the roads, and a half-a-dozen surrounding pastures bordering my land. We should be safe to bury Bear and hold his ceremony without interference from hostile forces."

Ben pointed in all four directions of the compass. "Though you might have the creepy crawlies, to the south, we have the massive buffalo herd. To the west, we have the creek, and along its banks are several snipers perched in deer stands. To the east, we have the high ridge, the woods, and Cooper Steading, where several soldiers of fortune walk those grounds. And to the north, is open land stretching to Salt Creek winding its way across the Nebraska plains."

"And," Wolf said, eyeing the tree line running along the bank of the creek a mile distance, "that is the direction I am getting the creeps from. Someone is watching us."

***

Ben placed the urn with Bear's ashes on the plating attached to the headstone, turning it until it clicked, indicating it was settled into place. He removed sage from a pouch around his neck. He used a Bic lighter to burn the sage, sang a soft Native song in the Oglala Lakota language, the tongue of his people, and tossed pinches of the burnt sage into the four directions of the wind. He then removed a stone arrowhead from a thong around his neck. He turned and placed the arrowhead against Wolf's chest. "May this open," Ben said, "the fabric of the Otherworld, so that you may give Bear a final farewell."

Lucas eyed the arrowhead, remembering the story Ben had shared with he and Cora Red Cloud one winter night this past year:

"This talisman," Uncle Pete said, as he draped the necklace over his nephew's head, "once belonged to Sitting Bull. It is a token of power that will shield you from the Dark Ones of the night. It is endowed with big medicine."

And memories of Ben when he was just ten-years-old, came to Lucas, when Ben had rescued his Uncle Pete's pit puppy from the Tall Man: Even as Crazy Horse moved to close with him once more, the Tall Man spun away from him and vanished into thin air. Crazy Horse collided with an invisible barrier as he tried to follow the Tall Man. He swiped at the air with his tomahawk, and at once, a doorway opened into the Otherworld. The Lakota Warrior turned to Ben, fixed his eagle-proud gaze on the arrowhead he wore around his neck, and said, "Whoever gifted you with that did you a great favor."

Ben feebly lifted the arrowhead from his chest. It gave off a faint violet glow, and he could still feel it thrumming with big medicine. "Uncle Pete said it once belonged to Sitting Bull."

"Tatá ka Íyotake," Crazy Horse said, nodding solemnly.

Crazy Horse stared at him for long moments. He then stepped through the rip in the fabric connecting two worlds, and was gone.

Wolf closed his eyes, sank to his knees, and wept. "I can't see him," he whispered. "There are just clouds, sparkling and shimmering, looking like a misty rainbow, but no Bear."

The big Lakota lowered his head, his huge shoulders shaking. He "I. Can't. See. My. Dog. Bear is not there."

Yes, he is, Goblin sent to Lucas just a foot away from him. *I can see him resting beside a mountain stream. Use the feather, Lucas. Guide this Native to his dog.*

Lucas stepped up behind the Native who mourned the passing of his dog. He removed the eagle feather dangling from the thong around his neck, and placed it on the back of Wolf's neck. And both Lucas and Wolf gasped as visions exploded in their minds:

A black buck with a 14-point spread, burst through swirling threads of swiftly falling snow. The buck's antlers glistened, casting specks of power off into the moonlit trees he ran through. Behind the stag, a pack of white wolves ran, their green eyes glowing in the dark woodlands. They were closing fast, some of them weaving in and out of the saplings on either side of the buck. An enormous grizzly appeared to one side of the trail. His sudden roar caused the entire pack of white wolves to veer off from the hunt. The buck continued to run through the winter night.

When he emerged from the edge of the tree line, the morning sun greeted him. The buck approached a sparkling stream. He lowered his crown of antlers and drank deeply from the waters. A hawk swooped down to perch on his antler tines. Brief words passed be-tween buck and hawk. Nodding, the hawk mounted the winds and flew over the stream, his sights set on blue mountains far ahead of them. The redtail flew on over a lush, green landscape, dotted here and there with thick forests, high hills, and three rivers that crossed through the land like silver threads holding it all together.

Fireflies speckled his beak, his face, his breast, and his wings as he entered into a wooded dale situated at the foot of the mountains. Specks of lime-green and lemon-yellow whirled around his gracefully flapping wings as the fireflies illuminated the dale with flashes of light. It was by their dazzling light that the hawk spotted below him in the glade, a red fox, basking in a haze of golden sunlight streaming down through the overhead branches. The hawk spoke to the vixen, and she bolted off through the glen.

There at the end of a high trail overlooking a steep canyon, the fox came to a Brindle pit bull sleeping beside a stream. The vixen sniffed gently at the big dog's nose, waking him up. At once, the pit sat up on his haunches. The fox barked at the figure standing on the far side of the stream, and the dog darted to the edge of the waters.

"Bear!" Wolf called to his dog. "I've come to say good-bye!"

The dog bounded to the left, then darted to the right, and yet his paws never touched the waters separating him from his master. Bear gave one last heart-piercing howl, his voice echoed across the rocks of the mountain and engulfed Wolf as he stood there, softly crying. "Bye, boy," the Lakota soldier said. "I'll see you on the Otherside one day. You were loved greatly, and will not be forgotten."

Bear barked one last time, then slowly faded from sight.

23

Wolf rose to his feet, tears running down his face. He rubbed his neck where the eagle feather had just been. "Thanks," he said, smiling through his tears.

Lucas nodded silently.

"I seen him," the big Lakota said. He placed a large hand on top of Lucas's shaggy blond head, "thanks to this Thunder Dreamer. The feather that once belonged to American Horse holds great medicine."

The big Native soldier began to share with the rest of the Ghost Company all the things that they had seen. The six Cheyenne stood there, listening attentively, their eyes thoughtful and filled with reverence. Native medicine was not to be taken lightly. And not one of them doubted Wolf's words.

Wolf caused all of them standing there to peer at him in alarm. He spread his arms to reveal the red dot dancing across his chest. "Told you I felt eyes upon us!" he whispered, cryptically.

The others knew at once it was the red dot of laser beam, more than likely coming from the scope of a high-powered rifle. Rather than try to take cover behind any of the headstones surrounding him, Wolf spread his arms wider and assumed a position to let his enemy know he was prepared to take the shot that would end his life. In truth, the unknown sniper had him dead to rights, and his death by bullet was inevitable. A second red dot flittered around, then drifted over to zero in on Lucas's chest. He looked down at the bright red laser beam. Without looking up, he whispered, "Oh, no!"

Three sudden bangs were heard from some distance away.

Unaware of the laser beam hovering over Lucas's chest, Ben dove at Wolf, taking him down with a flying tackle. It was Goblin who saved Lucas. The pit pup lunged up, planting his forepaws on his stomach, causing him to topple over to the ground. A second later, a hot lead projectile struck a granite headstone ten feet behind where he had just been standing. The bullet shattered the granite, sending pieces in all directions. Two more bullets struck the headstone behind Ben and Wolf sprawled on the ground beside Bear's resting place.

The next few minutes were chaotic. Lucas could hear the crackle of walkie-talkies as the ranch came alive with former soldiers, all trying to communicate with each other at once. Some were shouting commands, while others spoke calmly, and even as Goblin kept him pinned to the ground behind the headstone of Bear, Lucas could see the Ghosts had all vanished. He didn't even see them leave the dog graveyard, yet he knew they had gone into action, trying to discover who had been shooting at them.

Beef and Reason came from the north end of the ranch to check on Lucas there in the cemetery. Reason looked Lucas, Goblin, and Lobo over, making certain they had not been grazed by flying shrapnel from the shattered headstone.

Beef spoke quietly to Ben.

"Five of them?" Ben asked, his dark eyes straying to the creek some distance away to the north. "And caught by Cora?"

Before Beef could answer him, the four of them looked across the field in the direction of the creek where a female Lakota dressed in an Animal Control uniform was marching five young boys toward the graveyard. Lucas could see it was Cora Red Cloud, and she prodded at two of the boys with a rather large 44. Magnum pistol.

A deep furrow creased Lucas's brow as he locked eyes with one of those boys being herded toward him by Cora. It was Jabar walking with four other Muslim boys, all dressed in camo. Exchanging a puzzled look with Reason, Lucas said, "How the hell did he get released from detention? Judge Sully must be losing it to let him go after the crap he pulled yesterday."

Cora led the five Muslim boys through the arched opening of the graveyard. Jabar and the four boys struggled with the zip-ties around their wrists. Wolf grinned. "Good thing," he said, "my niece was here, Black Bull. Ghosts? American Vets? Five biker clubs? All guarding Wounded Arrow, and it still took her to stop the terrorists."

Ben said, "Yeah, too bad she didn't catch them just a few seconds earlier. It might have saved the Ghosts and I from having a coronary over being shot at."

Wolf glanced behind him to the Ghosts coming up from the creek. All six soldiers carried the high-powered rifles that the assault team had been armed with. It was Beef who pointed out the obvious as the Ghosts brought the heavy fire power with them into the graveyard. "That is some serious weaponry. You boys are in deep trouble."

Jabar snapped, "Allah will protect us! We do his will!"

Lucas sneered at Jabar and said, "Just like he protected you from taking that dart to your forehead, right? Where was Allah then?"

Wolf fixed his gaze on Lucas. "You know these Muslim boys, Lucas? They are friends of yours?"

"Not hardly, Wolf," Lucas said. "Evidently, assaulting Ali and attempting to shoot Khalid did not keep Jabar in detention. But how about this? Trying to take out former US soldiers?"

Beef said, "Possession of these guns as minors is a serious offense. But what my superiors are going to want to know is, who supplied them with the guns?"

Lucas said, "Achmed Waziri."

Jabar spat over his shoulder, "Prove it, American! Besides, Waziri has diplomatic immunity. So, ha ha!"

Beef herded the five boys out of the cemetery and walked them to his cruiser at the center of the ranch. Once the Ghosts had the guns loaded into the trunk of the police cruiser, and the boys secured in the backseat, Beef drove them away from the ranch. As Beef left Wounded Arrow, Lucas shared with Ben, Wolf, and the Ghosts all that had taken place at Khalid's house the day before.

Since each member of the company knew Khalid as the Phantom captain who had escorted them safely out of Mosul several years ago when they had been sent there to secure the x-rays machines that could have been used by extremists to make dirty bombs, Lucas knew they were hanging on his every word. Lucas tried to downplay his role in foiling the assassination of Khalid, and yet Ali spoke up, sharing with the soldiers that it was Lucas wielding his father's cane that had made all the difference yesterday.

It was Ali who told the story, leaving no doubt in the minds of the Natives that Lucas had really stepped up to the plate. After hearing this, Cora gave Lucas a warm hug, whispering, "Welcome back to Wounded Arrow, Little Luke."

Which made Lucas feel all weepy inside.

He would have liked to have spent more time with this company, but the Ghosts had guard duty to see to as the sun began to sink in the western sky. The Cheyenne soldiers politely bid Lucas and Ali goodbye before taking leave of them to walk the perimeter of the ranch.

Ben looked at Reason, saying, "We didn't get much time to talk about the ranch with all the excitement taking place. Why don't we share a fire before you all head back into Havelock?"

24

Chapter Twenty-Four

Reason agreed to Ben's suggestion, and soon Wolf, Ben, Reason and the two boys sat around the blaze of a campfire situated between Ben's underground home and the dog barns some distance away. Wolf and the boys whittled at sticks to make marshmallow and hot dog skewers so that they could eat a fire-cooked dinner beneath the moon and the stars. Goblin ended up getting more than half of the hot dogs Lucas burned over the fire. "He deserves a steak," Lucas said.

"Yes," Ali agreed. "I saw him pounce on you when that red laser danced across your chest. He saved your life."

Lucas said, "But what made him do that? How did he know that a bullet would follow that red dot? Maybe my guardian angel guided him to do what he did to save me from getting shot."

At this, Ali looked at Lucas in disbelief. "Why would an angelic being even consider using an unclean dog for such a deed?" he asked.

Wolf blurted, "Unclean? You think dogs are unclean?"

"He does," Lucas said, shaking his head. He looked across the fire at Ali. "So, you believe in angels?"

Ali finished eating a toasted marshmallow. He smacked his lips as he said, "Angels are part of Islam. The Arabic word for angel, malak, means messenger. According to the Quran, the angels duties are to share revelations from God, record each person's actions, and gather a person's soul when they die. Another being in Islam is the Jinn, who are invisible to humans, also known as djinn or genies. Jinn are supernatural creatures. However Islam considers angels, jinn, and demons as three different types of entities. Jinn were worshiped by many Arabs before Islam began. In ancient Arabia, they were entities among many religions. Zoroastrian, Christian, and Jewish angels and demons were also called jinn. Some scholars claim jinn were at one time pagan gods who became lesser beings as other gods grew more important. According to Arabian belief, jinn caused mental illnesses."

Wolf took a long, silent look up at the star-filled night sky.

Lucas watched him earnestly, wondering what he was going to say next. Even Goblin seated there beside Lucas, peered up at the Lakota Dog Soldier, his head cocked to one side.

Wolf asked, "Do you know how Mohammad came to receive his message from the angel Gabriel? He had a seizure due to his epilepsy.

And you base your entire religion on what one man claimed an angel told him after recovering from an epileptic seizure?"

Ali offered him a haughty look. "Muslims identify the prophets of Islam as humans chosen by God to be his messengers. According to the Quran, the prophets were instructed to bring the will of God to the peoples of all nations. Prophets are human and not divine—"

"That's why," Wolf interjected, "in the beginning it was changed from Mohammadism to Islam, because the first gave too much credit to the prophet Mohammad, who was only a man, not god."

Ali said, "Islam says that all of God's messengers preached the message of Islam—submission to the will of God. The Quran mentions the names of other prophets in Islam, Adam, Noah, Abraham, Moses and Jesus. Muslims believe that God finally sent Mohammad, the last prophet to convey the divine message to the whole world to finalize the exact word of God. The example of Mohammad's life is called the Sunnah, meaning the trodden path. Muslims are to copy Mohammad's actions in their daily lives."

Tossing the last of his hot dog across the fire to Goblin, Wolf asked Ali, "Did you know Mohammad was sent as a prophet to both human and jinn communities? Surah 72 mentions Mohammad's revelation to the jinn. Perhaps, because they are subject to judgment and will be sent to heaven or hell according to their deeds? Another Islamic prophet, who interacted with jinn, is Solomon, a king in ancient Israel that God granted authority over the rebellious jinn. King Solomon forced them to build the First Temple."

Still looking puzzled, Ali said, "Islam traditions says the angels were created on Wednesday, the jinn on Thursday, and humans on Friday. The jinn became corrupt and God sent his angels to battle the infidel jinn. Only a few survived, but with the revelation of Islam by the prophet, the jinn were given a chance to find salvation."

Wolf said, "Kind of a lofty position this last prophet had, to share Allah's revelation to the creatures made of fire. Jinn, demons, and angels are all beyond this realm."

Ali sat up straight on his log seat. "Do you insult the prophet?"

Placing his hands up, Wolf said, "Don't get your dander up, son. I only ask questions. Isn't that what all religions are? Man trying to figure out God? How could anyone get that exactly right?"

"Islam," Ali said, stonily, "is a religion of peace."

Wolf frowned sadly, and said, "There is very little proof that yours is a peaceful religion. Where Islam is dominant, religious minorities suffer persecution. Where Islam is the minority, there is violence if Muslim demands are not met. Either way provides a justification for religious terrorism that haunts Islamic fundamentalism.

"There are 109 sword verses in the Quran that do not square up with religious tolerance. Islam is a religion of peace when Muslims do not have the numbers on their side. Once they do, things change. Many Muslims are peaceful and do not want to believe what the Quran really says, preferring an interpretation that is closer to the Christian path. The sword verses of the Quran have played a key role in very real genocide: The brutal slaughter of tens of millions of Hindus. Buddhism was nearly wiped off the Indian continent. Judaism and Christianity met the same fate in lands conquered by Muslims, the Middle East, North Africa, and Europe. Violence is so ingrained in Islam that it has never really stopped being at war, either with other religions or with itself. Sunni and Shiite."

Long moments of silence passed between them. The fire crackled and wood smoke drifted up into their faces. Lucas shielded his eyes with an arm thrown across his face. Wolf turned his head to one side, allowing the ghost-like smoke to slither off of him and be on its way.

Ali ignored the smoke and offered the old Lakota a glare of defiance.

Ali huffed heatedly, stuck out his chest, and said, "So what do you believe in? How is your religion any better than mine?"

Offering the little Muslim boy a slight grin, Wolf said, "The Great Spirit AKA Wakan Tanka, is the supreme being among the many Native American cultures. He also takes a personal interest in us and intervenes in our lives. According to the late activist, Russell Means, Wakan Tanka is the Great Mystery."

He grinned and looked across the fire at Ali and said, "Similar to your prophet, Mohammad, who had a seizure and afterwards was visited by Gabriel, the angel, a Ghost Dance Religion was founded by Wovoka, a Northern Paiute. The Ghost Dance was meant to serve as a connection with traditional ways of life and to honor the dead. In 1888, Wovoka, the son of a medicine man, fell sick with a fever during an eclipse of the sun. Upon his recovery, he claimed that he had visited the spirit world and the Great Spirit predicted that the world would soon end, then be restored to a pure state. All Natives would inherit this world, including those who were already dead to live eternally without suffering. In order to reach this reality, Wovoka called for meditation, prayer, singing, and dancing as an alternative to mourning the dead.

"This Ghost Dance spread to many tribes on reservations, the Shoshone, Arapaho, Cheyenne, and Dakota, Lakota, and Nakota. They brought their own understanding to the Ghost Dance, predicting that the white people would disappear. A Ghost Dance gathering at Wounded Knee in December 1890 was attacked by the Seventh Cavalry, who massacred unarmed Lakota people, fearful that their dancing would cause many more Natives to go into a murderous rage.

"The Lakota are a Native American tribe. The seven bands of the Lakota are:

"Sichaŋu, meaning burned thighs.

"Oglala, meaning they scatter their own.

"Itazipcho, meaning without bows.

"Huŋkpap, meaning camps at the end of the circle.

"Miniconjou, meaning plants near water.

"Sihasapa, meaning blackfeet.

"Oohenuŋpa, meaning two kettles.

"Lakota leaders were Sitting Bull, American Horse, Sword, Touch the Cloud, Red Cloud, Black Elk, Spotted Tail, and the legendary Tašúŋke Witkó, Crazy Horse from the Oglala and Miniconjou band."

Wolf paused, offering Ali a cold-stone serious look.

He then said, "And the All Father, the Great Spirit, has not once asked us to kill anyone who does not accept him as their god."

25

It was past midnight when Reason loaded both sleep-dazed boys into the backseat of his van. After making sure they were both sprawled out comfortably as they shared the seat, he placed Goblin and Lobo in the passenger's seat. Reason turned to say good-bye to Ben and Wolf. "Thanks," he said to Ben, "for sharing the history of the ranch with me. I'll write up a piece and post it on the Storm Haven site. Lots of kids will enjoy reading about the rescue work you do with pits."

Ben nodded and said, "Be sure and give my vets credit for the work they do out here. They often serve an ungrateful nation, and many take them for granted. It would do them mighty wonders to be bolstered on the Internet with your story. A little nudge to their self-esteem would go a long way in keeping their heads held high. Please, at my request, give them the credit they deserve."

Reason assured him he would follow through with his request, and as he turned to climb into the van for the return trip to Havelock, Wolf stepped up beside the van. "You have your hands full," he said, gesturing at the two sleeping boys inside the van. "The Thunder Dreamer is not an easy boy to live with, as Ben often found out dealing with him and his anger issues. But this Ali?"

Reason waited for him to say more.

Standing there, shaking his head, the big Lakota offered Reason a deep frown. "So conflicted. So turned inside out. This religion he was born into has him far outside the Sacred Hoop."

Reason said, "I'm sure Ali and his father, Khalid, have never had their faith described that way before. Do you know by most people's standards, both would be considered Moderates, preferring to live here in peace with the rest of us?"

"Moderates," Wolf said, a glint in his dark eyes, "are irrelevant when it comes to the Extremists. These people have killed more of each other than they care to admit. Moderates are extremely cautious not be to be called apostate or heretics by the Extremists. Or, they too, will find themselves on some kind of religious hit list."

In an attempt to show the old Lakota his deepest respect, Reason kept a smile on his face. "Religious hit list?" he said. "I really don't know how conflicted Ali is over his belief, but I do know his father is a good man, with a good heart."

Wolf peered at Reason, his eyes narrowed in thought.

Before either of them could continue, Ben looked out to the road. "Now what the hell is that all about?" he said in alarm.

A black Ford van went speeding past the front gate of Wounded Arrow, heading north and doing about 90 mph. Its headlamps lit up the roadway ahead, while twin red taillights marked it's location in the swirling fog and the darkness surrounding it.

Once it disappeared over the top of a rise, its driver braked hard, gunned the van's engine, and turned around at the bottom of the steep roadway to come roaring back over the hill it had just descended.

At the wheel was Crow Harper.

The president of the Apaches grimaced in pain as he cradled his bandaged stump at the end of his left wrist against his chest. His right hand was attached to the steering column with a short length of chain, leaving him just enough room to steer the van. He cursed Waziri for cutting his hand off to free him from the handcuffs securing him to the dumpster. He cursed Waziri again for forcing him to drive with him to cut a deal with the Powder King. The scraggily, bearded biker had pleaded with the Muslim man to drive him to the local ER to have him sedated while a surgeon sewed up his stump. But Waziri refused and kept them on track to purchase the load of Deep 9 powder he planned to destroy the US service dogs with.

Crow blubbered incoherently as he gunned the van and took it helling down the roadway, once more passing the gateway of the ranch. He fully expected at any moment to be blown to kingdom come, for the vest he wore was hooked up to a number of explosive devices. In his rage and hatred for the Muslim man, Crow drove the van defiantly and with reckless abandon. Waziri had ordered him to race up the driveway of the Wounded Arrow ranch, plow directly into the main dog barn, and crash through the doorway. And then, Waziri would detonate the bombs strapped to Crow's chest.

And four kegs of powder would be dispersed into the air, leaving the dogs inside the barn to die a slow, painful death as the chemicals evaporated the air in their lungs, instructing their brains to shut down.

If he failed to drive through the gateway of the ranch on his first run up to the place, Waziri promised he would unleash the fiends on him. "What fiends?" Crow had asked as Waziri chained him to the steering column inside the van.

Snickering, Waziri had said, "If you do not drive straight to your goal, Crow Harper, you will suffer a most horrific death!"

Grimacing with pain, Crow had glanced behind him to the four plastic drums filled with the deadly powder. The Muslim man had waved his hands above a small wooden crate situated in the van beside the four barrels, uttering words in a foreign language. Crow looked on in bewilderment from his place in the front seat. He hissed in terror as a green mist leaked out of the crate, leaving a crackling emerald cloud in the back of the van.

Waziri smirked at the strange conflagration and said, "You will suffer the feeding frenzy of hungry fiends. The bad news is, they will be tainted from feasting on your black soul. The good news for you is, the excruciating pain will last for only seconds as they feed on you like blood-crazed sharks, tearing your soul to pieces!"

Crow actually whimpered as he went speeding past the gate of the ranch, for the crate behind his seat rattled noisily, then burst apart as four wisps of black-green smoke coalesced into the air in the back of the van. His eyes wide with fright, Crow glanced over one shoulder to see four brutish apparitions that could only be described as Middle Eastern ghosts, for they all were bald with the exception of scalp-locks hanging down the back of their clean-shaven domes. They wore no shirts, and were heavily rippled with thick, powerful muscles. And that, to Crow's horror, is where their human qualities ended, for their legs and feet were nothing more than wisps of black, oily smoke that undulated beneath them as they began to drift toward the front of the van. Stomping hard on the brakes, Crow brought the van to an abrupt halt in the middle of the road. Whipping the steering wheel around, he peeled out and headed back toward the gateway of the ranch.

Wolf brushed past Reason and Ben, his .44 Magnum raised in both hands. As the van came speeding through the front gate of Wounded Arrow, the big Lakota dropped to one knee at the edge of the driveway, closing one eye and drawing a bead on the oncoming van. He first sighted on the driver, but then a twinge of his conscious caused him to lower his sights to the driver's side front tire.

A thunderous shot rang out and the large pistol bucked in Wolf's grasp. His first shot missed the tire, but the second follow-up shot was dead-center and the rolling tire popped with the impact of the hot lead passing through its rubber casing.

The van veered wildly toward the left side of the driveway and the driver nearly lost control of his speeding vehicle.

Wolf's third shot took out the passenger's side front tire, ripping through the hard rubber like a warm knife passing through butter.

Standing as the van careened past him, Wolf took aim at the driver, then paused to determine who he was about to send out of this life with the shot from his .44. Upon seeing the biker with the scraggily beard and the wild dreadlocks, Wolf held his shot.

Crow Harper didn't even glance in the Dog Soldier's direction as he sped past him. He was gibbering loudly and continuing to glance over his shoulder at the four green-tinged beings drifting his way in the back of the van. The two front tires, badly damaged by the two bullets from the high-powered pistol, fell away from their rims in shredded pieces that flew through the air and landed on either side of the driveway. Down to his rims, Crow stomped on the accelerator. Mad with terror of the ghostly beings slinking up behind him, he gave out one last guttural cry as he shot past Ben's underground home and then went crashing into the front entrance of the main dog barn.

A number of things all happened at once then.

Two of the greenish ghosts encircled the biker president, both wrapping their arms around him, the tips of their fingers sinking into flesh where their hands latched onto him. One of them sank long fangs into Crow's neck and began savagely mauling him. The second one slid around to the front of the biker, and tore a chunk of flesh out of the center of his chest, bright red blood exploding in its mouth.

Then, Crow heard the sudden click as Waziri from some distance away detonated the explosives strapped to his chest.

The thunder of hellfire followed, and the van, its hapless driver, and the four plastic barrels were ripped to shreds by the powerful detonations . . . and an enormous cloud of white dust filled the inside of the dog barn.

26

Chapter Twenty-Six

As Wolf's first shot echoed through the air, Goblin launched himself from the front seat and into the back, pouncing on the sleeping form of Lucas. *Wake up!* the pup sent into Lucas's thoughts. *Evil is coming! You must wake up and send it back!*

The roar of Wolf's gun had caused both boys to wake up, but as Lucas sat up, Goblin came hurtling into him there on the backseat. He reached out to catch the pup before he slid back and off the seat. Beside him, Ali cringed at the sound of Wolf's second and third shot.

The two boys looked outside the van to see Crow Harper fly past them in a black van. "Crow's still alive," Lucas whispered, watching as the van wobbled crazily up the driveway.

Ali watched the biker president take the van directly through the double doors of the dog barn's entrance. He gasped out loud as the van exploded. Tears spilling down his face, Lucas muttered, "All of those dogs! All of those poor, damned dogs!"

He sat there watching the enormous white cloud burst from the bomb-shredded van, then transform into a dragon with coal-black eyes and an open red mouth. The cloud-creature viciously hissed at the two dozen bikers who came running toward the barn. Despite the fact that they all were heavily armed, the smoke-beast dismissed them with another hiss, then slithered deep inside the dog barn.

"That demon," Ali cried, "is going after the service dogs!"

Lucas leaped out of the van and headed toward the barn, determined to do something about rescuing the dogs trapped now within it Ben latched onto him. "But, Ben," he cried, "we've got to get the dogs out of there! It will kill them sure as hell!"

"No," Ben said, "it won't."

Lucas looked up at the Lakota dog handler in bafflement.

Ben said, "The dogs are not in there. Cora had me remove them two days ago. They are safe in the underground kennels of Kooper's Steading. Remember when we discovered them, Lucas? Cora thought it was a perfect place to temporarily settle them. And they are guarded well. That is the nightly station of the Ghost Company. They would each die before they allowed anyone to harm those dogs."

Reason asked, "Kooper's what?"

"Steading," Lucas told him, his eyes locked on the smoldering barn where wisps of smoky white powder leaked out through holes in the structure. "Just beyond that hill to the northeast is an old farmstead where Old Man Kooper used to hold dog fights in an underground bunker. I found it when I lived here with Ben in foster care."

Lucas looked to Ben. "But what if that demon can track by scent?"

There came a cry from the yard before the demolished barn. Bikers gathered there began to scatter as the cloud-dragon emerged from between two charred beams that had once served as the center posts for the dog barn's front door. The creature's mouth opened in a vicious snarl. At once, whippets of blue-white lightning burst from between its jaws. The zephyrs of lightning passed above the heads of the twenty bikers, causing them to beat a hasty retreat to the nearby second barn.

"What is that thing?" Reason asked.

Wolf said, "A wanagi from the Otherworld."

The ghost-dragon turned its gaze on the field beyond the shambles of the destroyed barn. It was the field of Ben's neighbor, a rancher who owned a large herd of buffalo. It was the field that lay between the dust monster and the US service dogs tucked away in the under-ground kennels of Old Man Kooper's former fighting arena.

The dragon of dangerous particles and deadly chemicals sniffed at the air, and began tracking the dogs by scent. Concentrating fully on that scent, the creature sent out a savage roar, sizzling branches of blue-white lightning jetting from its wide open mouth. It began to move forward, away from the ruins of the barn, and directly across the field beyond. There, gathered in a huddle, were a herd of nearly a hundred shaggy buffalo, staring in alarm at the ghost dragon slowly drifting their way.

The herd huddled together beyond the electric fence in its path.

Suddenly from the driveway, Ben cried, "Cora! Get out of there!"

Lucas looked to the field of the buffalo ranch one-hundred yards distant and saw Cora Red Cloud riding a black and white Appaloosa directly in front of the herd. Her long raven hair streaming over her shoulders, she jerked on the reins of her horse, bringing it skidding to a stop before the advancing creature from the Otherworld. Her dark eyes gleaming, she offered the dragon a defiant glare.

The moment the ghostly roiling white smoke of the dragon came in contact with the electric fence, a loud crackle filled the air, and traces of the creature's blue-white lightning sparkled along its wires shooting at once to the left and the right. There came one resonant Zap! and the four strands of the fence snapped and curled back to leave an open pathway for the dragon to pass through.

At the sound of the electrical implosion, Cora's speckled horse let out a terrified scream and reared back, her front hooves thrashing at the air. The sudden movement, sent Cora sailing from her saddle, and she landed heavily on the ground not five feet from the lead bull of the buffalo herd.

Wolf cursed and started to run toward his fallen niece, but Reason stopped the big Lakota and guided him over to his van. Ben and Lucas were quick to follow them. Inside the van, Ali looked to the smoldering barn and the four green ghostly forms slithering out from between the burned and broken boards of the barn behind it. All four large beings resembled the genie in the Aladdin cartoon Ali had once watched when he was younger. All were bald with the exception of long, dark scalp locks, and they all had buffed up chests and arms, much like the wrestlers from the All-Star Wrestling team.

"Jinn," Ali said. "Those are the jinn we were talking about earlier. Waziri must have transported them across the sea and set them free here on American soil. They are far more dangerous than terrorists."

They all watched the four jinn minions drift in behind the dust monster, their own sights fixed on the milling herd of buffalo. Reason headed the van straight through the opening the dragon had left in the fence, then veered in between the beast and Cora sprawled before the buffalo. Goblin and Lobo let out a fierce barks.

The cloud-dragon turned its head like a slow slithering snake and peered down into the van at the pit bull pup, extreme menace in its shark-like black eyes.

Goblin and Lobo barked again.

"No," whispered Lucas, in an effort to calm the feisty dogs.

Use the feather magic, Goblin sent into Lucas's mind. *The eagle feather of American Horse was given back to you for a good reason, Lucas. Wield its magic, or those buffalo are going to die!*

Goblin let out a third bark, which was cut off halfway as Lucas clamped a hand over his snout. "Shhh!" he hissed between clenched teeth. "Look, you've got that cloud-demon glaring at us!"

In the back seat, Wolf opened the side door of the van and hopped out to see to Cora. Ben was right behind him. Goblin lunged out of Lucas's grasp and bolted out of the open door, running in between Ben and Wolf.

Cora's horse bolted and ran as Goblin reached her side. The pup snuffled at Cora's limp form. He growled into the faces of the many buffalo inching their way forward to examine the fallen rider. He actually nipped at the nose of the lead bull who had lowered his head, sticking his wet nose directly on Cora's face. As Wolf lifted her into his arms, the bull backed away, refocusing on the advancing cloud-dragon on the opposite side of the van. He huffed a bold challenge to the ghostly apparition from the Otherworld. "No, my brother," Ben said to the bull. "Take your herd elsewhere. We will deal with this wanagi! Go and be safe, brother!"

Snorting defiantly, the bull buffalo peered up at the Lakota and huffed and wheeled around, his herd following him across the field catching up to Cora's fleeing horse. Ben made sure Wolf had Cora inside the van before he shouted to Reason, "Go, follow the herd to a safe distance! Go now, and I will deal with this!"

27

Springing out of the van, Lucas reached down inside his shirt, latched onto the eagle feather, and ripped it from the leather thong around his neck. He caught a quick glimpse of Reason turning the van toward the herd. Honking furiously on the horn, he managed to get the entire herd of buffalo to turn and run back across the field, where Cora's Appaloosa was already fleeing to the relative safety of the distant pasture.

Realizing the van was no longer between him and the demons from the Otherworld, Lucas skidded to a stop beside Goblin in the dew-slick grass. He wheeled around, his eagle feather crackling with Big Medicine. A burst of multicolored light beams streamed from his raised fist clenched tightly around the token of power. Each beam attached itself to the rainbow of color Ben had already conjured with the arrowhead he held in his own clenched fist.

The light beams transformed into the ethereal forms of raptors. In an explosion of glittering feathers, an entire flock of eagles, hawks, falcons, owls, and ravens sped toward the ghostly white dragon in a full-blown aerial attack. Beaks and talons ripped and tore through the beast's form, shredding portions of its wings, breast, and horned head. Momentarily stunned by the bird barrage, the dragon reared back, snaking around the many winged forms hurtling into it.

Upon seeing the brilliant-colored raptors relentlessly assaulting the cloud-dragon, the four jinn suddenly armed themselves with green glowing curved scimitars. At once, they began to attack the magical flock of winged creatures, felling them with extreme accuracy.

Lucas stared down at the eagle feather clutched in his hand. "How did I do that?" he asked, bewildered by the magical flock of raptors.

It was Goblin who reminded him of the tokens of power: *Remember the talisman Ben's Uncle Pete draped around his neck? The arrowhead once belonged to Sitting Bull, a token of power that would shield Ben from the Dark Ones. It is endowed with big medicine.*

Lucas remembered the encounter Ben had had when he was ten-years-old back on Pine Ridge: The Tall Man had come to steal Uncle Pete's pups. Ben had summoned the spirit of Crazy Horse to defend him, and afterwards, the Lakota Warrior said to Ben, "Whoever gifted you with that did you a great favor."

Goblin stood there, peering over at Lucas and he sent, *My first encounter with the Otherworld took place on that parking garage that you nearly jumped off of. That's when I saw a band of hooded figures in red vapors swirling around you. They reached out their hands clutching at you. I barked. I could not help myself, for the ghosts hovered four feet from me, enraged that I had interfered in their stalking of such a troubled young boy. The spirit creatures prepared to launch themselves at you. I darted in front of you and let out a fierce bark. You had to wake up before they invaded your soul. If they were allowed to do that, you would never be the same. Ben drew out his stone arrowhead attached to a leather cord beneath his shirt. He held it up and shouted, "Trouble this boy no more! Go back to the Otherworld, wanagis of woe! By the power of the sun! By the power of moon! By the power of the stars! By the power of the Light, I command you to leave this child alone!"

The ghosts wailed in distress and drifted away through the sky, snarling, growling, and hissing like mad cats. They then vanished.

Ben afterwards had said, "Wanagi is what the Lakota call demons. They hail from the Otherworld. We live in a tri-fold world, past, present, and future, yet a thin veil separates us from the unseen realm where good and evil wage an ancient war that impacts all of us. Those who can see the workings of this realm have the Sight. Uncle Pete claims dogs see the spirit realm more keenly than we do. Goblin is attuned to both worlds. Lucas, you carry a load of anger inside of you, one that creates red-hot waves in the aura that surrounds you. I am no medicine man, like my uncle Pete, but I have a gift when it comes to seeing the auras that emanate from dogs. I see this same aura surrounding you. You have gone on unchecked for so long that it has attracted destructive spirits to you. If you don't learn to control your furious rage, they will continue to harass you, feeding off your anger, lending their own madness to your fits, consuming pieces of your soul."

Standing there, Lucas watched in horror as the cloud-dragon blew breaths of sparkling particles at the raptors. At once, owls, falcons, eagles, and hawks were caught in the blasts. Smaller birds fell to the sweeping blades of the four jinn who swung their scimitars, literally hammering them from the air.

It was a terrible slaughter, and Lucas knew that the buffalo herd would be next in line. One whiff of the chemicals wafting from the dragon, and the buffalo would suffer an agonizing death.

"Lucas!" Ben cried. "I know how to stop this thing! But we need to combine our magic to do it!"

Ben raised the arrowhead that had once belonged to Sitting Bull. He was surprised to see a violet glow emanating from the stone arrowhead, as if some power beyond knew of the danger the dragon and the jinn presented.

Goblin barked a challenge to the dragon of dust and smoke, then sent to Lucas, *Kick it up a notch, Little Luke! Instead of a flock of birds, send it a force of brutal strength and damaging power!*

Glancing down at the feather clutched in his hand, Lucas said, "What makes you think I have any say so in what this talisman brings through from the Otherworld?"

Goblin sent: *By activating the arrowhead, you opened a doorway into the Beyond. What comes through it to help us, has a lot to do with the images you conjure, just like Ben when he summoned Crazy Horse to defend him from the Tall Man when he was just a boy. You must concentrate now to stop this thing.*

Ben held the violet-glowing arrowhead up to the four directions, north, west, south, and east, and at once a lavender-shaded field of force draped itself over him, Lucas, and Goblin. The warding encased them in its transparent shell just as the dragon blew a frosty breath of the Deep 9 chemicals down at them.

The violet shield took the brunt of the dragon's breath, caving inward, and then repelling the smoky cloud so that its devastating particles slid off the warding. Lucas drew the feather back and over his shoulder and thrust it forward. He conjured an entire barrage of images in his mind, and let them loose with a fierce shout. Spectral creatures of the wild burst through the rip in the fabric between this realm and the Otherworld. More than a dozen of the shimmering, transparent beasts closed at once with the dragon and the jinn.

In this first wave there were badgers, wolverines, wolves, cougars, bobcats, and deer with wide-spread antlers that glittered as they made a full on charge at the five opposing mystical monsters conjured by the extremist, Waziri.

The wolves and cougars swept the four scimitar-wielding jinn off their feet. The spectral badgers and wolverines closed on the fallen spirit-warriors, mauling them, clawing at them, and creating a dog pile all over their prone forms, preventing them, for the moment, from rising to attack.

The dragon roared and a burst of snow-like crystals exploded from his mouth. And although they were all creatures from the spirit realm, the chemicals caused many of the shimmering beasts to disintegrate, turning them into sparkles that fizzled and dissolved as the turbulent cloud washed over them.

Lucas decided he needed help from the wildest of the wild. "I'm trying one more thing," he said to Ben. "And if that doesn't work, then it's going to be up to you, Ben."

Ben, however, was looking over his shoulder behind them to some unseen force or figure. Lucas shook his head and said, "Here goes!"

He swirled the eagle feather through the air and stabbed forward, an image appearing on the ethereal plains of the Otherworld, one that Lucas had conjured to wreck havoc with the dragon. A thunderous roar came from the shimmering silvery mist and an enormous supernatural grizzly bear came charging through the rip in the fabric. The brawny brute did not hesitate to attack the dragon, plowing into him with incredible speed and power.

Upon seeing the ethereal grizzly locked in combat with the cloud-dragon, Goblin let out a howl. "Shhh, Goblin!" Lucas hissed, looking ahead of them to the jinn as they flitted from side to side, sweeping their blades through the astral forest creatures battling against them.

The dragon roared and another burst of chemicals exploded from his mouth. The bear locked the dragon in a savage embrace, sucking in the deadly cloud so that it could not drift any further. The massive grizzly roared in pain and fury, then buried his fangs into the dragon's neck. He shook his shaggy head from side to side, tearing the life out of the cloud dragon, which imploded into a sparkling mist.

28

Even as the silvery mist evaporated, Waziri appeared there above the field, hovering in the astral plain. From inside the warding, Lucas looked above the field to Waziri dressed in his purple robes and shimmering turban, resembling a Medieval wizard. He appeared to be standing on a floating carpet.

Four riders came hurtling out of the Otherworld behind him, war cries echoing across the field as they fixed the jinn in their eagle-proud gazes. They rode scintillating horses of star dust. They shimmered as they carried their Native riders directly at the four jinn.

Ben said, "Sitting Bull, Touch the Cloud, Gall, and Crazy Horse!"

Sitting Bull thrust his spear through the chest of the jinn he attacked. With a wild war whoop, the great medicine man shoved his weapon deep inside the glowing jinn. It exploded as the Native magic sent the jinn back to another realm.

Touch the Cloud cried out in surprise as the jinn before him swung his scimitar and cleaved through the chest of his dazzling horse. The massive warrior's mount broke apart beneath him. He came back up, to drive his tomahawk into the skull of the jinn before him. It, too, exploded into a sparkling green mist.

Gall sat back on his glimmering horse and drew a bead with his bow. He released the string, sending his pulsating arrow into the chest of the jinn. The arrow imploded, sending thunder ripping through the green ghost of the jinn, leaving it mere tendrils of smoke.

Crazy Horse's raven hair rippled over his shoulders as he rode at the jinn. White war paint covered his face, a scattering of blue hail stones on one cheek, a yellow lightning bolt down the other. Trailing from his left shoulder was a stone tied with a leather thong. He swung his tomahawk and buried it in the chest of the jinn, who disintegrated, its form sluicing away like a watery substance.

All four Lakota warriors wheeled around to watch as the bear ambled up to them, his head hanging low, his shoulders slumped.

Crazy Horse dismounted. He and Touch the Cloud knelt beside the great bear, both resting their hands on its bulky shoulders. Sitting Bull and Gall soon joined them, both singing softly.

The bear vanished in a cloud of sparkling blue particles that drifted up and joined the silver stars.

Crazy Horse looked at Waziri drifting away on his flying carpet. "You are a twisted soul, who will never reform or change."

The war chief looked to Ben. "Warrior of the Lakota, one day you will send his soul wind-riding. Keep your medicine close."

A few moments later, Reason drove back around to the place where the supernatural battle took place. By then, Wolf had roused Cora and held her up in her seat as Reason brought the van to stop. While he hopped out and ran around to the side to open the door, Wolf and Ali helped Cora to climb out. She was still a bit dazed from her fall from her horse, but she smiled cordially as Wolf introduced her to Reason and Ali.

The four of them stared in wonder at the sight of the four great Lakota war chiefs sharing a fire with Ben and Lucas. They joined them, taking their place before the crackling blaze. Ben gestured at Cora to kneel beside him, and as she did, Lucas nodded at her, offering her a slight smile, but then he turned his full attention to what was being said by the four war chiefs. Sitting Bull held his arrowhead that he'd taken from Ben. Gall held Lucas's eagle feather that had once belonged to American Horse.

Ben said, "You once claimed that each time you rode into battle you entered into the Otherworld. On dozens of battles that you rode in, you rode directly through a hail of bullets and was never struck by one. It was nothing short of a miracle that you survived, preferring as was your way, to ride at the front of your fellow braves."

Sitting Bull laughed at the perplexed look on Crazy Horse's face. "Tell him about the time," he said, "during the Custer massacre! You rode directly into a storm of white soldiers' bullets fired from breech-loading rifles! You survived without one scratch!"

Shaking his head, Gall said, "Yes, and during the Wagon Box fight you rode through a hail of bullets. I say, it was because of the stone you wore at your left shoulder."

"I say," Sitting Bull said, "it was the medicine from being chosen as a Shirt Wearer. Red Cloud badly wanted that shirt when the Big Bellies removed it from you."

Shaking his head again, Gall said, "His shirt was decorated with over 200 paintings and medallions, marking his many great deeds. But it was the small stone he wore into battle that protected him."

Crazy Horse said, "That first time I had a vision, my horse was wild and spirited, and thus, I took the name Crazy Horse as my father before me. I loved that man. He allowed me to take his name, while he resorted to being called Worm, stepping aside so that his son might know greatness. I was surprised when I rode through a hail of bullets, and yet in each battle, I would imagine I was in the Otherworld. This one thought kept me from taking any bullets from my enemy."

"So," Lucas asked, "you trigger the power of the medicine through your mind?"

Sitting Bull asked, "How did you summon the bear?"

Lucas said, "I just thought of him, all powerful and fierce, and he came roaring out of the seam in the fabric between the realms."

"Then," Crazy Horse told him, "that is how to activate the medicine of the eagle feather. With your thoughts."

And with that said, the four Lakota chieftains began a storytelling session that lasted into the wee hours of the morning. Each man had a glorious history to speak of. Each man had ridden into so many battles, conducted so many buffalo hunts, bravely led their people on the path of their enemies, and each had hundreds of stories to tell.

The last thing he remembered, Lucas looked across the fire at Reason and Ali, who were both staring in rapt fascination at the four chiefs, and then, he snuggled up beside Goblin and fell asleep.

That next day, Lucas kicked himself mentally. He really wanted to bid the four Lakota chiefs a proper good-bye as they returned to the realm beyond. As it was, he did not wake up until the next morning back at Reason's house.

Reason invited Ben, Wolf, and Cora over to the house for breakfast. As a writer, he was fascinated by the fact that all three Natives seemed convinced they had all experienced a supernatural encounter. He wanted to pick their brains about why the four legendary chiefs intervened against the magical beings Waziri conjured. Reason spent the major part of that breakfast asking questions and taking notes.

Wolf explained that the Lakota were visionaries, that they were a spiritual people, and that a visit by legends from the Otherworld were to be accepted with gratefulness as a gift from the All Father.

Slipping pieces of bacon to the dogs under the table, Lucas said, "Now that Crow is dead, what about my dad?"

Reason poured a round of strong black coffee into the mugs of his three guests seated at the table, before saying, "Beef and his captain are squaring up facts on what Khalid witnessed when he spotted Crow leaving that powder in Stone's truck. The county attorney claims Khalid's recording proved it was Crow. Beef thought that once Waziri was arrested, the county attorney would have a clearer picture about the players involved in this plot to kill service dogs, but . . ."

Lucas turned in his chair as Stone came through the front door. "Dad!" he cried, springing from his chair to embrace him. Allowing for only a brief hug, Stone turned him around and sat him back down in his chair. "I was released an hour ago," he said. "However, now that Waziri has fled the country, Khalid made plans to go after him. He contacted his superiors in the Middle East, informing them that as an ex-Delta Ranger, I have contacts overseas that will help in the hunt. Our flight leaves in two hours. I'm sorry about such a short good-bye, but you and I can keep in contact daily over the Internet."

Well aware that Lucas was about to have an emotional breakdown after hearing such news, Stone quickly said, "If it's any consolation that you're stuck in foster care a little while longer, Ali got the worst end of the entire deal. Khalid asked two old friends to take him in while he's stalking Waziri. They happen to be your old foster parents, the Yardleys. Remember? You ran away from them back when—"

"Just the two of you?" Lucas blurted, his eyes filling with tears. "Two to take on Waziri and an entire band of terrorists? What if Waziri sets a trap, and an army of extremists removes you and Khalid from the face of the earth in one bloody gun battle?"

Stone said, "Khalid is a highly qualified anti-terrorist agent. He knows what he's doing. He saw the potential in me helping him. He will not take any unnecessary risks having your dad along with him. We both know how dangerous this man is."

He paused, then said, "Demoted at Homeland Security, Agent Raynes is joining us on the hunt."

"Great!" Lucas said, sarcastically. "An agent with an attitude! I feel better about this already!"

29

Chapter Twenty-Nine

Alex Thorn, a shaggy-haired 14-year-old, stood in the alley behind the house. In the darkness, he resembled a Goth raccoon, black face paint around his eyes, black hair hanging in a tail down his back, black trench coat swallowing his slender frame.

He actually gasped when a small monkey-like creature skittered past him, its claws scraping across his black Cargo pants, tugging at his black Keds. The bug-eyed creature scurried up the side of an oak tree in the middle of the yard. Alex knew he should not have come on this venture. Even without this burglary, he clumsily tottered his way into the juvenile justice system. Like thousands of angry, lost, hurting boys before him, he considered his "court list" a knotted club held over his head. His mom used it every morning as leverage to get him out of bed, so that one more truancy did not get added to his list.

He crept past the tree, glancing warily at the creepy monkey. He could feel its black-eyed gaze on him as he sidled up to the house. Atop a layer of white powder, Alex had a yellow lightning bolt down the left side of his face, and scattered across his face were hailstones. Earlier that day, Lucas had given him a lecture on the significance of Indians and painted faces: "Protects them from being recognized by demons! Native warriors painted their faces for battles. The designs held magic! Every mark on the face and body had meaning. The hand symbol meant that the warrior was great in hand-to-hand combat. The zig-zag across the forehead symbolized lightning. Red was war."

Lucas had enlisted Alex to do the sneaking he couldn't do at the moment. Since moving into foster care with Reason Nelson, Lucas had opted out of any lawbreaking activities, and burglarizing an old man's house was crossing a line. Therefore, Alex was out in the middle of night, trying to reclaim the two rings Lucas had given to the old relic collector, Gus Howard.

As his friend, Alex was determined to get them back. Even as he inspected the cat-trap in the door before him, he could hear Lucas saying, "Besides, you are not burglarizing Gus's house. Just taking back what's mine."

Alex's eyes widened when he saw the monkey advancing on him across the backyard. Splayed against the back door of the house, he felt something brush against his leg. He cried out in alarm as a gray cat hurtled out from between his feet. The cat went careening into the spindly body of the black monkey. It screeched angrily, lashing out in a spastic attack. The monkey wheeled away to avoid sharp claws. Put off by the fury of the mad cat, the creature ran back to the tree, scurrying up into its branches. The cat raced across the backyard toward the open gate, and darted down the alley, disappearing into the night.

Kneeling down, Alex crawled through the opening of the cat door. He stood up and crossed a small kitchen, and entered into a shadowy bedroom, pulling his tazer from his duster pocket. He moved to a dresser situated against the far wall. He opened all three drawers, revealing an entire cache of weapons resting on velvety pads in each drawer. The little kid gaped at the assortment of pistols. "Who does this guy think he is, James Bond?" He reached down into the top drawer, touching what appeared to be a gold cross. It snapped open to become a short sword. "And, Van Helsing thrown into the mix?"

A quick search of the drawers resulted in a frustrated sigh. Alex turned to the still form in the bed. Gus appeared to be asleep. Tightly gripping his tazer in a two-fisted grip, Alex focused on the old's man's thin chest, his eyes widening in horror when he spotted the railroad spike buried in Gus Howard's breast.

Wheeling around, Alex ran directly into the hooded figure moving out of a shadowy corner of the room. Pushing himself away from the dark form, he darted out into the hallway. Nearing its end, he barreled into the kitchen, his sights set on the cat-trap at the end of a patch of slick linoleum floor. Picking up his pace, Alex was moving so fast he slammed head-first into the solid metal door. He saw stars. He saw blackness. He staggered back. He stumbled and fell, fighting hard not to pass out.

He sighed in relief when he spotted the hooded figure passing through the living room and exiting through the front door.

Suddenly, the back door struck the kitchen wall, causing the entire house to shudder. Nate Holland stood there before him, and Alex scrambled to his feet and frantically jabbed at him with the tazer. Dodging the crackling prongs, Nate slapped Alex, causing him to drop the tazer. The biker grabbed him by the throat. A voice came from the end of the hallway: "Let him go, Uncle Nate."

Struggling to breathe in the big man's vise-like grip, Alex turned to see a dark-haired girl stepping out of the kitchen. "Celeste!" he managed to whisper, relieved to see Lucas's older sister standing there looking like a Vampire Mistress clad in her black duster. Her short raven hair gave her a boyish look, but nothing could tamp down the catlike glare in her she-lion gaze.

Celeste scooped up the tazer, driving the snapping prongs into Nate's neck. He did the funky chicken, crashing back into the wall. Alex darted into the bedroom and snatched up a pair of glowing handcuffs from one of the drawers. The twin metal bracelets crackled as he placed one of them around Nate's right wrist, and locked the other end to the floor radiator.

"Did you get the rings from Gus?" Celeste asked Alex.

"Gus is dead," Alex quietly said.

"What?" Celeste gasped. "Dead? How?"

At once, Celeste darted into the bedroom. She was terribly saddened by the sight of Gus Howard pierced through the heart with the railroad spike. "Some one," Alex said from the doorway, "got here before me!"

Consumed by grief, she bent and planted a soft kiss on Gus's forehead. She gave a sigh. "We have to get out here, Alex!"

As she spun him around toward the living room, Nate drew a .22 pistol from a holster beneath his jacket. He leveled the gun at the chain connecting the handcuffs to each other. Six shots rang out. Two of the bullets trailed sparks as they flew across the room. Startled by the whizzing hot lead, Alex ran into the wall and slid to the floor, unconscious from his collision. Celeste slapped Nate as she raced past him, sending his gun flying from his grasp. She glanced helplessly back at Alex sprawled on the floor. It was then that the black monkey latched onto the tail of her long, black duster, and pulled her out through the back door.

Reason sat staring at his computer screen, when Rumor sprang onto the edge of his desk. Startled by the cat's appearance, Reason attempted to coax it to walk the last few feet and into his lap. But the feline refused. Still ruffled from his encounter with the monkey, Rumor's fur was sticking up and his widened eyes were fixed on the nearby open window.

Reason did not dare pick him up in the agitated state he was in. He knew better than to attempt his hand at cat-wrangling. He knew that Rumor belonged to Gus Howard, a retired security specialist who lived down the street, and yet the cat had somehow discovered the dog-trap in his own back door and managed to creep stealthily past the two dogs sleeping in the kitchen. Reason went to the kitchen and set out a can of tuna. After finishing the meal, Rumor darted into Reason's den. He sprang up into his lap, and proceeded to fall asleep.

Fanning away tuna breath wafting up from the cat in his lap, Reason was startled by the muffled gunshots from four houses away. He placed Rumor on his desk, and headed for the back door, dodging Lobo and Goblin who sprang up into his path.

Peering through his screen door, he was startled when Celeste ran up to his house. "Gus Howard has been murdered!" she said. "Alex is trapped inside his house with my uncle Nate. If you call the cops, please get Alex out of there first!"

He stared at her as she turned and ran off across his backyard, a small black monkey trailing behind her. He then hurried back into the kitchen and called Detective Beef Tory to report the shooting.

Ten minutes later, Reason sat watching from his back porch, Rumor snuggled in his lap, Lobo and Goblin sprawled at his feet. Red and blue lights rotated from the nearby alley. A yellow flashlight beam cut through the shadows as Detective Tory moved away from his car. The lemony beam strayed down the alley.

Reason sat watching as the large, blond detective made his way into his yard. Rumor gave a hiss and tore off for the dog-trap.

Beef approached the porch, a frown creasing his well-trimmed golden beard. He said, "Gus Howard is dead. Evidently, Nate Holland went there to steal the rings from Gus. He is determined to have all four of them. Told you we should have returned them to your grandfather. He's the only one who can keep them safe."

Reason cursed softly. "Billy wants nothing to do with those Templar rings, claiming they are cursed. If Nate persists in getting them for himself, I'll go to the Den and tell them it was Nate who chopped off Crow's hand from that dumpster in my alley, in order to get Crow to the buy from the Powder King. He turned Crow over to Waziri, along with four barrels of Deep 9 he used at Wounded Arrow.

"Remember last year when Lucas was removed from his home, due to the domestic between Stone and Maggie? He ended up in foster care at Ben Black Bull's dog rescue ranch. Stone went to court three times, trying to get Lucas back. That same year, Maggie was killed in a car accident. Soon after, Lucas was back at home. Rumor has it Maggie witnessed Nate having a meeting with you. When she confronted him about being a snitch, Nate felt threatened. If Stone ever found out his dirty little secret, Nate would end up dead. He ran Maggie off the road and planted a bottle in her car. I made him look bad because of my story about Grunge, but for him to steal those rings, little does he know of their history."

Beef said. "Alex Thorn has Nate cuffed to a radiator. He has his gun. He refused to let me inside. He wants to speak with you."

Reason said, "The kid hates me. I make him go to school. I make him stick to his contract. Why me?"

Beef said, "I called in there. Alex answered the phone. I asked him who he trusted. Alex said his truancy tracker. That would be you."

Reason rolled his eyes and muttered, "Sweet Jesus."

30

At the end of a heated debate with Beef Tory, Reason agreed to wear a bulletproof vest to appease him. Beef said, "Wear the vest, or we find another way."

The moment he stepped in through the back door, Reason slipped out of the bulky vest and dropped it on the kitchen floor. "Alex?" he said. "Where are you?"

"The little bastard is in here!" came a thunderous voice from the front room. "The damned psycho raccoon!"

Cautiously, Reason stepped out of the kitchen to enter the living room, dimly lit by a table lamp. Nate was handcuffed to a floor radiator. Alex sat huddled in a recliner, staring warily at the scruffy biker, tear streaks marring the war paint he still wore. Reason looked down at the pistol the kid held. "Is that loaded?"

Alex tossed the gun on the floor. "No. I got knocked out. When I came to, I decided to stay put to explain to the cops that I didn't kill anyone. Nate didn't either. It was someone else."

Reason looked down at the cuff linking the biker's right wrist to the radiator. It held a faint glow to it. Nate gave another strong pull, yet sparks shot from the band of metal, causing him to cry out.

Alex said, "Just get me out of here, will you, Reason?"

"Working on that," Reason said.

Reason stepped into the bedroom. He stared in horror at the sight of Gus staked through the heart. He had not known the man well, just a casual wave when he'd seen him puttering around in his yard. It seemed impossible that he'd died in such a gruesome manner, the railroad spike barely visible in the blood clotted around the wound.

When he reappeared in the hallway, Nate lunged at him. The band secured to his wrist emitted a loud hum, and the biker was reduced to having some sort of spasm on the floor. It was then that Reason saw the maps plastered above the wall beyond a computer workstation. He admired Gus's meticulous attention to details. The research appeared to be thorough. Sadly, Reason shook his head. Damn, he thought, to have a book just aching to get out, and then to have all that work cut short before it could be finished?

He offered Alex a most sympathetic look. "Sorry," he said, "but cops will want to question you. Do you know Detective Tory?"

Alex nodded. "Known as the Viking when he rode with the Outlaws? Yes, he might nail me for being an accessory, right?"

Nate squinted his eyes, looking up at Reason. "Heard Viking and Rain Nelson got into it over dogs. The very issue the Den has to deal with because some writer put a bug in the ear of the ATF! They have bugs planted in our clubhouse, Writer Man."

Reason nodded slowly, yet said nothing.

The sudden beep of the nearby phone caused the three of them to stare at the desk where it was situated. Reason bent forward to read the caller ID on the answering machine. "Is it Tory?" Alex asked.

Shaking his head, causing his long tangles to fall into his face, Reason said, "No. It's from someone named Wolf."

Reason picked up the phone. "Hello?" he said.

Click! The caller hung up. "Cryptic," Alex said, softly.

Reason looked down at the answering machine. It continued to blink indicating there were messages left behind earlier that night. Disregarding those for the time being, Reason called Beef, assuring him the situation was under control.

Minutes later, Beef stepped inside the house. He had Lobo, Rea-son's award-winning sniffer dog with him. The big pit greeted his master warmly. Beef offered Alex a sad smile. "Sorry, you are to be taken into custody, kid."

Alex said, "I didn't murder anyone. All I did was sneak in through the cat door. What are you charging me with?"

"Depends," Beef said, pulling him up out of the chair. "Best case scenario, I'll return you home later tonight."

Alex said, "And worst case scenario? Lock up at DC, right?"

"We shall see," Beef said. "What's the story on Gus?"

"Gus," Reason said, "has a railroad spike through his heart."

Beef moved over to Nate seated there on the floor. Studying the illuminated handcuffs binding him to the radiator, he said, "Where might the key for these be?"

Darting into the bedroom, Alex reappeared seconds later, holding a glowing key. He handed it to Beef, who slipped the key into the slot on the cuff around the biker's wrist and opened it. Nate lurched forward, head-butting the blond detective. Beef staggered back. He fell to his knees. Nate ripped the pistol out of his holster. He wheeled around, raising the gun to fire at Reason.

Even as the biker lunged toward him, Reason sidestepped, flinging his arm out, clotheslining Nate across his throat with his forearm. The brawny biker flew off his feet, landing hard on his back. Reason sank to one knee, driving his right hand into Nate's nose with a palm strike. The pistol flew out of Nate's grasp, and Lobo walked over to him and stood there, a soft growl burbling deep in his throat.

"Sheesus!" Alex cried. "Where'd you learn those moves, Reason?"

Beef fumbled dizzily with the radio at his belt, managing to say, "Back up."

Seconds later, two cops came through the front door.

Nate was escorted away by the two uniformed cops, while Beef led Lobo to the crime scene in the bedroom. Reason went to the kitchen to retrieve a wet washrag. When he returned to the living room, he washed the paint off of Alex's face. Alex endured several swipes of the damp cloth. "Anything you can do for me, Reason?"

Reason said, "Your contract states four months of school attendance. You've ditched me so many times in the past two weeks, I don't think I could recommend you as the poster child for my truancy program, do you? I can't outright lie to the judge, Alex."

Tears welled up in Alex's eyes. "Yeah, I know. I'm a royal screw up. If do get sent away, look in on my mom. She'll be all alone."

A few minutes later, Beef exited Gus's bedroom, Lobo trailing behind him. He turned to examine the maps on the wall and the papers scattered on the desk before him.

"Gus was writing a book," Reason said. "Officially, I know you can't involve me in this investigation, but unofficially, would you be willing to let me take a look at his files, Beef?"

Beef said, "Thanks, Reason. If we need a consultant to decipher the old man's writings, I'll mention your offer to my superiors."

Reason asked, "Why do you have Lobo involved? Thought I made it clear, he was permanently retired."

Beef said, "I wanted to see if Lobo could find those rings. Rumor is, they ended up here with Gus. However, he didn't find them."

Beef turned to place Alex in handcuffs.

Just before stepping outside, Reason shooed Lobo out the door and said, "Let me know what you decide to do with Alex."

31

Late the next day, Nate made his one phone call the cops allowed him down at city jail. They could not tie him to Gus's murder, and so they released him. He had payback on his mind the moment he returned home.

Celeste lay curled up in her bed, Grunge sprawled beside her, when she heard the commotion Nate made in the kitchen. She stared at her bedroom door, prepared for the explosion that would follow.

Nate shoved her bedroom door open. He stood there, his bald head gleaming, his green eyes radiating rage. Grunge peered up into Nate's eyes, detecting the red-hot rage he was nailing Celeste with. A low growl rumbled inside of his chest. Slowly, the big Brindle stood up in the center of her bed. "Check yourself, Uncle Nate," Celeste said.

Nate realized in that instant that one word from her, and he would not make it back out into the hallway. In an eerily quiet tone, he asked, "Why did you go anywhere near that writer's house, Idiot Child? Get the dog in the truck. There's a fight tonight. Some killer pit up from KC."

Celeste cried, "You will never put this dog in another fight. Lucas loves this brute, and to break his heart like that would be cruel!"

At 17, Celeste Holland was a force to be reckoned with. Having been through treatment, twice, she had battled her addictions to both meth and K2. She was now drug free, and as such, opposed to her

Uncle Nate's business, and how it might impact her future. She was disappointed that her father had chosen to leave the country to join Khalid and Raynes on their search for Waziri in the Middle East. Especially, now that she had just finished treatment in Omaha, and ended up in the care of her Uncle Nate.

Nate always had trouble dealing with the wild, angry, impulsive girl, oftentimes resorting to hard slaps to her face and head. He claimed he was just toughening her up so that one day she could ride with the Den. The good little Celeste had died the night her mom died. She had been hell on wheels ever since. Up until a year ago, Celeste had been dealing with her pain over the loss of her mother by using great quantities of drugs. Oblivious to the rest of the world around her, she started using any drug she could get her hands on to cope with her grief. She started with weed, but after a stint on probation where she had to give UA's every week, she had switched to K-2, the man-made substitute for weed. The agency keeping track of her did not have the finances to test for K-2, and therefore, it never showed up on her tests. She became addicted to the stuff, and used it consistently for the rest of that year, until her best friend, Crystal, suffered a collapsed lung from smoking one evening. She suffocated right there in front of Celeste, and paramedics got there too late to save her.

After such a tragic experience, Celeste wanted no more to do with K-2. So, she progressed to meth. She discovered that was a dead-end, too, one night when she smoked a lethally potent batch cooked up by a member of the Den. Ripper, the biker who had produced the stuff ended up dead that night. Celeste went to the ER and spent the next four months at an inpatient treatment center. When she was released, her caseworker had her placed at a dog rescue ranch in the small town of Seward. It was there that she discovered her gift.

Colton Lone Wolf, the Lakota dog handler who owned the rescue ranch, told her it was known as Spirit Talking.

Her gift: She could talk to dogs.

Nate forced Grunge into his Blazer at gun-point. In a last ditch effort to rescue him, Celeste climbed into the Blazer and was relieved to see Ben Black Bull approaching the house. Behind the Lakota dog handler was Rain Nelson of the Outlaws. The two men confronted Nate, and

Nate challenged Rain to a fight.

Even as Rain rained down fury on him, Celeste ushered Grunge out of the Blazer and took off running down the driveway. Moments later, she and Grunge reached Havelock Avenue, the business district of the small suburb. She had someone specific in mind to talk to about putting a stop to Nate's insistence that Grunge die a painful, bloody death in the fighting ring. Someone who would either put Nate in a world of hurt if he persisted with his efforts to throw the poor dog into a last-stand fight, or someone who would put him in the ground.

Celeste had become that desperate in her quest to save Grunge.

Five minutes later, she and the Brindle stood staring at the enormous stained-glass window of the Emerald Pub. It was a central focal point of the five-block business district of Havelock, depicting a black dragon, red flames shooting from his mouth, and an emerald clutched in his talons. Celeste narrowed her eyes for she could have sworn the flames slowly unfurled as she faced the building, and if she squinted just right, she detected a slight flutter of the dragon's wings.

She had heard that the Emerald's iconic stained-glass window had been gifted to Billy Connors back in Ireland years ago. The rumor was that Old Billy, an Irish gunrunner, was owed a debt by the Hidden Ones, and each shard of colored glass had been crafted by the skillful hands of the Wee Folk of the Misty Isle. The window was no small piece of work either, being six-feet wide by eight-feet tall.

She had once asked, "Why such a large window for a pub, Billy? It's bigger than the stained-glass windows of Saint Patrick's church."

Billy had said, "It's a beacon, lass, for those braving the seas of the Otherworld. The bigger, the better for them to find their way."

He talked that way quite often, in riddles that only he seemed to get, but the Irishman was highly respected by the local biker clubs, and his word was law amongst them. Celeste was hoping Billy could at least get Nate's attention when it came to a hand's off approach with Grunge.

As she reached for the ornate door handle in the center of the large oak door, the strange black imp appeared on the sidewalk beside her. "Why?" she gasped. "Do you keep following me, monkey?

The bald-headed imp sent back to her: *Not a monkey. Mogrim, I am from the realm of Valasar. Jango is my name, or at least the name my old master called me before he was no more. Have you come to attend the White Council?*

Taking one startled look at the bug-eyed creature crouched beside Celeste, Grunge went into attack mode, and yet even as he charged across the sidewalk, Celeste sent her thoughts out to the overprotective dog: *Grunge! Stand down! He means us no harm!*

Grunge skidded to a halt, his sights shifting from the hissing goblin-like creature to instead meet Celeste's gaze. In the seconds that both could have erupted into a fight, Celeste sent her thoughts to Jango: *Calm down! Let's keep the peace, okay?*

Keeping a close eye on the fierce pit bull before him, Jango scampered across the sidewalk, and with surprising agility, he clambered up Celeste's back leg and ended up perched on her left shoulder. The mogrim reached out with a very human-like hand, his tiny fingers gently caressing her cheek.

Are you, the little imp asked, *prepared to enter into a war that has been raging for centuries? Have you come here to join with the Servants of Light to stand against the Darkness? If so, I claim you as my new master and will serve you faithfully.*

Before Celeste could respond, the oak door before her seemed to open of its own accord. She and Grunge both peered into the shadowy alcove beyond. Celeste glanced down at the strange little imp seated on her shoulder. Jango stared back at her, his overlarge eyes changing from dull black to a brilliant shade of blue as he gestured at the darkness inside the pub.

Placing one hand on Jango's head, Celeste and the dog entered a dimly lit room, complete with an oak bar on one side and a stone fireplace on the other. Above the mantle of the fireplace were the heads of seven mounted stags, all illuminated by stringers of tiny emerald-colored lights.

Celeste continued on down a hallway stretching before her. A low growl came from Grunge beside her and that's when things really took a strange twist.

In the chamber at the end of the hallway, a moonlit river stretched before them. Beside the river, was a Gypsy encampment complete with brightly painted wooden wagons. Celeste was greeted by a tall, dark-haired man who introduced himself as the Cingane Chieftain. The man kneeled to pet Grunge. At first, the dog seemed surprised by the man's forwardness, then he panted excitedly as the man urged

Celeste to join him beside a nearby campfire. On her shoulder, Jango chortled with glee, clapping his hands in applause.

In the next instant, Celeste fell asleep next to the campfire.

When she woke up, she saw Grunge resting peacefully nearby in the faint glow of the smoldering fire.

However, the entire encampment of Gypsies was gone.

Jango urged her to follow him over to the silver-tinted river.

Celeste looked down at her reflection and gasped when she saw the tattoos on her throat and neck. The stag in the hollow of her throat had antlers that evolved into twin wolves snaking up on either side of her neck. The wide-antlered stag held a fierce gaze in his dark eyes, and the two wolves were facing sideways, their lips set in mid-howl. It was a fascinating piece of work, and yet she had no memory of the ink being applied to create the images on her neck and throat.

Jango sent, *The Chieftain said those tattoos are talismans that will come to life when you most desperately need them.*

Celeste said, "Awesome ink work, but why me?"

32

Chapter Thirty-Two

A voice came from beneath the trees beside the river: "It is your destiny, lass. You were called to this long before you were born. If you want to blame it on anyone, the Star Children played a big part in not only losing the Lionstone, but the Star Fire crystal, as well."

Celeste looked to the tall, lean figure beneath a stand of pine trees beside the river. Old Billy Connors stepped out of the blackness there, the cherry in his pipe illuminating the weathered features of his face. Dressed in a three-piece suit, his long, silver hair fell loose about his slender shoulders, while beneath his hawk-like nose was a thick, white mustache. His amazingly blue eyes pierced Celeste where she stood. Greatly reminding her of Mark Twain, the old Irishman quietly asked, "Will you become a new Keeper of the Flame?"

She looked deep into the old man's lion-like gaze, and then behind Billy, where an iron gateway was revealed. The elaborate gate made no sound as it swung open, revealing a sunken garden beyond. Inside a circular pit was a round wooden table where a pair of white-robed women sat. Celeste stared at the two ladies in stunned surprise. "Cat? Cinnamon?" she said, "Owners of the Roaring Lion bookstore?"

Cat's hair was shaved on one side. Cinnamon had long auburn hair that cascaded past her slender shoulders. The robes they wore gave off a slight illumination. And yet it was the torcs at their necks that glowed brightly, lighting up their features.

Three enormous grizzled men stood at the table behind them, one with white hair, the second with raven hair, and the third with shoulder-length golden hair. All three had long beards and despite the fact that they wore sleeveless Harley T-shirts, they greatly resembled Norse Vikings from ancient times.

Billy said, "Our hometown of Havelock is known amongst the White Council, the Tuatha De Dannan, the Unseen Court, the Sidhe, and the Web of the Wise. In our small suburb are Waystations between alternate realms, where Guardians of the Gateways are located: The Emerald Pub, owned by me. The Roaring Lion, owned by Cinnamon and Cat. The Trainyards Bar, owned by the three Bears, Kodiak, Winter, and Griz. All of us are Mage Lords who are committed to battling the Unseen who are bred of Darkness."

"Wizards and witches?" Celeste said in disbelief.

He took a long, slow drag on his briarwood pipe. Through a haze of blue smoke, he said, "That is one name for us, but trust me, we are much more than that. And we need your help."

Celeste reluctantly took a seat at the round table, and even more reluctantly accepted the steaming cup of tea Cat offered her. *Things are weird enough*, she thought. *I don't need any mind altering herbs to take me further south than I already am!*

Cinnamon said, "You know Billy's grandson, right? Well, Billy's discovered a way to be involved in Reason's youth work that has just been approved by Judge Sully at juvenile court. It took a lot of legal wrangling by therapists as proof that it might succeed."

Billy blew three perfect smoke rings from the bowl of his pipe at the head of the table. He said, "All the things that plague at risk kids is what Reason has been dealing with for the past ten years. Drug abuse. Teen suicide. Runaway and throw away kids. Anger and rage management. Truancy which leads to probation. Probation that leads to institutions. Institutions that lead to parole. Parole that leads to prison. These are all just endless Celtic hoops that many kids find themselves trapped in once they enroll in the juvenile court system."

Cat smiled warmly at her and said, "So, Billy's proposed a new program, using one kid as a test pilot, to instigate a program that not only curbs delinquent behavior, but builds self-esteem and character through leadership skills. Something new in the field of youth work."

After three more smoke rings drifted from his pipe, Billy said, "Virtual reality. Alternative realms. All the video games you played, you've certainly heard of Virtual gaming. It's the computer-generated simulation of a three-dimensional environment that can be interacted with in a real or physical way by a person using special electronic equipment, such as a helmet or gloves fitted with sensors. The environment is similar to the real world or a Fantasy realm, creating an experience not possible in physical reality. Augmented reality systems are considered a form of VR that layers virtual information over a live camera feed into a headset giving the user the ability to view 3-D images. This information is known as forced feedback in medical, gaming, and military training apps."

Celeste asked, "What does juvenile court have to do with gaming? I thought most video games were frowned upon by therapists and parents. Violent video games tend to make kids more violent. That was proven during the Columbine shooting trial."

Looking down the hallway to the oak door where only moments earlier the moonlit river had been, Celeste said, "Wait a sec. This secret chamber? There's an alternate dimension beyond this door? And you're thinking of putting a kid in there?"

Billy said, "No kid is being sent to Middle Earth. But remember what I said about the screens? The effect is created by VR headsets with a head-mounted screen, but can also be created through specially designed rooms with multiple screens. Inside the chamber are six windows depicting scenes from different locations of another realm."

Celeste leaned forward, placing her arms on the table where her steaming cup of tea remained untouched.

A silence permeated the garden.

Billy took another toke of his pipe.

Cat reached down beside her to pet Grunge's head.

The three Bears looked down the hallway to the oak door.

Billy finally said, "Reason's not the only writer in this family. I created a game script that aligns with the scenes that appear on those windows inside the chamber. I submitted it to Game Wizards, and the techs there designed a virtual reality game that can be played with the use of a headset and hand controls, all connected to that room by a single connector cord—"

"The sword fighting is to die for!" Kodiak said, his gold beard creased by a white-toothed smile. "Billy's still a kid at heart, so it's little wonder he came up with such an intense game for kids!"

Celeste said, "And you want me to be the test pilot for this cure for delinquency? Why not use an avid gamer?"

Billy seemed to be reading her mind. "We seriously considered Lucas for the initial gaming session, but you and I both know of the boy's urges to go absolutely ape in a moment's notice. In that respect, Lucas would make for an unstable guinea pig, possibly sabotaging the entire game, earning the disapproval of Judge Sully at juvenile court."

Cat said, "Proving the point that violent video games makes kids more violent. No, Celeste, we are seeking someone with a calmer demeanor, yet someone flexible enough to rise to some very peculiar challenges in order to make the game a success."

The three Bears all looked at Billy. Cat and Cinnamon, too.

"Are you gonna," Cat asked, "tell her the kicker, Billy?"

Fifteen minutes later, Celeste and Grunge stood on the sidewalk in front of the Emerald pub, both of them illuminated by the stained-glass window glowing with some inner source of mysterious light.

Jango scampered out through the oak door of the pub, glancing back curiously at Billy trailing behind him. The old Irishman puffed away on his pipe, creating a cloud of bluish smoke. Billy offered her a rather sheepish frown, fanning away smoke as he did so.

"Okay," Celeste said, "do you want to run that last part by me one more time, just so I get this straight?"

With a nod of his head, Billy blew out a frustrated sigh that caused his thick white mustache to flutter at both ends. "The kicker," he said, looking off down the avenue, "is we're killing two birds with one stone in this realm and the one beyond. In this realm, our cause is noble: Creating a virtual reality game that will help delinquent youth. In the realm beyond, matters are much more serious. There is war raging there that we, the White Council, is now a part of. If you chose to join us, your true gifts will be awakened. Dealing with dragons and demons tends to take a lot of skill. You are much more than you know,

Celeste Holland. You may have considered yourself a worth-less little druggie a few months ago, but you have much more potential than that. Will you join us and awaken your powers?"

Celeste said, "One would think that maybe I am still tripping after hearing you talk, and this tattoo is a little much to figure out."

She paused, then said, "I came here tonight to get you to have strong words with Uncle Nate about Grunge, but now..."

Billy removed his pipe stem from between his teeth. "I'll deal with Nate, lass. All I ask of you is you think this over. Agreed?"

She gave a shrug, and as Grunge followed her down the sidewalk, she said, "We shall see, Billy. We shall see."

33

A few minutes later, staring at the alley stretching before them, Celeste said, "I'll take you to Reason's place."

Grunge looked over at her. *Reason? I thought you hated him for being Mister Truancy Tracker.*

"I do," Celeste said. "But he's the only one who would stand up to Nate if he comes to take you. Besides, Lucas is staying there."

Reluctantly, Grunge passed through Reason's back gate. Celeste waited, making sure that the dog had gone inside through the dog door, and hoping Lucas was still awake to greet him. She reached Gus Howard's back porch ten seconds later, listening to the sounds coming from inside. A police radio gave off annoying static. A robotic voice relayed information. There came a thump from the bedroom inside. Footsteps across the linoleum floor in the kitchen. More noises from the front of the house. Car doors slammed. An engine started. A fire truck drove off, a steady grinding of gears echoing in the night.

Snapping her fingers, Celeste stood there waiting. Three seconds later, Jango scampered out of the nearby shrubbery. The small, bug-eyed creature stared up at Celeste, puzzlement in its gaze. Kneeling down beside it, she gently stroked the fur at the base of its neck.

The mogrim chortled with glee, craning his small, bald head to the left and right, pleased with the attention Celeste was giving him. She whispered into his ear, then stepped off the porch as Jango crawled in through the cat door.

Blending into the shadows, she listened intently as footsteps could be heard inside the kitchen. Jango came shooting out through the cat door. The back door swung open. Detective Beef Tory followed the black mogrim across the yard. In the alley ahead of him, Jango wheeled back around. Beef clawed at his holstered pistol. Before he could draw the weapon, Jango hurtled into him taking him to the ground. He perched on his chest, doubled up his tiny fists, and gave Beef a furious pounding.

By then, Celeste had slipped inside the house. She went directly to the computer workstation. Keenly aware that she was not alone, she listened several seconds to the murmur of two female voices coming from the bedroom. When certain the two forensic officers were busy going about their work, Celeste removed a thumb drive from the coin pocket of her black jeans.

Celeste worked quickly to download information from the C drive of the computer. The moment the files she wanted were downloaded onto the thumb drive, she removed it from the USB port and slipped the drive into her shirt pocket. She started to get up, when the red flashing light on the answering machine caught her eye.

Silently, she removed the machine from the cord attaching it to the plug in the nearby wall, hurried through the kitchen, slipping through the door. The moment Jango spotted her, he sprang off of Beef and scampered away, leaving the cop dazed from the beating he took.

Tucking the answering machine beneath her arm, Celeste raced away toward the open back gate.

Rumor suddenly sat up, going from a sound-sleeping ball of gray fur situated on the edge of Reason's desk, to alert beast mode, letting out a guttural meeoww! A faint sound came from the kitchen, and Rumor stood up on all four paws.

Still shaken from the murder of Gus Howard the night before, Reason opened his desk drawer and drew out a .380 Lorcin pistol. Back in the 90's, when his writing career first started he'd authored a book about a female informant who had been murdered. Her name was Kelly Drake. She was as an informant for Jessie Dalton. Having been responsible for dozens of narcotics busts, she had been shot at the Emerald Pub's outdoor café by Jack Holland of the Elder's Den. Despite a thorough investigation, her murder had never been solved. And that's when Reason stumbled his way into the middle of the conspiracy. During the bust of a party, he escaped only to grab the black leather jacket of Brooks, a dealer involved with Kelly. He'd discover-ed a mysterious blue key in the pocket of this jacket. The key belonged to a safe deposit box at a Havelock bank. Inside this box was a CD of Kelly being shot there at the Emerald by Jack. Later, Reason had written a book about the murder. Reason was less than friendly to the anonymous caller who phoned him several months later at 3AM.

The man had asked, "You the guy who wrote that book?"

"Yeah," Reason answered.

"Where'd you get your information?"

"Why? What's it to you?"

"Well, the information in your book is fairly accurate."

"I wrote it as a piece of fiction."

"Truth is sometimes stranger than fiction."

"Any accuracies were purely coincidental."

"There is a network of people involved in that narc's murder. If they contact you one day, you're gonna want a gun."

Click! The caller chuckled and hung up.

The .380 Lorcin had been purchased that next week.

The pistol held in a two-handed grip, Reason quietly made his way into the kitchen, missing the presence of Lobo and Goblin. The two dogs were getting fresh air by bedding down in the kennel in the backyard. If not, they would have provided the perfect burglar alarm, alerting Reason to any strange sounds or any would-be intruders.

He was strangely relieved that the two were gone from the house when he saw a Brindle pit standing before him in his kitchen. The big dog curled back his lips in a low growl. Stepping out of his bedroom beside Reason, Lucas latched onto Grunge's collar.

"You already know Goblin," Lucas said. "This is Grunge."

Reason lowered the pistol. He set it on the nearby kitchen counter. "Alex was arrested last night. After Beef grills him, he's gonna want to talk to you. Besides, two of my rings are still missing."

Grunge detected the anger in the man's words. His dark eyes met Reason's. They held each other's gaze for several seconds, and Reason realized his direct stare was a challenge to the pit bull. He looked away, raised one hand, his fingers tucked in. Grunge walked toward him, sniffing at his outstretched hand.

Lucas said, "Uncle Nate used to make him fight."

The fact that Nate Holland had forced the dog into a dog fight did not set well with Reason. He had reported Nate to Animal Control two months ago, when he'd found a dog wandering around the neighborhood. The pit bull had been injured and he bore several old scars. Before the officer arrived, Nate and several of his bikers from the Den had showed up. "Here to get my dog you stole," Nate said, as he loomed before him on his front porch.

Sizing up the four other bikers, Reason said, "He was hurt. I took him in to try to find his owner. He is at the Humane Society."

Reason knew the man was not about to lose face with his men. He had glanced down at his clenched fists. As it was an Animal Control officer showed up before things went south. After taking it to a vet to have its wounds tended, the officer was just as frustrated as Reason over the plight of the poor dog. There was no proof Nate had abused the pit. By law, he was the rightful owner, and therefore the dog had to go back to him. Two months later, the officer returned to Reason's house to inform him the dog had been found with two bullets in his head out by Stephen's Creek. It was one of the reasons he was determined to take Nate down. His cruelty to animals was difficult to prove. Dogs did not talk. And yet, people did. It was the weak link in Nate's enterprise, and why Reason wrote the story.

A knock came from the back door. Reason snatched up his pistol from the counter. When he opened the door, Celeste stared down at the pistol. In a mock gesture of surrender, she raised one hand in the air, juggling the answering machine in the other. Reason placed the gun on the kitchen counter. Celeste handed him Gus's machine. She said, "Maybe it holds a clue as to why he was murdered."

She reached inside her shirt pocket and produced the thumb drive. "I know what Gus was working on. It will take those cops months to sort through his material. And even then, they won't have a clue as to what any of this means. How much do you know about paranormal activities? Ghosts? Demons?"

Reason simply stood there, holding the machine. "Yeah," Lucas said, "it freaked me out, too, first time she started talking this way."

After setting out a bowl of water for Grunge, Reason joined Lucas and Celeste in the living room where she plugged in the answering machine. The two were seated like two book ends on the couch, the machine situated between them. The kid had made himself at home, removing his shoes and socks. After noisily drinking water in the kitchen, Grunge wandered into the living room. He walked over and sprawled out before Reason now seated in a recliner.

"I'll be damned," Celeste said, in disbelief. "Grunge said he liked you, Reason. He's usually wary of everyone, but he completely trusts you, and that's a compliment coming from him."

The pit bull settled his chin on top of Reason's crossed feet, slowly closing his eyes.

34

Reason and Lucas watched Celeste as she depressed the button on the machine. After a sharp beep! a clear voice said:"Gus? It's Colton Lone Wolf. I finished the research on the ghosts of the Dead Kings. In the Hebrew Bible, Rephaim refers to either giants, or to dead ancestors of the Netherworld. Rephaim were an ancient race of giants in ancient Israel.

"In the Bible, the Israelites were instructed to exterminate the inhabitants of Canaan, including some large individuals. Several passages in the Book of Joshua suggest that Og, the King of Bashan, was one of the last survivors of the Rephaim, and that his bed was 13 feet long! This guy was big!

"In Deuteronomy 2:18-21 the Ammonites called the Rephaim Zamzummim, which in Hebrew translates into Buzzers, or 'the people whose speech sounds like buzzing.'

"In Deuteronomy 2:11, the Moabites referred to them as the Emim. They are also mentioned in Genesis 14:5 and their name translates as the dreaded ones, horror or terror.

"Ancient Semitic texts refer to the Rephaim as the Dead Kings. The many references to rephaim in the Hebrew Bible involving dead spirits suggests that many ancient Israelites imagined the spirits of the dead as playing an active role in the lives of the living.

"The link between these Giants and Ghosts comes from the word, raphah, which means to sink, to withdraw, to abandon or forsake. The Rephaim may loom large, only in the sense of a metaphor. They are gigantic precisely because they have withdrawn into the mythic past, they've become, as the saying goes, mere ghosts of their former selves. Gus, you're on to something! Dreaded Ones? Horrors? Terrors? Your theory about these Dead Kings is spot on!

"However, I delved into the thing about Molech. Leave it alone. You could be unleashing something that should be sealed away forever. Molech is the name of a Canaanite god who demanded child sacrifice. Molech is based on the root mlk 'king'. There are a number of Canaanite gods with names based on this root, the name of a god surnamed the king, lord, ba'al, or master, instead of Melek which is also frequently given to Yahweh the god of the Jews.

"Remember how God asked Abraham to sacrifice his son, Isacc? Child sacrifice was so prevalent in those times and the gods of Canaan asked those who believed in them to sacrifice their very own children to appease them.

"Jeremiah 32:35: 'And they built the high places of Baal, to cause their sons and their daughters to pass through the fire unto Molech.' 'Passing through the fire,' became the name for child sacrifices. In the Carthaginian religion, they practiced the burning of children as an offering to Baal. There was a bronze statue, its hands extended over a bronze brazier, the flames of which engulfed the child. When the flames fell upon the body, the open mouth seemed to be laughing. The Carthaginian nobles attempted to sacrifice 200 children of the best families, and in their enthusiasm actually sacrificed 300 children! Those who had no children would buy little ones from poor people. Molech was made of brass. They heated him from his lower parts; and they put the child between his hands, and it was burnt."

Colton muttered something inaudible, then Click!

Reason looked to Celeste. "Do you know this Lone Wolf?"

Celeste said, "He's a Lakota dog handler, yet he has doctorates in both theology and psychology. His paranormal work with the Dark Ones of Pine Ridge made him the one professional in a five-state radius who didn't think Gus was a royal nut case."

Reason asked, "Who exactly was this Gus Howard?"

Celeste quietly said, "Gus was a Demon Hunter."

The next morning, after receiving a call from Beef Tory down at the police station, Reason drove downtown to meet with him. Against his better judgement, he'd allowed Celeste and Grunge to stay the night at his place. She had come to him seeking asylum and a safe haven for the dog. If he'd turned her away, their uncle just might make good on his threat to toss the dog into a fight.

Reason would not allow that. He knew to keep the kids or the dogs safe from Nate, he really had no choice. As Celeste's legal guardian Nate was a mean-spirited man who didn't take her because of love. No, Celeste as a ward of the state, came with special needs payments. Reason imagined Nate was taking in three-thousand per month, and all he had to do to earn that was to show up at each six-month court hearing, pretending to be the kind and caring uncle who just wanted what's best for his niece.

Nate Holland was playing the system.

When Reason arrived at the police station, he noticed the bruising on the left side of Beef's face. "Did you get into a fight?" he asked.

Beef grinned sheepishly. "You ought to see the other guy."

He ushered Reason into an interview room, and was greeted by Alex Thorn seated before them. Beef said, "The County Attorney is not going to charge Alex with any crime in regards to the murder of Gus. As he sees it, Alex wasn't responsible for Gus's death. Judge Sully is placing him on a suspended sentence to the Youth Development Center on charges of trespassing. Six months probation with the sentence hanging over his head to help him keep his nose clean."

Reason looked over at Alex. The raccoon was gone. The war paint washed away. The kid sat there, his long, dark tangles of hair hanging to his thin shoulders. He did not meet Reason's gaze. Instead he looked like he was about to cry.

The suspended sentence meant Alex had lucked out. Having been in his courtroom on numerous cases, Reason knew that Judge Sully only did that at the end of the line. He easily handed down six month probation terms to first time offenders, but saved the suspended sentences as a last minute scare tactic to some of the repeat offenders. It was a wake-up call to the more hardened little criminals, to let them know they were on the edge of bigger and badder placements.

It had a fifty-fifty success rate.

Some kids left the courtroom in shock and awe. Having been sure Judge Sully was going to send them away to treatment or some other institutional setting, the doomed kids wept with relief with the second chance Sully gave them. The others were just too stupid to recognize mercy when it was offered. Reason had sat in court, exchanged sad looks with Sully, and listened to him say, "Sentence revoked," way too many times. Reason labeled them the Kamikaze kids. Despite the trespassing charge, Judge Sully was giving Alex a break with the suspended sentence.

So why, Reason wondered did the kid look so sad.

"Alex's mom," Beef said, "refuses to take him back. Per a phone conversation I had with her, she is flying back to her homeland in Wallachia. Though she is breaking the law by abandoning her son, the entire family is well aware of her struggles with Alex these past two years. Alex's grandfather demanded she cut all ties with the rogue, ruffian, and scoundrel."

Alex sadly muttered, "My grandfather is of the Cingane, a clan of Gypsies who would rather tie kittens up in a gunny sack and toss them in a river, rather than spare their lives."

Beef offered the kid a sympathetic look. "I tried to convince his mom she would be charged with reckless abandonment if she left him to fly overseas. But this grandfather of his commanded her to leave Alex here to fend for himself."

Alex looked across the table at Reason. "The Cingane have their own system. A cat has nine lives, right? Cingane give you just so many chances to succeed. And then, if you fail, you are shunned. Grandpa Petrov has ordered me shunned."

35

Chapter Thirty-Five

Alex Thorn was one of Reason's truancy cases, and as such, had been failing to fulfill his contract in regards to attending school. After missing three months of school, Alex had been court ordered by Judge Sully to adhere to Reason's truancy program. He would either succeed or fail. Reason was just there to be a tracker. So far, Alex had refused his help. Reason knew at the rate the kid had been going, if it hadn't been the burglary, he would have stumbled his way into some other tragic situation sooner or later.

A knock came on the door of the interview room, and in stepped caseworker for the state, Connie Douglas, a slim, middle-aged woman with short-cropped blond hair. In the past, Reason had provided foster care for three state wards under her supervision. He liked her as she was one caseworker who went the extra mile for her troubled cases.

Connie said, "Would you take Alex in on an emergency stay?"

Reason gave her a puzzled frown.

"I get it," Alex said. "You don't want me either. I failed you, too."

"Failed me?" Reason said. "Failed yourself! I gave you a hundred chances to prove to Judge Sully you could comply with his attendance order. You blew all of those."

In the past, Reason had taken in some of the most hard-core kids. Kids who had reached the end of the line. Kids who burned everyone who had ever taken them in before. He once took in a kid who had ran away from forty-six other placements. He had remained with Reason for two years after his placement there, not running once. In the course of ten years, he had taken in kids who had hit him, kicked him, bit him, and spat on him. Each one he saw as the one star fish he was going to make a difference with. And he put up with what few foster parents in the system ever would. He endured every assault, every failure those kids brought upon themselves. And he never called it quits. Never once called a caseworker and said, "Come, get this little monster. I've had enough."

It just wasn't in his nature to quit.

Reason nailed Alex with an unrelenting gaze. "You've got a lot of potential, but somewhere along the way you lost hope. I tried repeatedly to give you direction, to steer you down the right path, but you sabotaged every effort I made to help you."

Reason peered into Alex's dark eyes for long moments, then said, "Alex of the Roma, a nomadic ethnic group, spread across Europe. Romani are known as Gypsies. Not to be confused with Romanians. The term Gypsy comes from gypcian, derived from Egyptian. This title owes to the belief that the Romani were itinerant Egyptians. In fact, the Gypsies of your line, Alex, were exiled from Egypt as punishment for harboring the infant Jesus during Herod's reign in Jerusalem, when he had all male infants killed to keep the prophecy of a Jewish Messiah from being fulfilled. Another title of the Romani is Cingane, derived from a Christian sect the Romani were associated with in the Middle Ages.

"Alexander, born in Wallachia, the Gypsy child of an American biker and a Romani archivist, grew up among a pack of wolves. His father adopted an injured, pregnant wolf, and she had a litter of seven pups. Little Alex was in charge of those pups for the next three years, living in a Gypsy encampment. He and his pack roamed the wilds together, forming a bond. Alex loved his wolves. And then his mother left his father and moved here to America. Alex was eleven. And he has been struggling to find his true center ever since."

Alex stared at Reason, his brow furrowed deep in confusion.

Reason said, "I am a writer. I research. Last year, when you were assigned to me through juvenile court, I contacted your mom, hoping she would work with me. Your mom shut me out, refusing to tell me anything about you. And so, I contacted your grandfather—"

"Grandpa Petrov?" Alex asked, incredulously. "You called him all the way over in Wallachia?"

"Yes," Reason said. "And what I told you, is what he shared with me. He asked me to do one thing."

Alex sniffled. "What was that?"

"He asked me to restore your honor."

"My honor? I have no honor."

He fell silent. Several minutes passed.

Reason said, "Why don't we see if we can fix that?"

Connie Douglas invited Alex to ride with her so he could gather up his personal belongings. Once done there at the Thorn residence, she would drive Alex over to Reason's house a few blocks away. Her second mission would then begin, for she had statements to take from Celeste Holland. Reason had shared with her why the girl had showed up at his house last night, and she was concerned for her welfare. She needed to set up an emergency placement meeting with Judge Sully. She knew Nate wasn't about to lose his monthly payment. He would have his lawyer contacting Sully, as well. So, Connie needed to be a step ahead of him.

As Connie and Alex left the police department, Beef said, "I spoke to Colton about the war paint, and he said it provided the perfect disguise for Alex, so that spirits would not recognize him here in the real world."

"The Dog Soldier?" Reason said. "Colton Lone Wolf. I met Wolf out at Ben's rescue ranch."

Beef said, "Alex told me about this contract Nate has out on you. Something to do with the article you wrote making the Den look bad. Nate wants you dead. That's why Wolf has agreed to watch your back for the next several weeks. He also set up a meeting with the Den and the Outlaws in an attempt to get this contract rescinded. His word carries weight in the biker world."

Reason offered him an incredulous look. "A bodyguard?"

"Yes," Beef said. "I told him about Gus Howard's murder. That greatly concerned him. He was assisting the old man with some type of paranormal research. He said both of your paths were destined to cross, in some sort of Celtic knot-work woven by fate."

At the sound of thunder coming from outside in the street, Lucas and Celeste cringed inside Reason's house. Nate revved his Harley several times before killing the engine. Lucas peeked out the peep hole on the front door, continuing to watch his uncle start up the sidewalk toward the house. "What if he breaks in?"

"Shhhh!" Celeste warned. "We'll go into stealth mode. Maybe he'll go away."

Nate's massive fist pounded furiously on the front door. Grunge gave a low growl. *Yes,* Celeste sent out her thoughts, *he means you harm. His plan is to throw you into a fight, with Duct tape wrap-ped around your muzzle so that you can't fight back. All for twisted men who relish such sport. He's a dark man.*

Grunge let out a soft growl at this. Furious pounding came from Nate on the front porch. Lucas glanced back at Celeste. "Where did Reason put his gun?"

"You shoot him, he'd go to the morgue. You'd go to prison."

"For what? Protecting my dog?"

"No judge or jury would see it that way. Hold it together, Lucas. Don't get over dramatic on me."

The pounding on the front door stopped.

Lucas rose to his feet to peer out the peep hole. "Oh, crap!" he gasped. "He's heading around to the back door!"

Nate spotted the dog door, and dropped down to his knees on the back porch. He knew he could not get his large frame through the dog trap, but he could reach up once he stuck his arm through to unlock the back door. Celeste, Lucas, and Grunge watched as Rumor shot past them, a horrendous growl erupting from her mouth.

Nate cried out, taking two nasty scratches down both cheeks as Rumor spastically raked him with her front claws. He banged his head, extracting himself from the dog trap. Bleeding from the gouges on his cheeks, Nate headed back to his bike in the street. Just before starting his Harley, he shouted, "This ain't over! I will be back!"

By the time Reason arrived home, Connie had the placement of Celeste

Holland approved by Judge Sully. Celeste was court ordered to remain with Reason, until her dad returned to the states to resume taking care of his kids. Resigned to what fate had in store for them, Celeste remained silent, refusing to say one word in protest of being placed with her least favorite truancy tracker. In the past, Reason had been a living hell as she defied him in her endless quest to get high. And now that she was clean, she found it ironic that she would be living with him.

Lucas took the news that they would be staying at Reason's just as hard. After hugging the dogs, he looked up at Alex. "Best keep an eye on these guys. Nate vowed he'd be back. Meanwhile, you, Celeste and I will have to get used to living with the new warden."

Reason overheard this from his place in the kitchen. He stuck his head around the corner, grinning impishly. "Oh, it could be worse. I could send you out to the backyard to do poop patrol."

Rolling his eyes, Lucas said, "Did enough of that out at Ben's ranch. Besides, I'd rather do dishes than use a pooper scooper. I call dibs on the dishes."

36

An hour later, after Reason fed the three kids on the Isle's pizza, he went to his den, slipping the thumb drive into his desktop computer to snoop through Gus's files. Rumor planted herself in his lap. In seconds, the cat was purring as Reason stroked her be-neath her chin. Seated nearby on a big couch, Lucas and Alex played a video game, keeping the sound low so as not to disturb Reason.

He had just opened the first file, when the dogs came into the den. Grunge head-butted him on the leg. Goblin sniffed at Rumor, sending the cat springing from Reason's lap. She leaped up onto the desk, peering at Lobo staring in at them from the hallway. Reason said, "We have guests. You and Grunge are related. Same sire and dame, just different litters. That makes you brothers. So behave yourself."

Reason held up the ring he wore and flourished it in the direction of Lobo. At once, Grunge and Lobo touched noses, and in seconds, the three dogs were settled in the den, staring calmly at Jango as he capered into the room. He carried a leather bag in his small hand. Trailing behind the mogrim, Celeste said, "His name is Jango. I sorta adopted him after meeting him down at the Emerald."

Reason asked, "What's it got in its bag?"

As soon as he said it, he grinned. The words so reminded him of Gollum's words in The Lord of the Rings when he and Bilbo were swapping riddles, he was immediately aware of how much the little black creature resembled Gollum. Gently, Reason took the bag from him. He loosened the drawstrings, turned the bag over, and dumped out two gold rings into the palm of his hand.

Lucas said, "The lost has been found. Jango got them from Gus."

Celeste read the screen: "Cryptic Connections. These files have to do with the book Gus was writing. Ever heard of the Celtic hoop? Where one line is drawn in a continuous loop to create a symbol?"

"The Cingane believe," Alex said, "in the fates like the Celts did, that several segments are connected in one continuous hoop."

He paused. "The rings."

He ran a finger around one eye. "The face paint."

He gestured at the words on the monitor. "These files."

Celeste said, "Gus seemed to think these Ring Smiths had to do with your four rings, Reason. Care to elaborate?"

Reason sighed, offering her and the two boys a sad frown.

He then said, "In Ulster, in the 12th century, their was a slave trade inspired by a demon known as Molech. He and his thirteen minions were responsible for the abduction of thousands of children in many lands. Hundreds of Sacred Bands had been sent out to destroy Molech and his minions, but their ability to disappear had allowed them to savagely attack any who came against them, and they became known as the Unseen Ones. Invisible they became invulnerable.

"Ring Smiths had been called to forge rings that allowed their wielders to see demons from the Otherworld. The rings were given to a Celtic swordsman, a Saracen archer, a Hebrew spear-maid, and a Norse axe man. The four warriors set sail to the Isle of Skye, where they used the magic of the rings to kill Molech's minions. However, Molech escaped.

"Many years later, the warriors were buried in Ulster, their names etched on markers: Ian McNial. Sara Ali. Rachel Abrahams. Ragnar Thorson, condensed to Tory, one of Beef's ancestors. McNial, meaning Niall's son AKA Nelson, my own last name. Beef and I are both descended from these two ring masters who battled against evil in ancient Ireland. And yes, I have been a reluctant ring master all these years, using its power to benefit me, not taking up the battle as my grandfather, Billy Connors, asked me to do. As a boy, he took me to the Grand Lodge of the Templars one evening, where men in white robes with red crosses on their chests performed a ritual. I was approached by a man wearing a goat mask. The Goat Man declared, 'I am Baphomet the fire god! I require a sacrifice!'

"The Goat Man removed his mask. It had been my grandfather, Grand Master of the Templars representing Baphomet, a god who the knights opposed since their order began in the 11th century. At 16, I was terrified by the drama acted out before me. After witnessing that ceremony, I refused to join the order of the Templars. Instead of a Templar, I became a writer, determined to fight evil in my own way.

"One evening when I thought I'd put my grandfather's strange order behind me, I received a package from the old Irishman. It contained the rings. My grandfather warned me of an impending doom, and he urged me to stand up as a Templar Knight. Even though I scoffed at such nonsense, I took to wearing one of those rings, and discovered it was endowed with a power. Any time I wore it, I was able to do whatever I set my mind to. Writing. Dog training. Youth work. Investigating. The ring not only inspired me to accomplish many great things, it empowered me to pursue them, with each goal like a milestone on a long journey."

Reason fell silent, his tale having been told.

Lucas and Alex stared down at the two rings he held.

Celeste ran two fingers over her intricate tattoo and solemnly said, "Perhaps it's time you allow others to share what you obviously consider a burden. After all, what could it hurt?"

An hour later, assuming the three kids were all fast asleep in their separate rooms, Reason ushered Beef into his den. The detective had called a few minutes ago, telling him he had information to share with him. Lobo, the only dog still awake, greeted Beef as he and Rea-son stepped into the den.

After accepting the soda Reason offered him, Beef said, "The autopsy on Gus revealed that the railroad spike driven through his heart was used in another murder years back when William 'Freight Train' Guatney, caved in the skull of an 11-year old boy in Illinois. Freight Train rode the rails. For forty years he traveled the US in box cars, picking up odd jobs in towns where he was known as a likeable hobo. But Guatney also had a darker side.

"The special target of his anger was young boys. In August 1979, Guatney was arrested in Illinois, charged with three counts of murder. Homicide investigators suspected Guatney might have murdered fifteen children in the past five years alone. Nebraska charged him in the deaths of 13-year-old Jon Simpson and 12-year-old Jacob Surber, abducted from the state fair at Lincoln, in 1975. Jack Hanrahan, 12, disappeared from his Topeka neighborhood May 20, 1979. Molested and murdered, his corpse was found in a creek bed ten days later; on August 20, Guatney was charged with first-degree murder. In Illinois, Mark Helmig, 9, was murdered at Pekin, in 1976. Marty Lancaster, 14, was killed two years later. In several of the murders, Gautney used a railroad spike to render them unconscious."

Reason said, "Someone broke into the evidence room and stole the murder weapon used by Guatney? Who in the hell would do that?"

37

Huge and grungy Mange, warlord of the Den, sat there in his old Ford van parked in the shadows on Logan Avenue. From his vantage point he had a straight shot, one-hundred yards to Gus Howard's backdoor. His night-vision goggles turned the outside world into green and black images.

Seated beside him, Nate said, "You've had the place covered for the past two days. Give me an activity report."

Sliding his goggles up to his forehead, Mange removed a pen light from his shirt pocket and flicked it on. In the dim light, he read: "10:10: Gypsy Kid entered the old man's house. 10:15: You entered. 10:18: Celeste entered. 10:22: Celeste exited. 11:00: Viking visited Writer's house. 11:15:Writer went inside. 11:30: You escorted out in cuffs. 11:40: Gypsy Kid led out in cuffs. 12:00: Writer returned to his home. And tonight, Celeste sneaks back inside the geezer's house and went down to Writer's carrying something in her hands."

Nate responded, "Still no rings? The Arab paid us to find them. What the hell happened to those rings?"

A second later, Mange's cell phone rang. He answered it, saying, "Got both places covered. The dead geezer's. The Writer's place."

Silence came from the other end of the line.

Mange said, "We appreciate the cash you deposited in both our accounts. But could Nate and I maybe get a bonus?"

Again, only silence came back over the line.

A flashlight beam suddenly bathed Gus's back gate in a lemony aura. The flashlight went out. Two boys opened the gate and entered the old man's yard. Mange whispered into the phone, "Golden Boy and Gypsy Kid are back!"

Snick! came over the phone line. Snick! Click! Click!

"Was that a lock blade?" Mange asked. "Do you have a knife?"

The line disconnected, leaving Mange to stare at Lucas and Alex entering Gus's home, unaware that someone was in there with them.

"Lucas," muttered Nate, "is gonna get himself killed. This dude who hired us is one creepy spook!"

With that, he exited Mange's van and headed for Gus Howard's back door. Watching him from his place in his van, Mange heard a sudden noise at his driver's side door. He turned to find himself staring into the eyes of a figure with slanted catlike eyes.

"What do you want?" Mange asked.

The figure said, "A remnant of your soul."

Lucas and Alex moved silently through the dark kitchen. Having eavesdropped earlier on Beef sharing information with Reason, the two boys had waited for the detective to leave. Ten minutes later, Lucas crept into the den and stealthily removed two of the rings from the chest where Reason kept them.

After quietly slipping out through the backdoor, he handed one of the rings to Alex and said, "The railroad spike driven through Gus's heart was used in another murder? And Freight Train Guatney caved in the skull of an 11-year old boy? If that doesn't give you the creeps, I don't know what would?"

Alex said, "It creeps me out totally that a killer of kids used the spike found buried in Gus's chest. But what do we know about demons? Or weapons to use against them?"

Lucas said, "It was you who told me about all the weapons—"

"Most of them were guns. Who said lead bullets fired from guns can kill a ghost? A demon? Or even a vampire?"

"It was you who said the Cingane fashioned silver bullets to slay vampires with. So, maybe these special-made weapons—"

"Special weapons in the hands of two ignorant kids?"

"Don't call me dumb, Alex! Told you names piss me off!"

"I said, 'Ignorant,' not dumb!"

Lucas shrugged, wanting to change the subject. "What did Reason mean by these Templars?"

Alex answered, "Founded in 1119, the Poor Knights of Christ was one of the most skilled fighting units of the Crusades. After the First Crusade in 1099, Christians made pilgrimages to sacred sites in the Holy Land. Saracen bandits preyed upon pilgrims, slaughtering them by the hundreds. In 1119, King Baldwin of Jerusalem created an order to protect these pilgrims. He granted them a wing of the royal palace in the ruins of the Temple of Solomon. The new order took the name Templar knights. They were the advance troops in the Crusades."

But by then, their arguing ceased for they had reached Gus's backdoor. Seconds later, they were inside the house.

Wearing the rings, they chose not to turn on the lights. As they entered the hallway leading to the bedroom, they froze.

Cocking his head to one side, Lucas listened.

He heard the swish of fabric from somewhere ahead of him. Either at the end of the hallway, or coming from inside the bedroom.

They waited a full minute before proceeding.

The moment Lucas and Alex entered the bedroom, they knew they were not alone. Someone was lurking in the shadows. The bed before them was stripped of its bedding, but there was a dark spot left behind by the blood from Gus's chest. Lucas felt a warm breath on his neck a fraction of a second before a strong arm wrapped around his throat. A sharp prick came from just beneath his left jaw, and a trickle of blood ran down from the tiny puncture hole the knife had made, even as a voice whispered, "I see you wear the rings that have been passed down from the 12th century. Templar rings! Or do you American boys even know who the Knights Templar were?"

Lucas recognized the voice of the man behind him. "Waziri!" he blurted. Alex offered the Arab man a defiant glare, saying, "A Templar Knight is truly fearless, and his soul is protected by the armor of faith, as his body is protected by the armor of steel. He need fear neither demons nor men. And especially not you, Saracen."

Lucas stared in disbelief at Alex. "I'm the one with a knife to my throat," he said. "And you're talking smack to this nutjob?"

"I am a Saracen Warrior!" Waziri declared. "I have a direct bloodline to the Gate Keeper, Mohammad Bin Aziri, who in the 10th century opened a portal in Bagdad to Molech. My family has served the Ghost of this Dead King ever since. On a Babylonian cylinder seal representing child sacrifice, Molech is listed as the abomination of the children of Ammon. In the Hebrew Bible, seven instances of Molek were regarded as the term for child sacrifice."

Surprising Lucas, Alex quoted, "Leviticus 18:21 'And thou shalt not let any of thy seed pass through the fire to Molech, neither shalt thou profane the name of thy God.'"

Waziri growled, "You see, you are Huntsmen, who mean to do my master harm! For that, you must die!"

He moved swiftly, driving the knife directly in through the collar of Lucas's jean jacket, slicing through the shirt beneath. The sharp point scraped on metal, skittering away.

An electric shock traveled up the blade of the knife and into Waziri's hand. Lucas, who had slipped his ring hand up between them at the last possible moment, spun out of his grasp, revealing the glowing green ring he wore.

Waziri snarled, "Damn right you're an associate of the Templars! The ring has protected you!"

Alex threw a punch, planting his fist directly in the center of Waziri's face, crushing his nose and sending the dark-haired man down to both knees. A moment later, Nate appeared behind the two boys, latching onto them by the collars of their shirts. He herded them back down the hallway and outside the house.

As he sent them running toward Reason's house, he glanced back to see Mange being drawn out through the window of his van. The figure with the catlike eyes sank his canines into the tender flesh of the big biker's neck. He inhaled, sucking the life out Mange, causing both of his eyes to loudly pop. His soul sailed out through his empty eye sockets, and the creature captured a remnant of his soul. He then roared in triumph, "Molech, King of Dead Ghosts is back!"

The roar was reminiscent of a hunting lion on the plains of Africa. It was a haunting sound, and as Lucas and Alex ran, it made them look for the nearest tree, as if some primordial instinct kicked in and had them wanting to be up off the ground out of harm's way. Alex said, "Let's get back to Reason's house, Lucas!"

Lucas found himself craning his neck so that he could look to the sky. He gestured toward the western skyline. There, moving across the moonlit horizon was a mass of multi-colored figures, greatly resembling Mongol warriors. Some sported ram-horns on their helms. Others wore chain mail coifs that trailed back over their shoulders as they rode their turquoise winged-horses through the skies.

"God!" Lucas cried. "Demons!"

Alex said, "Fallen angel type demons, whose king is Lucifer?"

"Yes!" said Celeste as she appeared on the front porch. "Get inside the house! Inside now, and don't give me any crap!"

38

Chapter Thirty-Eight

Amazed that the boys obeyed her, Celeste made a mad dash for Gus Howard's house, hoping to find a suitable weapon to combat Molech with. She knew from months of working for the old relic collector that he had an arsenal of strange and exotic weaponry stored in his bedroom. She'd once heard the demon hunter speak about tokens of power that could ruin a demon's day.

She entered the kitchen and tore down the hallway and into the bedroom. She reached into Gus's chest of drawers, and her hand closed on the hilt of a bladeless sword. The moment she picked it up, a slight humming came from the leather-wrapped hilt, and a shimmering lavender blade sprang from the mouth of the falcon engraved on the hand guard.

Jango crept up beside her and sent a vision inside her head: Old Billy Connors stood before a rustic inn. Bagpipe music came from inside and the front doors swung open. Two lean figures clad in black came racing down the front steps of the inn. One wielded a sapphire blade that reminded Celeste of a snowy winter night, while the other wielded a red-bladed sword that spoke to her of sunsets.

The female Elf with the short, gold hair, twirled her red blade over her head, then brought it down to rest on the upraised sword of the raven-haired Elf with the blue blade. Locking their swords together, the two Elves glided forward to connect their luminescent blades with the dull blade Billy Connors held out to them.

The Irishman said, "Lady Kerrin Skye, Sword Mistress of the Unseen War! Creed Blackstag of the Wolf Lords of Shadow! I thank you for your aid in forging this sword! May both of your skills be transferred to this newly-made blade that whoever wields it be endowed with your prowess and mastery of blades!"

Lady Kerrin took hold of her hilt with both hands and pulses of sparkling light traveled down her blade. Scintillating flashes of dark blue light slithered down Creed's blade, evolving with Kerrin's red light beams, turning the gray blade Billy held, into one that was a bright lavender shade. As the vision began to fade, Celeste caught a glimpse of Billy handing the purple-bladed sword to Gus Howard.

Gus, in turn, placed it inside his dresser drawer.

Drawn to the loud roaring coming from Molech, the demons flew their steeds to a place in the sky directly above the suburb of Havelock. There, they hovered, glaring down at the Ghost of Dead Kings looming over the body of his victim beside the Ford van. Molech growled fiercely and the entire mob of demons recoiled, at once recognizing his place in the hierarchy of demons. One demon with horns crowning his head, said, "How may we serve you, Lord?"

"Where," Molech snarled, "can I feed? I need sustenance so that I can come into my full power? It has been over hundreds of years since I've walked this plane. I need to feed!"

The horned demon jerked on the reins of his turquoise steed. "Follow me, my Lord," he called down to Molech. "We have an excellent feeding ground! One with an endless supply of the mentally ill, the deranged, sexual deviates, murderers, rapists, psychotics, the very dregs of society. We have staked out the State Prison."

Molech was just taking to the air to join the flight back to the State Pen, when Reason and Beef came running down the street.

Reason could see Nate standing beside the van, looming over the hapless form of Mange. The biker lashed out and slugged the cat-eyed, noseless creature before he could take flight.

Drawing his gun from his shoulder holster, Beef slowed as he approached the creature there in the street. "Hands in the air!" he demanded, brandishing his pistol in the face of the demon. "Now, put your hands in the air!"

Molech chortled softly.

Beef lowered his gaze and studied the features of Mange sprawled in the street next to the van. It appeared the muscles, the nerves, and his eyes, had been sucked into a powerful vacuum sweeper. Molech drew a long knife from a sheath at his side, the blade glowing red. Beef gave the creature before him one last chance to surrender. "Drop it!" he ordered, raising his gun in a two-fisted grip.

Molech lunged at him, the knife extended before him.

Beef fired.

The red-hot lead projectile sped from the muzzle of the gun and punched a hole in the breast of Molech. He staggered off balance from the force of the bullet, and yet he recoiled quite suddenly, and came on, the blade a red blur in his grasp.

Beef fired his remaining five bullets at point-blank range, each one striking Molech in the center of his chest.

Sidestepping to avoid the red blade, Beef felt his attacker brush past him. Molech stumbled forward, moving woodenly. At the end of four paces, Molech wheeled back around, an angry scowl on his face. He sucked in a great gasp of air, his cheeks bulging. He spat six times, sending all six lead bullets from his mouth. Beef recoiled as the projectiles hit him with terrific force, punching him off his feet.

Molech paused, his shiny head cocked to one side, his black eyes narrowing shrewdly. He sniffed the air, his noseless face contorting. "You," he growled at Reason, "are the ring bearer of a Celtic King!"

And suddenly, Jango was there between the Ghost of Dead Kings and Reason. He launched himself at Molech, using one tightly balled fist to pummel him upside his head, while bringing his other hand down in a swift chop, sending the long knife flickering out of his grasp. The fight that followed was lightning-swift as the two combatants erupted into a whirlwind of brutal attacks. The two fighters exchanged dozens of strikes, punches, and round-house kicks that would have leveled lesser opponents. One moment, Jango went on the offensive, delivering swift strikes toward Molech's face. In the next, he went into a defensive crouch as Molech reacted with strikes of his own, growling in frustration as each was deflected with efficient blocks. Both fighters appeared to be evenly matched.

Molech delivered an overhand strike down at the shiny black head of Jango, when the mogrim ducked, swerved to the left, wheeled back to the right, and threw a swift upper cut into the chin of Molech. The blow was sudden and savage, delivered with such brutal force that Molech's head snapped back, causing him to reel backwards.

Jango followed through with a devastating punch to Molech's throat. The King of Dead Ghosts dropped to one knee. Jango was just preparing to finish the fight, when the horde of demons came down from on high. Knocked off his feet by the mad swarm, Jango went down beneath them and their turquoise steeds, barely avoiding their slashing swords.

The mob of demons were so preoccupied with trying to slay the fast-moving mogrim, they failed to notice Celeste come racing up behind them, the tattoos on the side of her face and down her neck blazing bright blue. Skidding to a stop, Celeste quoted, "Ephesians 6:12: Our struggle is not against flesh and blood, but against the rulers, against the authorities, against the powers of this dark world and against the spiritual forces of evil in the heavenly realms."

The horde recoiled, an amber cloud roiling out around them, creating a blood-red fog that covered the street behind them. Latching onto one of Jango's arms, Celeste quoted, "Ephesians 6:10, Be strong in the Lord. Put on the full armor of God to stand against the devil's schemes. Stand firm then, with the belt of truth buckled around your waist, with the breastplate of righteousness, and with your feet fitted with the gospel of peace. Take up the shield of faith to extinguish all the flaming arrows of the evil one. Take up the sword of the Spirit, which is the word of God."

Shoving Jango toward Reason, Celeste shouted, "If you want to live, run to the vacant lot! I'll be right behind you!"

With Jango clinging to his neck, Reason helped the fallen detective to his feet. Beef stumbled his way across the street, weaving his way onto the lot. Following behind them, Nate glanced back to see Celeste stand before the wild pack of demons, the tattoos of the twin wolves and the antlered stag pulsing with a luminous blue light. Nate stood there, watching in astonishment as the stag peeled away from her neck, transforming into a large white creature. It bowed its head, then dropped to its knees before Celeste. She quickly mounted the stag and it lurched to its feet, raking the air with its antlers, now pulsating with a strange blue light.

The twin wolves peeled away from her face, materializing as large creatures, sparkling with blue light. A violet-bladed sword appeared in Celeste's right hand. She gestured toward the demon ranks with it, and the wolves moved like quicksilver, appearing in several places at once as they flashed through the midst of the demons. Narrowly avoiding their rising and falling red blades, the pair killed dozens of the demons in a burst of savage fury. Celeste guided the stag into the mob, and wielding her purple blade, slew demons in great numbers.

39

A war horn was winded from within the demon ranks. The demons jerked on the reins of their turquoise steeds, wheeling away from the wild sweep of Celeste's blade.

The demon horde formed a semi-circle before her. Celeste sat on her mount, her luminous blade wavering in the air before her. The wolves spun away from the watching demons and took up guarded positions on either side of the stag. She gasped, then froze. A small, but muscular figure appeared there, striding boldly out of the mass of demons. He stood barely five feet tall and yet his furry chest and shoulders were massive and rippling with corded muscle. He had the body of a human, and yet the face and head of a yellow-eyed goat.

"Baphomet!" Celeste snapped.

The goat-headed demon cackled.

"Yes!" he howled, his long white beard sticking out from his chin, twin horns upon his head glistening. "Fire gods crossing over from the Otherworld! My master and I have returned! Our banishment is ended! Time for soul reaping! And no Templar is going to stop us!"

He gestured with a cloven hoof, and at once dozens of the demons gathered around Molech, still weakened by his brutal beating he'd taken from Jango. As Molech was carried away, Baphomet drew a shiny black blade from a sheath behind his left shoulder. "Come, Brethren!" he crowed. "Let us feast on souls!"

Celeste gave a nudge of one heel, and the stag turned at once. Followed closely by the two wolves, it carried Celeste to the center of the vacant lot. Sliding off the stag's back, she said, "A warding is our only chance. I cannot stand against the power of a fire god."

While the wolves took up guarded positions in front of Reason, Nate, and Beef, the stag darted out in front of Celeste, dipping its head and digging the ends of its tines into the soft ground. An eerie violet light skittered down the length of its antlers, slithering into the grooves it had created in the earth.

Popping and crackling with magical powers, the violet shaded force evolved into a shimmering field that began to spread as the stag wheeled around, running in a wide circle, dragging its antlers through the ground. "What the holy hell?" Reason said. "A force field?"

"Yes," she replied. "And if it holds, we are safe for the moment."

An enormous, purple transparent bubble formed over their heads and around them, creating a twenty-foot haven of safety for those within. Reason looked on as Baphomet and a score of raging demons struck the warding, their sword blades skittering off the barrier, their faces striking the electrically charged mass with stunning force. Many of them bounced backwards, while others slithered down the length of the force field, sprawling in crumpled heaps upon the ground. Baphomet repulsed by the protective ward, recoiled for mere seconds, then attacked the violet-shaded warding in a furious rage.

Celeste studied the effect of the warding for long moments, then, satisfied that it was holding, she turned to Reason. "Vacant lots like this," she said, "are scattered throughout Havelock. Most are staggered block by block, heading north above the route of the Havelock tunnels. If this one is the same, we have a way out of here!"

With a gentle sweep from right to left with her sword, she moved to the center of the lot, tapping with her sword at the iron grating that created an opening to the sewer system below. Glancing once more at the enraged demons attacking the warding with sudden ferocity, she slashed at the iron grating, her blade slicing through each bar of iron like a hot knife through warm butter.

Pieces of the grating fell inward and clanged loudly as they struck the concrete floor of the tunnel seven feet below them. "Reason? You first! Lead the way!"

Reason slowly lowered himself in through the opening and down into the dark depths below. "My gun," Beef said, turning away from the tunnel below them. "I can't just leave it there in the street."

Celeste snapped, "Leave it! Bullets are useless against demons! You need only to focus on saving your soul, not your gun!"

Sighing in frustration, Beef peered through the transparent warding, taking one last look at his pistol laying beside Mange. "But what if some kid wanders along here and picks it up?"

"Good God, Tory!" Celeste quipped. "Consequences on this plane of existence will mean nothing to you if your soul is devoured by demons from beyond! You could end up being tormented for the rest of eternity! This is, that serious! Forget your gun! Save your soul!"

She took a hold of Beef's forearm and gestured to the hole in the ground before them. Reluctantly, Beef kneeled down, then lowered himself down into the tunnel.

"You're not staying to play hero!" Nate said to Celeste as he moved up beside her.

She snorted, "Oh, hell no! Once that warding is dispelled, I would die seconds later!"

She gestured at the stag and wolves with her glimmering sword and quietly said, "Return to me."

Nate looked on in stunned amazement as the three creatures swiftly faded into ghostly images. They drifted through the air in a blue-tinged smoky haze, and returned to their places on Celeste's neck and face, becoming tattoos once more.

She tossed her head and smirked at Baphomet, and dropped down through the opening at her feet, her violet blade flaring brightly in the darkness below. Nate did not hesitate to follow her.

40

Reason and Celeste stood in the center of the nine-by-seven foot corridor. Both of them peered up to the white space of the hole above them, expecting at any moment to see demons come hurtling down at them.

Celeste lowered her gaze, locking eyes with Reason. She noted the ring he wore. "Is your imagination stretched out of proportion yet? Not every day an author like you encounters live ghosts or demons. By now, you probably have a million questions you'd like answers for, correct?"

Reason glanced worriedly up at the hole in the ceiling of the tunnel. "Right now, I have only one. Will that force field hold?"

As if answer to his question, there came a loud ripping sound from the air above them. The blackness inside the tunnel suddenly became illuminated by traces of purple light, as if remnants of the transparent force field had been shredded, and were now drifting down to the floor of the Havelock tunnel.

A moment later, the goat-head of Baphomet appeared in the hole in the ceiling above them, a smirk on his bearded features. "And now," he cackled, "your souls will quench my thirst!"

Celeste removed a glowing green gem from her belt pouch. She pressed on one if its facets, producing a solid clicking sound, and tossed the fist-sized jewel directly up at the fire god's astonished face.

"Holy shit!" Baphomet cried out in alarm as he hastily withdrew from the opening, instinctively catching the pulsating gem with his front paws. The goat-headed being tossed the green jewel away from him as fast he could, the gem sizzling as it left his cloven hoof.

Celeste gave a wild laugh.

Reason looked at her in puzzlement, not seeing how she could find any humor in their desperate situation. She saw his confusion and said, "My dad always used to say, 'You're enough to make a preacher cuss!' I just wonder what he'd say now that I made a god curse?"

A sudden explosion came from above them. A brilliant emerald light flashed across the opening, and a swirling cloud of green swept Baphomet off his hoofs, its fierce, tornado-like force carrying him away. "Run!" Celeste shouted. "If Goat Head overcomes this particular power point, it would be far too much for me to defeat a fire god!"

Jango led the way, launching himself down the tunnel heading north. Nate fell in behind the swift-moving creature as he scurried down the dark depths. "Four blocks," he told them. "Only four blocks to the north the tunnel comes out into the Burlington rail yards!"

As Celeste, Reason, and Beef broke into a run, Reason frowned. Despite the fact that nothing made sense since the moment he tried on the ring, he wondered if he was losing his mind. Ghosts of Havelock boys. Demons who fed on inmates at the State Pen. Two fire gods who had instigated child sacrifices. It was all a little much, even for Reason's writer's imagination to handle.

Keeping pace with Celeste, he said, "I know I sound crazy even asking this, but did we really just escape the attack of two gods? Wouldn't gods be a little more difficult to deal with?"

"Gods," Celeste told him as she ran, "is a figure of speech. In truth, Molech and Baphomet are demons, fallen from grace like their leader, Lucifer. If you study the names of Canaanite gods, you will find many are merely demons, who conned unsuspecting men and women into worshiping them. That battle of the Song Lord, the Chief Musician in Heaven? You know, Lucifer's story?"

Reason said, "Yeah. Lucifer rebelled against God, and he and one third of the angels tried to mount a coup. God cast them out of Heaven, and demons have been a pain in the ass ever since."

Celeste said, "Attention whores is all they are. Lucifer, Molech,

Baal, Baphomet, Mot, Seth, Anu, Enki, Enlil, Ishtar, Ashur, Shamash, Shulmanu, Tammuz, Hadad, Sin, Kur, Dagan, Tiamat, Bel and Marduk. All of these were demons, who set themselves up as gods to the people of the Middle East. In time, they became known as gods. And many of them demanded the sacrificing of children. In those days, any man who pleased his god by freely giving up his own child to be burned at his god's altar, was truly a worthy man."

Reason asked, "Why did they demand kids to appease them?"

"Some would say innocence," Celeste answered. "Some say purity, for children were prized for their innocence and purity, and therefore very appealing to these demon gods."

Shaking his head, Reason said, "I don't buy that. I've been doing youth work most of my life, and I've known some dastardly evil kids. Some I've known are self-centered, belligerent, mean-spirited kids. Besides, weren't wives and children considered by Male-dominated religions, even the Hebrews, simply chattel?"

Celeste looked over at Reason as they continued to jog down the tunnel. "Chattel?"

"Personal property," Reason told her. "In Old Testament times, Men were considered the dominant figure of all households, while women and children fell under the category of doves, lambs, and sheep, simply personal property."

"So," Beef said, "who elevated children to the position of valuable items worthy of sacrifice?"

Celeste tried to think of a plausible explanation.

"It has to do with the first-born sons," Reason said. "Remember the story about Abraham and God demanding he sacrifice his son, Isaac? Many of the Canaanite gods used psychological warfare on their worshipers, in order to control them and make them faithful subjects. Therefore, if any man in those days was willing to burn alive his own son in order to please his god, that man was a true follower."

They ran in silence for the next two blocks, all of them narrowing their eyes as they approached the moonlit exit of the tunnels ahead of them. "Yes," Celeste said. "A first-born son inherited the father's legacy, and carried on his line. It was a big deal to sacrifice him to a god demanding his death. It was a way to prove his loyalty."

No one spoke the next several minutes as they neared the exit of the tunnels ahead of them. Jango was the first one spring out of the tunnel. He scampered around the small pond beyond, and skittered up the trail to the train tracks running six lanes wide through the Havelock train yards.

Reason, Nate, and Beef followed the mogrim, and Celeste took up the rear position, glancing back to make sure no demons had followed them. "We need to seek shelter," Celeste said. "A safe-haven where no demon will dare to tread."

"A church?" Nate asked. "Usually, churches and holy relics are real turn-offs to demons."

Shaking her head, Celeste said, "No. Churches have been compromised in the past. We need to head to Sanctuary. There, no demon will trespass for there is a Guardian there who has sent dozens of them wailing back to the Unseen Realm."

Reason asked, "And where is this Sanctuary you speak of? And who in the hell is this Guardian?"

Celeste offered him an impish smirk.

And Reason and Beef both stared at her as she said, "The Emerald Pub. Your grandfather, Billy Connors, is the Guardian. With him, we'll be safe."

41

Alex followed Lucas and the dogs into Gus's bedroom. The dogs sniffed at the spot where Waziri had fallen to his knees after he'd slugged him in the nose. "What are you doing?" Alex asked as he watched Lucas rummaging through Gus's drawers. "We're just kids! We're not professional demon hunters!"

"I don't want to hear it!" Lucas snapped, his hand closing on a hand-crossbow inside of one of the drawers. "These demons killed my sister! They took out Uncle Nate! Reason? Beef? They are gone, Alex! So I'm gonna hunt them down and kill every last one of them!"

Alex reached down into one of the drawers and pulled out a short sword. He snapped, "I can't believe that you're that unhinged you'd go after these demons! This is just a plain, ordinary sword! What makes you lamely think it can be powered up?"

Lucas said, "They will activate the moment we need them! If they are not magical, why would Gus have collected them? Look at my ring! It's already lighting up!" He held his free hand up.

Alex's eyes widened as he saw that the ring Lucas wore was glowing faintly. "And look at this!" Lucas said, pulling the eagle feather from beneath his shirt. "Magic knows magic, Alex!"

The eagle feather of American Horse attached to the leather cord around his neck was pulsing with a blue light that lit up the words engraved on the stock of the bow and the blade of the sword. Reading them intently, Lucas asked, "Who is the Morrigan and Herne, Alex?"

Alex said, "According to Gypsy lore, the Morrígan is a battle-maiden from Ireland. Her real name is Mór-Ríoghain, meaning queen of phantoms. She often appears as a crow or raven. She encourages warriors to do brave deeds and is associated with the banshee of Irish folklore. Banshee means a woman of the fairy mounds and the barrows of Celtic kings. In English lore, Herne is said to have the antlers of a stag on his head. My Gypsy kin equate Herne, the Huntsmen with the Celtic god Cernunnos, the Lord of Wild Things."

Alex jabbed at the air with the sword. "Nothing happens," he said. "No light illuminates the blade. No fireballs burst from the tip. No light trickles down its sharp edges. What happens when we come face to face with these mad-dog demons, and no magic comes to life?"

Lucas turned and headed for the door, snorting, "That's not going to happen, Alex!"

And Alex muttered, "Famous last words."

Waziri led the two fire gods onto Ballard ballfield, a swarm of lesser demons trailing behind them. Green-skinned, frog-faced goblins. Bug-eyed, pug-nosed boglins. Sparkling and crackling, transparent demon-wolves, sporting badger-like heads.

"I need an altar," Molech weakly rasped. "I need to feed in my weakened condition on blood and hearts! The younger the better!"

Waziri gestured at the ballfield before them. "These young boys will do, won't they?"

The cat-eyed Molech peered at the team of boys in the middle of a glow-ball game on the ball diamond fifty feet in front of them. Unaware of the demons leering at them as they threw six phosphorescent baseballs back and forth across the field, the twelves boys continued to play. The brightly glowing balls zipped here and there, their luminous light only going dark when a boy caught one. No sooner did one boy snag a ball from the air, then a second kid tossed another, creating lines of florescent red light as the balls soared back and forth between them. "Their hearts will feed me," Molech said, smirking at the boys in their white uniforms. "The boys of summer play Little League. They become Boy Scouts. Go on camp outs. Take fishing trips. Take bike rides. Go skateboarding. Build tree forts. All the things that boys do, will come to end for this team. As I feed on their souls they will be no more and their young lives will be cut short."

Ali Karim, who had just joined the team of boys that night, spotted the demons running across the ballfield toward them. He shrieked in terror. Overwhelmed by demon horror rolling over them in waves, four of the boys wet their pants. Four more took off running for home. "Herd them!" Molech ordered. "The stone fireplace ahead of us in the park shall be an altar for the sacrifice!"

And so it was that Ali and seven members of his glow-ball team were forced to run before a mad pack of demons from the ballfield to the playground of Havelock park.

Grunge and Lobo led the way through the dark streets of Havelock. *They are directly ahead of us,* Grunge sent back to Lucas. *Molech needs to feed on souls in order to recharge after laying dormant for so many long years. Only in his weakened condition do you boys have a chance at stopping him.*

Lucas hefted the handheld crossbow. "Do you think I've picked the right weapon? I don't want to just wound him. I want to kill him."

Grunge looked back at the shiny black crossbow. *I detect an aura around the head of that quarrel. So I am assuming it is endowed with some sort of magic. Not quite sure about the potency of that sword, but I doubt Gus Howard would have kept it if it didn't have some sort of special powers when wielded against these demons.*

Running beside him, Lobo looked over at Grunge, sending, *Just what do you know about these evil spirits? You make it sound as if you've dealt with demons before.*

Grunge rumbled deep in his chest. *These eyes have seen things, old dog. Living with Black Bull this past year, I have witnessed first hand, these wicked entities. I've seen the tokens of power used by Lucas and Ben. I know there is a battle being waged by forces from the Otherworld. And the moment I followed the boys into that bedroom, I detected currents of power coming from the items stored in the dresser. My former owner, Pete He Dog, warned me that I had to keep an eye on the Thunder Dreamer. Goblin and I have known this day was coming. It is you, I wonder about.*

With a soft growl, Lobo sent, *I serve my master out of a deep love for him. If that service includes the hospitality he offers these two boys, then I extend my loyalty and love to them, as well. Is that good enough for you, old dog?*

Lucas, Alex, and the three dogs entered the park, coming to a stop fifty feet from the swarm of demons inside the playground area. As the demons closed ranks around the team of boys, Lucas said, "Ali? What's he doing here?"

Standing in the center of his team, Ali meekly raised his hand and hesitantly waved at Lucas, tears rolling down his cheeks.

Still weak from his long years of sleep, Molech harshly whispered, "Two boys? The White Council sends two boys?"

Blinking his slanted, catlike eyes, Molech reached out and stopped his goat-headed companion from charging forward. "Beware," he hissed. "See the engravings on the bow and sword? The marks of Herne and the Morrigan! What do Celtic legends have to do with us? This stinks of Merlin and Talesin! Curse all druids and enchanters!"

"And curse," Waziri snarled, "mangy dogs, the bane of all royal cats of our homeland in Egypt? Cats are the emissaries of the gods of Egypt, and they bring dogs to insult us? And the most despicable, disgusting breed among all dogs, pit bulls!"

Not true, sent Goblin, causing the entire swarm of demons to look to the small gray pup. *Love and loyalty. These are traits that Staffordshire terriers are noted for throughout history.*

These traits and virtues Goblin spoke of ignited a fire in the hearts of all three dogs as they took a guarded stance in front of the two boys. This fire broiled up from the depths of their souls, forming a blue-white barrier that spread outward from the chests of the three pit bulls, and created a transparent, luminous field of force.

A pack of demon-wolves detached themselves from the mob surrounding the two demon lords. They were mangy-looking with huge, transparent shaggy bodies. Their eyes shone with reddish light. Each of the luminous beasts howled, sending an eerie undulating call for battle through the air. The entire pack offered the approaching boys and dogs a menacing glare. They then charged forward.

Grunge, Lobo, and Goblin took up defensive stances behind the aura they projected. The demon-wolves barreled into the faintly visible barrier, their snouts and chests slamming directly into the shimmering wall. Many of the charging beasts swiftly evaporated with airy explosions as their shaggy bodies and furry faces connected with the magical barrier, extinguishing them like bugs flying into a bug zap-per. A few of the ghostly wolves slid off the field of force, and loped off and retreated back into the demon ranks, their lowered heads clear evidence that the traits and virtues activated by the three dogs resulted in their defeat.

Molech gestured with one hand, sending frost-white crystals at the warding projected by the dogs. The pellets of ice struck the barrier and it vanished. At his command, a mad swarm of goblins came howling from out of the midst of the demons gathered there on the playground. They were no more than three feet tall, but there were so many of them swinging swords above their black, greasy hair, that the dogs were soon to be shredded by the mob of small folk.

Lucas raised the crossbow and fired it directly at the charging goblins. The quarrel sprang from the tip of the bow, exploding and sending out a barrage of large, black-feathered birds into the faces of the oncoming goblins.

"Ravens?" Alex whispered as the flock of birds slammed into the front line of swordsmen. "The Morrigan?" he gasped as the ravens evolved into a black-cloaked woman, wild tangles of black hair spilling down past her shoulders. She landed on bare feet, twin swords whirling above her head. She then attacked, and fountains of bright green blood jettisoned through the air as her blades slithered into the ranks of the pug-faced goblins.

His eyes never leaving the wild dance of the dark-cloaked woman, Alex stood there in shocked silence, watching the swordmistress hack and slay with her twin blades.

42

The Morrigan sprang into the middle of the goblin horde, her swords whipping around her in a frantic flurry. Dozens of the greasy-haired warriors died, leaving wisps of black smoke drifting through the air as they evaporated, vanishing from sight.

Molech cast another barrage of icy-blue shards at the Morrigan. The particles of luminous sparks struck her, and she froze, one sword raised above her wild strands of raven hair, the other falling from her grasp. With a long, wail, the Morrigan disappeared, leaving behind a scattering of blue sparkles.

Molech gave a command, and a company of boglin spearmen darted through the ranks of the decimated goblins. They were larger than their goblin cousins, standing over five feet tall with broad shoulders and thick arms. Their heads were shaved with the exception of a single scalp lock trailing down from the tops of their heads. And they were all armed with wicked-looking spears, which they whirled down and around in unison as they ran directly at the three dogs.

"Alex!" cried Lucas. "Activate your sword!"

"One sword?" Alex said. "What use is it? We are dead!"

With terror in his eyes, Alex watched the boglins picking up speed as they raced across the playground. Upon hearing Grunge growl in defiance, Alex swung the sword up to defend the canines. And the ring on his finger connected with the emblem of the owl engraved on the hilt of the sword. "Ouch!" he cried as a flash of brilliant light erupted from the engraving of the owl. The explosion of light stung his hands, yet he kept his grip on the hilt and looked on in wonder as a greenish-black illumination slithered down the length of the blade and shot from its tip.

At once, a shiny black owl emerged from the ball of green light, and with a Swap! of sound created by his wide-spread wings, the black raptor launched himself directly at the charging swarm of boglins. The moment the owl careened into the spearmen, he evolved into a black-cloaked, hooded figure, wielding twin daggers. The hooded one rose up to a full seven feet tall, and with a whirl to the right, he took out three boglins even as they jabbed at him with their spears. Wheeling away from the fallen trio, he lashed out at four more of the oncoming foes, leaving tendrils of smoke in their wake, his blades slashing into them, sending them back to the Otherworld.

Flinging one dagger overhanded, he skewered one spearman, then heaved his second dagger into the breast of another. The two boglins evaporated at once, leaving this world to hurtle back to another plane of existence. The hooded man clapped his gloved hands together, and with a crack of white lightning, a long bow appeared in his hands. With a flurry of rapid movement, the large bowman fired off a dozen fiery arrows, leaving a red spray trailing through the air before plunging into the breasts of twelve more of the boglins.

Screaming in rage, Molech raised one fist and from it sprang a burst of fire that evolved into a winged serpent, wildly twisting and crackling as it sailed toward the large bowman. The moment its fiery fangs closed on the breast of the hooded man, the hood fell down about his shoulders, revealing the antlers he sported on his head.

"Herne the Hunter!" said Alex as the antler-crowned bowman vanished in an explosion of dazzling green light. "The charges on each relic have run out! What's the plan now?"

"Payback for my sister!" Lucas snapped, angrily.

Taking a sympathetic look at the boys, Alex gestured at the team still surrounded by Waziri and the two fire gods. The boys all wept hopelessly, certain they were about to die. Following his gaze, Lucas said, "I was once on their ball team but I got kicked off because of my temper. But, what do these demons want with them?"

Waziri said, "Their still beating hearts will be ripped from their chests that the fire god of the Canaanite faith can be fully restored."

Lucas snapped, "To hell with you and your weirdo gods!"

He raised his fist and from the ring on his finger a beam of scintillating light shot through the air, striking Molech directly between the eyes. He wailed in pain and crumpled in Baphomet's grasp. The smaller demon staggered beneath his weight and they both collapsed there on the playground.

"Did," Lucas whispered, "I do that?"

He looked down at the ring now glowing a bright green on his finger. He then felt a firm hand close on his shoulder. "Not bad for not knowing what you were doing, lad!" said Billy Connors as he stepped from the shadows behind the two boys. "Just think, if you had a little training. You would be a force to be reckoned with!"

The old Irishman raised a black staff in his hand. A blaze of white-hot lightning spat from the end of the oaken staff and struck the two fire gods. They were engulfed in a blue fireball that left traces of pulsing power drifting through the air, rendering Molech and Baphomet unconscious. Upon seeing them both sprawled there on the lawn, Waziri tossed a gold stone down at his feet, and an astral gate appeared before him. He reached out to latch onto Ali. "Khalid's son!" he hissed. "The Hound's little pup!"

"Not so fast there, Arab!" said Billy, jabbing his staff at the air between them. A burst of blue light shot from the end of his staff and struck Waziri in the center of his chest, catapulting him off his feet.

With a yelp of terror and desperate to escape the wrath of the Mage Lord, Waziri rose unsteadily rising to his feet. He then leaped through the portal and gated out of Havelock park.

Sprawled beside the closing portal, Ali looked up to see the rest of the boys on his team frantically racing out of the park, each of them certain they had escaped a horrible death. Watching the terrified boys running down the alley north of the park, Billy said, "And oh the stories those young lads will be sharing with their parents when they get home. Poor lads will more than likely need therapy for no one will believe their farfetched tale."

There came a shimmer beside Billy and all five mages of the White Council appeared there in the park, their long, black staves blazing. Cat and Cinnamon, flanked by the Three Bears, aimed their crackling staves down at the two fallen fire gods, sending waves of blue fire washing over their prone forms.

Billy turned from his five companions.

The old Irishman offered Lucas and Alex a weary smile.

"Off to home, lads," he said in a tone that brooked no argument. "I heard that you are staying with my grandson, Reason. He'll be worried about you, so skedaddle on home."

"Reason is alive?" Lucas asked. "What about my sister?"

"Yes," Billy said. "Reason. Celeste. Alive and well. Both probably wondering where the hell you two are. Head home, now."

Tearing up with relief, Lucas followed Alex and Ali out of the park, the three dogs trailing behind them. "I need to," Ali said, "get home to the Yardleys. Do you know where they live, Lucas?"

"Yes," Lucas told him. "I once lived with them. We'll walk you there, but this Morrigan and Herne, Alex?"

Peering down at the crossbow he carried, Lucas said, "Do you think we've seen the last of them?"

Shrugging, Alex looked down at the short sword and said, "Like I have a clue about how many charges a magic weapon has?"

Ali said, "Even your dogs created a force field with magic. I did some research on your dogs, Lucas. First known as nanny dogs, Staffordshire terriers had a reputation as loyal guardians of small children, guard dogs willing to throw down their lives for the children they were entrusted with. It was only later that pit bulls were bred for savage matches when cruel men turned noble Staffordshire terriers into rage filled, killing machines for their own entertainment. But your dogs sure showed nobility tonight!"

Grunge, Lobo, and Goblin looked over at Ali with a pleased look in their eyes.

When they arrived at the Yardleys, Lucas told Ali, "I wouldn't say a thing about what happened tonight. Knowing these two, they'll force you into therapy, just like Billy said down at the park."

43

Khalid was furious. His fury changed to disgust, then sickness. Had his emotions been displayed on a multifaceted jewel, with a color to represent each one, his soul would have been illuminated like a glistening rainbow. The shades of his aura were so strong, he put forth an incandescent blue glow that shimmered from the top of his turban-covered head to the tips of his sand-encrusted military-style boots.

He was afire with an inner light, and he stood there muttering foul curses at some unknown source that caused Stone Holland and Gloria Raynes to scan their surroundings as if they were able to see the figure or personae of his extreme ire.

"We killed the wrong man," Khalid said, sadly.

Kneeling beside the body sprawled between the three of them, Stone used the long silencer on his pistol to scoop back the hood from the face of the man gunned down only seconds ago.

"What the hell?" Raynes gasped when she saw the man's open eyes staring vacantly at the ceiling overhead. "Not Waziri? How is this so? We've trailed him since he left the airport back in Chicago!"

Still kneeling beside the dead man, Stone glanced up at Khalid. "Waziri pulled a switch on us. It could have been back in the States, or in Paris. Somewhere along the line, Waziri passed the tracking device off to this man. We've been blindly following this honing device from the States over here to the Middle East."

The three of them looked at each other, knowing how badly they had failed. It had been decided back at the Omaha airport how they would handle Achmed Waziri when they caught up to him. It wasn't a matter of if Waziri lived once he reached the Middle East, but how long he would be allowed to do so.

The quicker they accomplished their task, the safer the world would be. Waziri was a mad dog that needed to be put down. Stone and Khalid had been in complete agreement over this, with Raynes being conflicted on the grounds she was an agent of the United States, and as such, assassinating enemy combatants was not to be taken lightly. In truth, she knew it happened all the time overseas, it was just that she had never had to make that decision herself. Nor to carry it out.

The three of them had joined forces back in Lincoln to track down Waziri, with the understanding that the man was to be arrested for attempting to destroy US military dogs at the rescue compound of Wounded Arrow.

As a former agent of Homeland Security, Agent Raynes had secured an agreement with Khalid and Stone that the end of the road would not result in a dramatic shoot-out. Back in the United States, as they chased the man, they thought to be Waziri from one airport to another, her goal had been to arrest him quietly without incident and turn him over to the proper authorities.

During the week they spent in the States, trailing the man they assumed had been Waziri, Raynes had shared with the two men her own emotional attachment to the man. Stone and Khalid had listened in respectful silence as Gloria revealed the greatest heartache of her life. Her own parents, as emissaries to Africa, had been in the World Trade center on 911. Both had been killed when the planes struck the buildings. In that one terrorist attack, Gloria had lost her parents. And although, Waziri could not be tied to any involvement of the bombing of the World Trade center, she knew he was a member of the terrorist network who brought death to innocent victims like the three-thousand that had died during the 911 attack.

Gloria had joined Homeland to counter terrorist movements and be responsible for enforcing the laws that shut them down. Only she was committed to doing her job in a legitimate manner, nothing outside the box would be acceptable to her.

While Khalid and Stone took a hardline stance against showing mercy to Waziri, they did agree to abide by Gloria's terms during the first stages of the hunt. And yet, all agreements to bring Waziri in alive, were abandoned once he'd left American soil. Since it was made known he had flown back to the Middle East, Waziri was to be eliminated on sight in order to put a stop to his terrorist activities. In the end, ironically, it had been Raynes who had fired the fatal shot. And yet, she killed the wrong man.

We need to get a cleaner team in here," Khalid told them both.

Stone stood up, removing the silencer from his pistol. As he worked on the weapon, he moved swiftly down the tunnel-like hallway inside the tomb they were in. "Call in cleaners," he said. "But any second now, some unassuming tourists are going to discover our victim's body. We should be long gone by then."

Nodding in agreement, Khalid slipped his own gun back into a shoulder holster beneath his jacket. He went to one knee beside the corpse. After several seconds of searching through his jacket pocket, he produced a small red gem.

Stone and Gloria exchanged curious looks as Khalid tossed the gem down on the stones at his feet. At once, the red, dime-sized gem shattered and a roiling cloud exploded from its fragments. As the rippling reddish smoke parted, an iron gateway was revealed, complete with a lion-headed knocker at its center with a rusty iron ring in its mouth. "What are you doing?" cried Stone as Khalid reached through the smoky tendrils drifting before them and pulled on the ring within the lion's mouth.

"Getting rid of the body," Khalid responded. "We have allies just beyond the gateway."

The elaborate gate made no sound as it swung open, revealing a sunken garden beyond. Inside a circular pit was a round wooden table where a pair of white-robed women sat in deep discussion over a matter of grave importance. The ladies looked up at Khalid standing there within the gateway, startled looks on their faces. Surprised by the sudden appearance of the gate, the two cats seated before the lion-headed fountain at the center of the garden, suddenly bounded over to confront Khalid, who stepped back barely in time to avoid swipes of their sharp claws.

"Padraic! Eddie!" said a woman at the table. "He is friend, not foe! That would be Khalid, our emissary from the Middle East! And come just in time to advise us what to do with our problem!"

Stone stared at the two dark-haired ladies in stunned surprise. "Cat! Cinnamon!" he said, "owners of the Roaring Lion bookstore back in Havelock?"

Cat gestured at the prone body sprawled directly behind Khalid in the corridor. "Rain?" she said. "Be a dear, and please clean that up."

44

Tamping out his briar pipe in the shadows at the far end of the garden, Rain Nelson rose to his feet with catlike grace. As he approached the gateway, he gently scooted the two cats out of his path so he could approach the body. Dressed in leathers, he wore a torc around his neck, and it glowed as he reached down and drew the dead man back through the gateway. The glow became fainter as the Outlaw president carried the man into an alcove to one side of the garden. When he returned to the garden, he was shadowed by the Three Bears.

Looking at Stone, who looked completely lost as he stood there staring at the three large men, Khalid said, "Your hometown of Havelock is known amongst the White Council, the Tuatha De Dannan, the Unseen Court, the Sidhe, and the Web of the Wise. In your small sub-urb are way stations between alternate realms, where the Guardians of the Gateways are located: The Emerald Pub, owned by the Irish-man Billy Connors. The Roaring Lion bookstore, owned by Cinnamon and Cat. The Station, owned by Rain Nelson, president of the Outlaws. The Trainyards, owned by the three Bears, Kodiak, Winter, and the Griz. All are magic users of significant power. All are committed to battling the Unseen who are bred of Darkness and wage war on those who serve the Light."

"Wizards and witches?" Stone said. "Is that what you would have me believe, Saracen?"

Khalid nodded. "That is one name for them, but trust me, they are much more than that. And it appears, they need our help."

It was Cinnamon who told Khalid and his two companions about the conjuring of Molech and Baphomet. "Waziri," she said, "summoned the two demons. They are back, but not yet in their full power. It was your daughter, Stone Holland, who came to Billy, seeking his help. Billy confronted them at the park, summoning two imprisoning gems to anchor their souls, in order to dispatch them to another realm. Since you are at the Valley of the Kings, we ask you to place these gems inside the vault of Tutankhamun, where Molech and Baphomet can be imprisoned for perhaps ten more centuries."

Griz rumbled, "What is this Valley of Kings?"

Cinnamon said, "Also known as the Valley of the Gates of the Kings. It is a valley in Egypt where, for 500 years tombs were excavated for the pharaohs. The valley stands on the west bank of the Nile, and contains 63 tombs and 120 chambers. In modern times the valley became famous for the discovery of the tomb of Tutankhamun, with its curse of the pharaohs. Khalid has managed to open a pathway for us to send the souls of the two demons into this tomb, so let them deal with the curse of Tutankhamun, a potent dark magic for certain."

She calmly added, "Do you have any better ideas?"

Cat looked over at Rain. He shrugged and asked, "What about the Dog Soldier? Don't you think we should consult with him?"

The Outlaw looked at the three Bears, expecting an answer. It was Kodiak who said, "Wolf is dealing with a strange castle that has mysteriously appeared out near Wounded Arrow. He has left us in charge of the anchoring gems. I don't think he would oppose this plan."

Khalid stood patiently waiting in the corridor of the Great Pharoah, listening to a hushed debate between the six members of the White Council in the garden before him. Behind him, Stone began pacing up and down the corridor, while Raynes stood there looking baffled as to how Khalid had managed to open such a rift between realms. She was not easily accepting things at face value, and wondered how it was that Stone seemed to be dealing with the situation so well.

She was still overwhelmed with the fact she had shot and killed the wrong man.

After several long moments of more debate between those in the sunken garden, Griz lumbered over to the gateway, two glowing fist-sized gems in his hands. He passed them through, handing them to Khalid. The massive, golden-haired wizard said, "It took a lot out of the Irishman to subdue those two. As it was, the Bears were forced to call on Odin, Thor, and Freya to help imprison Molech and Baphomet inside the jewels. We barely managed to do so. Handle those carefully, Khalid, Lord of the Sands. Seal them away with caution."

Kahlid tucked the two pulsating gems into a leather pouch depending from his shoulder by a braided strap. He shared a long look with the seven members of the White Council, then nodded and turned away from the gateway.

Inside the sunken garden, Cinnamon heard the loud, angry hiss of her two cats, Padraic and Eddie. She turned to watch the two felines launch themselves at the mob of small figures racing past the round council table, their overlarge eyes fixed on the slowly closing gateway between the realms.

"Fair Folk children?" Cat asked, in puzzled tones.

"Damn!" cursed Cinnamon. "What mischief are they about?"

"Rebelling," Cat said, "against their Queen!"

With a swift flick of her staff, Cinnamon sent a sapphire fireball sailing across the chamber, directly toward the mob of wild-haired fairy children, all racing toward the closing gateway.

The brilliant ball of blue light struck the gate in front of them, and dozens of the leather-clad little figures ran directly into the center of the phosphorous flaming sphere. With wild cries of dismay, the fairy folk struck the barrier and were hurtled back into the garden. Some fell in stunned heaps upon the floor, while others dropped to their knees, holding their small hands out in a gesture of surrender. Some bowed their heads and wept openly, ashamed of their own actions.

A snigger of wicked laughter came from one wild imp, his strands of dark hair trailing over his bare shoulders as he dove through the closing gateway. Following behind the shaggy-haired imp, a child-like figure with the face and head of a coyote sprang up from the floor, slipping in through the gateway just inches behind the imp. And just as the gate was inches from closing, cutting off one realm from the other, a tall, slender red-haired boy tucked and rolled, as he, too, passed through from the garden and into the Valley of Kings.

The three misfit Fair Folk children danced around Khalid who stood in the center of the corridor, protectively holding the leather bag that contained the two gems imprisoning the souls of Molech and Baphomet. The Saracen's brow furrowed deeply as he named the fey creatures of myth that capered around him, saying, "Puck. Loki. And Coyote the Trickster."

Coyote snatched the bag, causing the strap to snap. With a burst of laughter, he tossed the bag to Puck, whose large blue eyes sparkled with mischief. He caught it and took off racing down the long corridor. Loki, red hair streaming, took off running behind Coyote and the blue-eyed Puck. The three continued to play a game of keep-away even as they sprinted toward the open gateway at the end of the tunnel like hallway.

"Damn them!" Stone snapped, drawing his pistol from the holster beneath his jean jacket. Raynes armed herself, as well, and yet before the two could pursue the small beings, Khalid said, "Put your guns away. Bullets can't harm them. They are just having fun. Once we catch up to them when this tunnel ends at King Tut's tomb, we can explain why we need those gems back."

Stone growled, "Fun with gems that holds the souls of demons?"

Khalid, who remained calm despite Stone nearly losing it over the interference by the three tricksters, said, "Puck, also known as Robin Goodfellow, is a nature sprite. He is well-known among the English, the Welsh, the Celts, the Norse, the Swedish, and Iceland, with the term pixie originating from the diminutive of Puck.

"In mythology, a trickster is a character in a story, god, goddess, spirit, man, woman, or animal, which exhibits a great degree of secret knowledge, and uses it to play tricks. Tricksters are archetypal characters who appear in the myths of many different cultures. Tricksters violate principles of natural order, playfully disrupting normal life. Often, the bending of rules takes the form of tricks. Tricksters can be cunning or foolish. In Norse mythology, the mischief-maker is Loki, who is also a shapeshifter. In many Native American mythologies, the Coyote stole fire from the stars, moon, and sun. I think by what I've seen of these fey jokers, we are dealing with Puck, Loki, and the Coyote."

He grinned despite the extreme seriousness of their situation.

"Come," he said, "let us go explain to these tricksters that they are literally playing with fire, whisking the souls of two fire gods away like they just did."

"And," Raynes asked, "if they won't give the gems back to us?"

Both she and Stone chambered rounds in their guns.

Shaking his head, Khalid said, "Come, let us bring reason to the unreasonable and the irrational."

A few minutes later, the three of them were just approaching the cavern-like opening into the chamber beyond the shadowy corridor they were in, when Raynes said, "I see them ahead of us! They've removed the gems from the leather pouch, and they are playing a very dangerous game of catch with both of them!"

A concerned look on his face, Khalid ran the last few steps into the tomb of King Tut, where Loki had just thrown one of the gems to Puck, who was suddenly jostled by Coyote. Khalid, Stone, and Raynes looked on in horror as the gem tumbled out of Puck's small hands and fell toward the hard, cold stones of the floor.

And all three tricksters spoke in unison, saying, "Ooops!"

45

Chapter Forty-Five
    Realm of Valasar Year 2000

Dusk banked above the radiant treetops of the Oakwood Kings, drifting for several moments on gentle currents. Winded from his long flight, the hawk wearily glanced down at an opening in the treetops beneath him. He passed over it, then circled back and plunged down between the branches.

In slow, graceful spirals, Dusk descended into the wooded glen below. There he gently settled down beside a small pond, dropping the small pouch he'd carried for so many miles.

He then said, "Tanner Silvertree of the Jewel Folk?"

Silence greeted him. Several seconds passed.

"Tanner?" he said. "I have a message from the Borderlord."

A moment later, a shaggy-haired woodland imp stepped into the clearing, his black leather shirt and breeches practically making him invisible in the shadows beneath the trees. He stood barely three feet tall, and with his silky raven hair trailing over his tiny shoulders and gold hoops glinting in the lobes of his pointed ears, he greatly resembled a young gypsy boy out to do mischief. But as he peered directly at the hawk, the fierce look in his blue eyes and the feral grin on his dark, elfin features, caused him to appear far more dangerous

The Saracen

than any wild kit of rogues or gypsies.

Dressed in his black leathers, belted at his thin waist with a thick band of leather, Tanner looked very much like a skinny, rambunctious eight-year-old boy. However, he carried an arsenal of weapons on him that no child would ever be skilled at using. Two short swords, a long dagger, and four small throwing knives.

"Borderlord?" Tanner said. "What would the Guardian of the Wilds want with me? Why, I am only–"

"Tanner Silvertree," Dusk said, "of the Fair Folk, descended from an Elven Queen and a Dwarven King. Famed Legend Weaver of the Jewel Folk, bright gem among the Chaykin race. Huntsman sworn to prevent Demons of Shadow from invading Valasar. Those are your titles, true?"

A troubled look on his face, Tanner asked, "Who are you that you know so much about me?"

"Dusk," the hawk said. "I serve the Borderlord."

He gave a sly grin and added, "You, as Legend Weaver, once had access to the royal archives, and your knowledge as a historian is needed. The matter is urgent, and the Keeper of the Lodge sent you–"

He dipped his head and plucked up the pouch. "Here," he said, dropping it on the ground between them. "Open that. The summoning ring inside will take you to the Lodge. Quite swiftly."

Eyeing the pouch warily, Tanner said, "I am leery of magical devices. Especially any token of power the Keeper sent. It's rumored his tokens came from a hoard cursed by the dragon Drakvoren."

"Fear not," Dusk said. "Is not the Keeper of the Lodge a fellow Chaykin? Certainly he would not offer this token if he thought it would send you to an unknown void. Especially not when those at the council need to hear your testimony."

"In regards to what?" Tanner asked, curiously.

Dusk looked down to the pouch on the ground between them. "The other item inside of that carrying case."

Tanner picked it up and opened it. As he stared down at the green gem that rolled out into the palm of his hand, Dusk told him, "The last messenger to carry that did not fare so well. The owl died upon arriving at the Borderlord's keep, peppered with darts by a flight of Morgoth who pursued him through the Northlands! But he managed to deliver that vision-gem sent by Lord Kennon of Hickory Hall."

Dusk fanned one wing, gesturing at the pond. "Toss it into the waters, if you wish to see why this council has been called."

Tanner did so, and as the green gem sank beneath the waters a tapestry of visions appeared on the surface of the pond:

A company of white-cloaked knights herded a large group of young boys directly into a mass of branches piled high on the crest of the hill. Another youth, a crown upon his blond head, stepped forward, a flaming torch in his grasp. A maniacal gleam in his eyes, he said, "Children of Star Fire, my Lords of Night have found you guilty, and therefore this fire shall consume you and put an end to your demon-inspired talents!"

As the vision faded, Tanner stood there, greatly unsettled. "And the Borderlord believes that I can change the fate of these lads?"

Dusk said, "It is why he has called for this council. If you wish to know more, simply use the ring to teleport to the Lodge."

Shaking his head, Tanner said, "I already told you, I'm not inclined to use magical devices. And as to attending this council at the Lodge? I'm not certain."

Long moments of silence passed between them.

Tanner refused to meet the hawk's gaze.

Dusk looked away from the Chaykin Huntsman and peered down at the bright red leaves floating on the mossy surface of the pond. "These leaves," he finally said, "resemble translucent jewels fallen from the crowns of the ancient Oak Kings. How ironic, since I came here searching for a gem among Jewel Folk, who has fallen from the grace of the king he once faithfully served. Farewell, Tanner."

Dusk then launched himself from the roots of the oak and soared away, leaving the Chaykin woodwalker staring down in bewilderment at the ring in the palm of his hand.

There beneath the Oakwood Kings, Tanner stood bathed in the pink light filtering through the branches above him. The sun was setting beyond the forest far to the west. Trying to keep at bay the images of the young boys the vision-gem had shown him, he held the summoning ring up, snorting in disgust at Dusk's suggestion that he simply use it.

After all, the ring was a token of power. In his opinion, magical items were too unpredictable. Especially a teleportation device which had the potential to malfunction and whisk him away to unknown voids, and cause him to disappear. Forever.

Tanner slipped the ring into his belt pouch. He then heard a faint sound coming from the nearby stream running adjacent to the pond, some thirty yards away. There the forest grew thick, yet a slender pathway wound itself out of the trees, connecting with a wooden bridge spanning the gentle flow. Tanner scanned the mist above the stream and saw a scattering of enormous fireflies drifting through the swirling vapors.

When the large company of white-hooded riders emerged from the trees to the west of the bridge, the white steeds of the ghostly riders appeared to be floating as they moved onto the bridge. The lead rider spotted Tanner standing there before them, and barked a command, bringing the entire band of riders to a halt.

"Woodwalker," the man said, drawing back his hood to reveal his bearded features and short red hair. "I am Sir Balan Dane, Commander of the Knights of the Flame. I hail from Kallador. King Rannen wishes to speak with you about your investigation regarding the bloodline of the Kings of Erin."

"Investigation?" Tanner said, puzzled.

"Yes," Sir Balan said, smiling pleasantly. "As a record keeper and archivist to King Ronan, you once had access to the legends of the heroes of old! Ah, the tales you could tell, little one! Come, share a fire with us! We'll discover the treasure trove you store inside your head, Legend Weaver."

Scanning the faces of the other riders, Tanner did not like the cold, hard stares they offered him. "I think not," he replied.

Dane stiffened in his saddle, clearly insulted. "I must insist," he said, snapping his fingers, and Tanner peered up in alarm as two of the white-cloaked riders spurred their horses forward. It was at that moment that a band of dark creatures descended into the clearing. Each huge, winged being had the thick, muscular body of a man, but the face of a bat, with shaggy manes running from their foreheads to the napes of their necks. "Morgoth Lords!" Tanner spat in disgust as the beings dropped down beside the stream.

Tanner ripped his twin jewel-blades free of his shoulder sheaths, then erupted into a deadly whirlwind, his twin blades glimmering with lime-green light. Turning and spinning, keeping in constant motion, he executed a series of lightning-swift strikes that caused the creatures to reel back.

One Morgoth sprang forward, his fiery blade descending in a killing stroke. Twirling one sword above his head, Tanner parried the blade of the tall Morgoth, yet was driven to his knees by the brutal attack. Blocking a second stroke with one raised blade, he thrust upward with the other, driving it deep into the Morgoth's breast. The bat-faced being burst into lemony flecks that vanished with a hiss.

Tanner slid his swords back into his sheaths and turned to see Balan Dane and his Wardens engaged in combat with the rest of the Morgoth Lords. He darted off the trail and veered into the mist rolling down the slopes of the high, wooded bluff before him.

At the top of the bluff, Tanner glanced back, listening. Swords clashed behind him. Voices of the riders were muted by the fog, but their shouting carried up the hillside. Silently slipping to one side of the main trail, Tanner darted onto a slender deer trail.

A second later, he discovered a grisly sight. "Oh, no," he groaned when he saw his wyndar stag sprawled dead beside the trail, deep gashes in his neck and shoulders. He kneeled beside the tiny, black stag. "Spry," he said, tears glistening in his eyes. "You served me well during many Hunts."

Removing a tiny pink gem from his belt pouch, he gently placed the gem on Spry's bloody shoulder. "May your spirit rise through the stars," he whispered. "Run free on the plains of the Far Realm."

The pink gem glowed brightly, spreading its light across the sleek black fur of the fallen stag. There was a sudden flash, and both the gem and the little wyndar vanished. Hearing a low hiss, Tanner peered up to see a Mogoth Lord looming before him.

A tall, dark figure stepped out of the shadows and intercepted the creature, his bright blue blade snaking out and under the chin of the beast so swiftly that the Morgoth's head went sailing away, its red eyes resembling hot coals whirling through the air.

Tanner looked on in wonder at the lean, raven-haired Elf standing before him, his blue jewel-blade lighting up his handsome features.

The Elf said, "Jewel Folk, woodland children, descended from an Elven Queen and a Dwarven King. For Chaylendriel and Graenor, going against the law set forth by priests of the two races, pledged their vows into the wind and married in secret in the realm of Valasar. And, a child was born to this Dwarven King and Elven Queen. Taking a portion of his Queen's name, Graenor gave title to the new race, and Chaykin entered the pages of Fair Folk history."

Sliding his sword home in the sheath at his left shoulder, the Elf quoted a poem straight from Fair Folk history, as well:

King Graenor of the Dwarf Folk,
    kneeled beside a moonlit sea,
    and there he pledged his heart,
    to a fair Wood Elf Queen.

Defying Ancient Law,
    beneath the stars they wed.
    The first forbidden union,
    their vows in secret said.

Then one autumn morning,
    to them was born a son.
    And two races of the Fair Folk,
    became joined as one.

Thus began the Legacy of
    the Children of the Woods.
    Bright shining Forest Gems,
    a race misunderstood.

For Dwarven sages wise,
    and Elven priests of Light,
    proclaimed these small folk,
    were demons of the night.

* * *

Hesitantly, Tanner said, "Many of the Elven race do not accept our kind, claiming interracial marriages are forbidden. If you don't mind my asking, what side of that do you stand on, Blade Master?"

The Elf offered him a slight smile. "Ah, you recognize that I am a master of the sword, but still, you don't recall my name?"

Scrunching up his nose, his brow furrowed, Tanner shrugged and said, "No, sorry, I usually avoid elves at all costs."

The Elf said, "And had I been one of those other kind of elves, I would have separated your head from your shoulders by now?"

This Elf with his long, unruly tangles of black hair, had an air of wildness about him. Tall, broad-shouldered, he wore a sleeveless vest, a shirt of black chain mail, leather breeches, knee-high boots, fingerless gloves, and leather bracers.

"Creed Blackstag," he said, "sent to you by Ravenhawk in case you refused to use the summoning ring Dusk offered you. He summons you to a council at the Lodge. If you wish to avoid Balan Dane and his Wardens, allow me to escort you away from here."

Blue eyes sparkling, Creed gave a sharp command, and Tanner watched in amazement as a small pack of white wolves raced off through the undergrowth. Creed then led Tanner away between the trees. The deer trail they were on soon led them back to a bend in the main trail, where they stepped from the wider path to a slender ribbon of trail winding away through the shadows. They moved hastily down an S-shaped curve, the trees on the slope behind them screening them. Soon the forest closed in around them. After traveling some distance down another deer trail, Creed brought them to a path running be-tween the black trees. Pressing the blue jewel embedded in his sword's hilt, he sent brilliant sapphire light spiraling down the length of the blade, illuminating the massive boles of the forest titans around them. In the luminescent glow, the giant trees greatly resembled pillars supporting the leafy ceiling of a forest cathedral.

They made camp in a small glen beneath these trees.

"No fire," Creed told Tanner. "The wolves will keep you warm."

Tanner fell asleep, a wolf on either side of him. When he awoke the next morning, the wolves were still with him, but there was no sign of Creed. He kneeled beside the stream running through the glen, and dressed as he was in his sleeveless vest, he saw his reflection in the waters, which revealed the tattoo of a snarling lion covering his right shoulder, while a dragon wound itself down from his left shoulder, the tips of both wings twining together to create a knot-work at his wrist. On his right temple and part of his cheek was the tattoo of a rampant wolf.

Swearing under his breath, he offered Creed a look of reproach as he stepped out from between the trees. "Is this your work?" he asked, rather testily.

Oblivious to Tanner's scowl, Creed said, "Ravenhawk asked me to apply the talismans. You will need them in the days ahead, for there is a boy coming to you from Outside the realm. To serve as his guardian, the lion, the dragon, and the wolf will aid you greatly."

To be continued in Book Three, Here there be Dragons.

Tom Frye
    6139 Kearney Avenue
    Lincoln, NE. 68507

46

About the Author

Tom Frye has worked for 45 years as an advocate for troubled youth. He began his career when still in high school, serving as a street contact for a runaway shelter. It was during his time as a worker at a detention facility, that he began writing stories for the residents. When kids began asking for sequels to his works, he knew he had discovered a way to connect with troubled kids. Tom has served as a mediator for his own truancy program, and once produced a substance abuse program which had an impact on 15,000 at-risk kids. He believes, though, that his greatest accomplishment can be summed up in the words of one boy who wrote to him while confined: "Discovered your book today. It was like reading a letter you wrote directly to me. Thanks for giving me hope."

The Havelock Emerald series . . .

Broken Road, the Prelude: 13-year-old Reason Nelson finds himself entangled in a web of treachery over the evidence that would solve the murder of a young female informant. As he flees from both drug dealers and a persistent private detective, Reason ends up at the Emerald Pub where he is confronted by the old Irishman, Billy Connors. Reason refuses Billy's help and continues to play a game of keep-away from those who murdered the narc. Despite the intervention of his mother, Rose, director of a drug program, and his brother, Boone, a youth advocate, due to his behavior disorders and his addictions, Reason remains defiant and refuses to accept help.

Book One: Wounded Arrow: When 11-year-old Lucas Holland, the son of the president of a notorious biker club, is placed in foster care he ends up at Ben Black Bull's dog rescue ranch, where the Lakota dog handler works with some of the most damaged dogs on the planet. Ben incorporates a company of veterans who suffer from PTSD, pairing each dog with a wounded warrior. It's there that Lucas learns that dogs and people all need healing of some sort.

Book Two: The Saracen: Shortly after his mother is killed in a car accident, Lucas returns home to Havelock to live with his dad. At his school, Lucas stumbles upon three boys recruiting another young boy to carry out a school shooting. Lucas comes away from the encounter carrying a pistol. Hidden in the butt of the gun is a flash drive containing the directives to terrorists to infiltrate Wounded Arrow, where 200 Military service dogs have been returned from the war overseas. Their goal is to place a chemical agent in the ventilators of the compound, eliminating these retired service dogs awaiting adoption as a reward for the service they provided to the US.

Book Three: Here, there be Dragons: In this Sci Fi thriller, the Emerald Pub is a way station between realms. Reason Nelson has finally grown up and is performing youth work with kids who are as troubled as he once was. In his role as a foster parent, he takes in Lucas Holland and Alex Thorn. Breaking into a relic collectors house one night to retrieve a set of rings that Lucas's older sister, Celeste, has stolen from him, the two boys set off a chain of events that releases a demon into the world.

To destroy this Prince of Darkness, Alex Thorn, a child of Gypsy blood, is chosen to enter the chamber inside the Emerald to retrieve a weapon that will annihilate the demon.

Book Four: Thorns of the Black Rose: Lucas, Alex, and Celeste find themselves back in the realm of Valasar. They find themselves in a quest to not only slay a dragon, but a conspiracy to save one, as well. When a lesser king and his two Sword Lords refuse to slay the dragon, Elendria, in order to steal her Star Fire, High King Manix declares them outlaws. When he orders that their three children are to be executed, Lucas, Alex, and Celeste become determined to rescue them, for one is to be a legendary Sword Lord, the other is to become the Lion Lord, and the third is destined to become the queen, Alicia the Black Rose.

Book Five: Jewels of Kandahar: Jenna McGuire is a specialist in the Mind over Martyr program used by the US Military. When faced with the reality of 500,000 Caliphate kids, she travels to Afghanistan to save a 14-year-old charismatic boy who may set off a raging firestorm. She is escorted by a group of Delta Rangers, who travel with her into the Kandahar Mountains. There, Jenna and her team discover a mysterious treasure of gems and jewels.

Milton Keynes UK
Ingram Content Group UK Ltd.
UKHW020813250224
438379UK00013B/1554